WINGS TO A NEW WORLD

WINGS TO A NEW WORLD

DAWN BLAIR

Morning Sky Studios
PO Box 5422
Twin Falls, ID 83303
Visit us at www.morningskystudios.com

ALSO BY DAWN BLAIR:

Dragons of Wellsdeep

Beat of the Drum

Stonecharmer

Stonecharmer

Stonebreaker

Stonesinger

Onesong

Palladium

Tangled Magic

Walk the Path

Sacred Knight

Quest for the Three Books

Manifest the Magic

To Birth a Destiny

History of a Dead Man (companion novella)

Prince of the Ruined Land

The Missing Thread

Sword and Shield

The Unicorn and the Secret (companion novella)

The Loki Adventures

1-800-Mischief

For Sale, Call Loki

For A Good Time, Call Loki

For More Information, Call Loki

For More Mischief, Call Loki

1-800-CallLoki (Omnibus of novellas 1-5)

1-800-IceBaby

Help Wanted, Call Loki

1-800-Lok8

Dressed to the 9's

Wells of the Onesong

Fractured Echo

Fall's Confession

The Doorway Prince

Stardust

Mystery of the Stardust Monk

Alexander's Den

Ninjas

By the Numbers

Space Ninjas Aren't Real

Children's Picture Books

Eggs at Play

It's not about saving the planet; it's about saving ourselves.

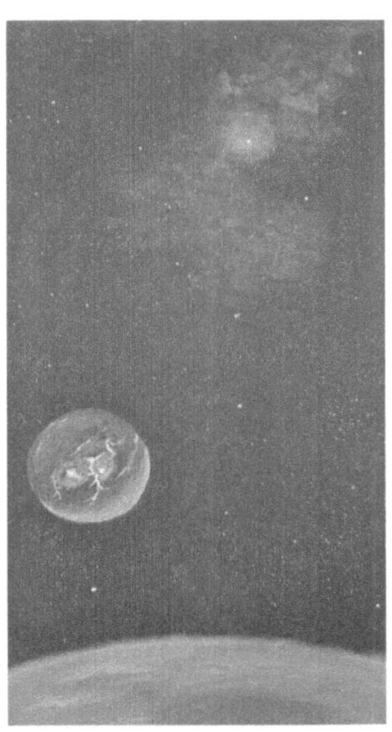

Artwork: Renewal by Dawn Blair
24"x12" acrylic on wood panel
See this and more at www.whisperedvoices.com

1

The land and kingdom of Myeller seemed out of place, as if it had stepped out of time for hundreds of years as the rest of galactic civilization grew around it. Silent peace reigned here, enough that Siva heard the birds singing in the forest beyond the bright courtyard glistening with morning dew. How long had it been since she'd heard the gentle songs rather than the stark cawing of ravenous crows defending their miserable scraps?

The dark sky she saw in her memory contrasted with the sunlight beaming down from the flawless blue sky onto the large expanse of the palace grounds. Everything seemed to sparkle, from the lusciously green grass, to the marble walkways, to the buttons on the servants' dark blue uniforms.

The lawn was split into two levels as it stretched out away from the white marble stonework of the palace. In every way, it looked like a perfect day for a wedding.

Metal chairs with white padded seat covers were set in

neat rows on the wide marble walkway before the stairway for the second level. They all faced the palace and had an aisle between them. It had been decided, by those who had given more thought to this wedding than she had, that Siva would come down the staircase like a descending angel from another world and approach the palace where she would begin her life anew. All very symbolic, she was assured.

An archway had been erected at the top of the steps and, earlier this morning, vines filled with fresh purple and white flowers were woven through the lattice work. The tent where she was to prepare for the ceremony was situated not far away on the raised tier of the courtyard.

Guests, mostly family members, were beginning to arrive in a steady stream now. Some took their seats, wanting a good view of the nuptials. Others languished in conversation about the lower tier of the yard under the sun. Servants were still filling the main canopy with refreshments which would be served after the ceremony, but there was also water set out for the guests sitting under the sun in the mild morning temperatures.

"My lady," the servant girl behind Siva called, reminding her that there was still much to be done before the ceremony. Siva withdrew herself from the opening of her tent, and her hands unwillingly released the soft leather hide as she turned.

The youthful girl smiled and motioned for Siva to return to the three-legged stool where she'd already been sitting most of the morning. Every time Siva sat on the low stool, she felt like her knees were up to her chest. But, it had to be short enough for the girl to work on Siva's hair and makeup.

Siva took to the stool with the same reluctance she felt about this upcoming ceremony. She understood why her father had chosen to betroth her to the prince, and she quite agreed with the contract it would set between the peoples of her planet and this one. It wasn't as if she'd ever expected to feel the sweeping emotions of romantic love often spoken about in stories. The complaining and weeping tales she'd heard told by the wives in the kitchens and laundry were truth about marriage. Even the men she trained with spoke of their exploits while not realizing she was in earshot. It frequently seemed that the best marriages were ones where the two lived in tolerance of the other person. Rutting could be done by any animal, whether for pleasure or reproduction. At least this marriage would provide food for her people. For that, she could be tolerant of a husband and rut as necessary.

So, Siva felt very practical about the matter of matrimony. She knew hers needed to be more than merely a simple match, but rather an arrangement that would provide for her country in a way that she alone could not. A wedding that would protect her people and safeguard their future seemed more advantageous than hoping she would find the truest of love most females dreamed about in their imaginations. Siva would save that for the stories.

Still, this left her feeling unfulfilled. No matter how practical and necessary it might be, something felt off. She'd picked up on these emotions last night during their rehearsal dinner, and she'd felt ill-at-ease since then. Siva had taken a midnight stroll around the palace after everyone else went to sleep and, while the silver moonlight had been enchanting on the white marble, it left her feeling chilled.

Yet morning had come, and she still had no logical reason for the way she'd felt. All she had to do was make good on the treaty's terms with the necessary arrangements. Then, she would do her duty and find her measure of happiness in this new land for the sake of her people. Children were starving back home. This world had abundance to share.

Siva paused the girl at her work for a moment so she could lean over for the nearby glass of water and take a sip. She poured more from a nearby white pitcher and took another drink. Since coming here to Myeller, her mouth had always felt dry, and she needed to have water close at hand. Clean water was the one substance her planet had plenty of. It had practically become a necessity Since sustenance of any other kind was scarce.

Realizing her thoughts drifted again, Siva put the glass down so the girl could continue.

"Your eyes are so beautiful and exotic," the girl said as she applied Siva's makeup. "It's a shame that they hold such sadness."

"What else am I to do? I am marrying a man I barely know and I certainly do not love." Siva didn't know why she was admitting these feelings to the simple girl. How was she to know about arranged marriages or the bargains made? Besides, Siva was betrothed to this girl's heir apparent who had always lived under his family's rule. Certainly she would not speak ill of her king. Not to mention that Siva knew she wasn't marrying for love, but for saving the people of her planet. The love she did this for wasn't a romantic one, but a greater one for country.

Instead, the girl broke out into tears.

Siva reached out and touched the girl's face. "What have I said to bring you to tears? I am so sorry if I have made you upset."

The girl grasped onto Siva's hands and held them tighter

than she imagined the girl would have the strength for. "Please, Princess Siva, please you have to try and look happy about marrying Prince Henris. Your very life could be at stake."

"What do you mean?"

Turmoil and confusion rippled across the girl's face. "Have you not heard?" When Siva could only shake her head, the girl continued, "Then you don't know about the prince's older brother and what happened on his wedding day?"

Siva tried desperately to think, but she couldn't even recall if the prince had an older brother. She could only recall meeting the two younger brothers. "What happened?"

The girl gripped Siva's hands even tighter. "Prince Bonrik's betrothed began crying during the ceremony. King Rolant lost his temper and had the bride and her entire family slaughtered. In the mayhem, Prince Bonrik was killed. I'm afraid the king's grief may still be deep from that incident."

Siva felt the new shiver run through her shoulders. She had never expected news like that, certainly not on her wedding day. How was she supposed to go out there now and stand before the king and beside his son knowing that her very life and that of her family was at stake? If catastrophe hit her and her father, what would happen to her world? Why hadn't Henris said something? Why couldn't the girl have just kept her mouth shut about the whole incident? Why had Siva spoken so harshly about her feelings?

"You needn't worry," Siva told the girl. "I don't often cry." She wasn't about to say that she had her reasons for being here. Her resolve to see this through was strong. She'd had her chance to back out … and decided to keep the commitment.

The girl released Siva's hands and brushed her fingers over Siva's cheeks once more. "You look so beautiful."

If becoming unsettled by this distressful news looked beautiful, then Siva knew she fit the bill. She wished she had more time to ask questions, but the trumpets were already signaling that her presence was required. She needed to compose herself.

As she made her way to the door, her father stepped into the entryway of the tent. "Siva, my darling, you look beautiful. A little pale though. I would've thought all this excitement would put the color into your cheeks."

Siva felt blackness crawling in along the edges of her vision. She couldn't breathe in this tight gown and when she did, the tent smelled like the makeup powder she'd been clouded in which made her want to choke. If she'd had her way, she would have married the prince in her black tee shirt and camo fatigue pants. Right now, reflecting on the girl's words echoing in her mind, she wasn't sure she wanted to go through with this. She knew, if she said the word, her father would put a stop to it. Their guards would lay down their lives to make sure they escaped. They could get away.

But where would that leave her people? One little negotiated arrangement to seal the contract and relief would come to her world. She could alleviate their suffering by merely surrendering to these circumstances.

Still, it went against her nature: to fight and win. This felt like surrendering.

"Please, at least let me take a weapon. I feel laid bare without it," she said with a forced grin and a shaky voice.

He leaned in toward her, giving a chuckle and a wink as he whispered. "I assure you that everyone feels that way on their wedding day. Let's not let the prince or his guards discover you with a weapon. They might think that you're trying to take his life. That wouldn't be a good way to join our two families together. Let there be good blood between us for now, and then later you can fill him in on the fact that you are more capable of protecting his life than his guards are."

She slid her hand around her father's offered arm and allowed him to escort her away from the tent. They walked out onto a massive lawn toward the archway above the many rows of seated people. As they reached the archway at the top of the marble stairs, she dug her fingers into her father's arm to get his attention and make him stop. "Let's make each other a promise right now," she said. "Promise me, if anything happens, you will get away. Do not stay for me. And I promise you that I will get away as well, and I will meet you at the old tree in the courtyard of our palace. Promise me."

He looked at her with concern. "Is there something going on that I should know about? I understand your apprehension at an arranged marriage, but I promise you that it will all work out."

"That's not the promise I want, Father. Please promise me that you'll stay safe."

He smiled and patted her hand. "Everything will be fine. It's quite normal to feel nervous and feel like your world is falling apart when you're about to tie yourself to a new life, especially when it involves needing to trust a stranger."

"I will try to have strength, Father, but did you know about the king's other son?"

Her question drowned out under the blare of trumpets sounding again. Her father just nodded and smiled, but she knew he hadn't heard her. He probably just assumed that she was saying she would be brave for him. That was, indeed, her plan at the moment. She had no desire to start a war and to risk the lives of the guests that were here to see the prince be married to the off-worlder. She would hold herself together.

Even if it killed her.

2

Rake glided down to the white marble balcony on the third floor of the palace, standing for a brief moment on the edges of his toes as his wings settled and released the air beneath them that had provided him with lift. As the wings tucked in toward him, he tipped his head to put his chin against his chest and rolled his shoulders forward. This allowed his specially tailored shirt the widest expanse in back that he could give it, as well as providing lots of room for the bones to hide and slip away.

Wings on someone like him were incredible, and some considered it magic. He considered himself unfortunate to have incubated long enough to allow for the difficult creation of his wings without the aid of the Crossing Ceremonies, which most of his kind had to endure if they wished to grow wings. Considering that his tucked all the way into his back to disappear when he brought them in, he knew he should be grateful. The ability to hide the dragon aspects were what allowed his kind to walk among humans unnoticed.

He'd probably feel more gratitude for his circumstances if he lived in a place like this palace and could allow someone else to take care of his problems.

Since that wasn't the case, he opened the door, one in a set of double doors which was kept unlocked for his return. He nodded to the armed guards waiting inside, knowing they would do no more than watch him with their stoic eyes.

The halls of Myeller's palace were abuzz with activity in preparation for the prince's forthcoming wedding ceremony. Servants – dressed in jackets with the official palace colors of deep blue and bands of red across the shoulders – appeared to be the most in a rush. They were the ones who would be on the front lines. Everyone else playing backup to them wore their everyday tunics of blue with red necklines. It was easy to see who to stay out of the way of today.

As Rake turned the corner to head into the east wing of the palace, however, all commotion seemed to stop. He paused, welcoming the reprieve. All the noise had been an overload on his senses.

Yet the hallway was filled with scents. A honey butter soap from the prince's bath. Ham and eggs from his breakfast, kept a little light today. Coffee. Cologne.

Rake's footsteps were the only sound as he approached Prince Henris' room. He raised his hand to knock on the wooden door carved with a rearing lion ready to shred its prey, but the door opened in front of him and the palace barber came out, nearly running into Rake and spilling the soapy water from the shaving bin.

As the barber swerved around him, muttering a low

apology, Rake entered. "Deciding to go old school all the way, huh?" Rake asked, calling out though he had yet to see Henris.

"A fortunate man only marries once," Henris said from behind the dressing screen. "Have you seen her, Princess Siva? Oh, she is a gorgeous one."

Rake hadn't seen her. So far, his duties had kept him away from the palace since the bridal party had arrived from Nungh Two. He'd heard that the bride-to-be was strangely exotic and that some had found her beautiful. Others were reserving judgment. Rake felt himself in the latter camp, though he had yet to see her. The last thing he wanted was to be guarding a poor starving waif who had been pampered as royalty with the last meager food her people had.

At least Prince Henris seemed taken with her. Rake supposed that should be enough, and, if Henris ordered Rake to protect her, then that was exactly what Rake would do.

"No, Prince Henris," Rake said, realizing that he should answer, "I have not had the pleasure of seeing your bride. Sapere Hig made it to the palace without incident, I hope."

Hig had been chosen to officiate the wedding. Rake wished he'd had the opportunity to bring the sapere from the shrine here to the palace himself, but had been correct in assuming he wouldn't make it back in time. Sapere Hig had been left to arrive on his own.

Henris came out from behind the screen, tugging at the bottom of the doublet to make sure it was fitting properly to him. "He's here. And you were able to put in a good defensive line?"

"Yes, all is quiet for several miles outside of the city." Rake bowed his head to his prince, not wanting to add that it was too quiet considering how news of this wedding had caused a stir of fanfare.

At least Henris had listened to him and kept the wedding down to family and close friends, a relatively small number considering that it was a royal wedding and everyone wanted to be there. The intimate gathering hadn't stopped Henris from pulling out all the stops on making this into a celebration.

"You really did go old school," Rake said.

Henris raised his head and put his hands out to his sides to show off the royal doublet. For the three years Rake had known Henris, the prince had always worn a short beard. Now that beard was gone and the prince looked so young.

"I go to my bride as a child so she may make me a man," Henris laughed. "I did forgo the goat milk bath, opting for a regular hot bath before I jumped in the shower to finish the job.

Considering the differing marital traditions on the planets in this galaxy alone, Rake figured that the woman from Nungh Two would scarcely understand the ritual Henris had gone through this morning. What bizarre practices was she putting herself through to fulfill the customs of her planet? Rake didn't even want to hazard a guess.

"What's her real title? I hear that she's not actually a princess," Rake said.

"You're right. Technically she has no title, which is why we bestowed an honorary title upon her. We can't have it appear that I'm marrying a commoner." Henris took a few bites of his scrambled eggs. "Her father is the primieret. I gather that he is the voice for their whole world. Imagine that. Ruling a whole world and not just a single country. They decide on a primieret by vote, as I am to understand, and the primieret rules for ten years at a time. Primieret Ozlem is in his second term. However, his daughter has no title or official capacity. She is no different than the rest of the citizens on her poor, destitute planet."

"Then why has she been matched for you, Henris?" It had been a question plaguing Rake's mind since he'd first heard about delegates from Nungh Two coming to establish a trade treaty. "They have nothing to offer us. How could a bargain even be reached?"

"They do have something we could use." Henris kept his eyes averted as he headed toward the window and lifted the curtain slightly to look out. "They have lots of people and weapons for advanced warfare."

Rake didn't like the flat sound of Henris' voice. But was it because Henris didn't like the thought of using people as fodder or because he was coming to terms with using another planet's population to fight his war and didn't want to hear Rake's objections.

"My bride is just the first," Henris said. "Sorry that you couldn't be one of the men at my side, but I wasn't certain if you'd make it back in time. I'd rather have you in the crowd anyway, especially after my brother's tragedy."

Rake nodded, knowing what Prince Henris expected of him if this ceremony went like the last. Or worse.

"But I don't expect weeping from Siva Candemir. She seems to understand her duty," the prince added. "Honestly, I swear that she seems to think it is her obligation. I hope she doesn't have a martyr complex. That will get boring fast."

Rake held his tongue at this. He often wished more people would take their actions seriously.

"How did your mission go?" Henris asked as he turned back to his mirror and fluffed a lock of hair that had fallen out of place.

"Do you wish a real answer to that?" Rake asked. "I still wish you would hold the ceremony inside the palace. It would be much easier to defend you, your family, and the guests."

"But it's a beautiful day outside." Henris pointed to the window. "Look at that. Would you deny my bride such peaceful calm? Do you realize that, during the day, Nungh Two is grey, as if it were in a perpetual fog? They no longer have a view of the blue sky."

Rake didn't know if the prince was really trying to impress his bride, or mocking her. With Henris, it could easily go either way. Some days, Rake wished the Dragon Council hadn't ordered his allegiance to the royal family of Myeller. But, now that he'd been sworn, he'd found himself biting his tongue more often than he had on any other assignment.

Henris was still awaiting an answer.

"I cleared as many away as I could. It's not as wide of a swath as I would like, but it should give you time enough for the ceremony. I will stop by and take a moment now before the ceremony to ask Sapere Hig not to draw this out. I still believe this is best done fast."

Henris smiled. "Good. I'm quite anxious to have my bride become my wife. Let's get to it, shall we?"

3

The smell of newly cut grass and lilacs wafted by Siva as she and her father walked down the long staircase to the lower level. Two boys had just finished unrolling a dark blue carpet down the aisle between the chairs as people turned to watch her descend. At least her shoes were flat, and she didn't have to worry about heels shaking under her ankles on the marble.

She stepped carefully onto the virgin carpet and began to walk down the aisle. Such an archaic tradition, she thought, this walking down the aisle and being given away. In her kingdom, no woman needed to be given away, for she was already free to make her own choice whether to marry or not. Often the woman decided not to marry at all. But on this planet, there was apparently a stigma attached to being unwed and sharing a bed chamber. Maybe that was why her planet was in the desolate state that it was while this planet thrived. She didn't understand why the gods should care about a piece of paper declaring a marriage bond, but apparently, for some reason, they did.

Her father paused as they reached the back of the aisles. The audience rose, seeming to turn as a single unit to stare at her. The music changed and her father began walking forward again. She had forgotten about the stop they'd rehearsed last night, but she was glad her father had remembered.

Siva felt her pulse in her throat, and her ragged, short breaths. She couldn't breathe in this gown. It had belonged to Prince Henris' late mother, and he'd wanted her to wear it to honor his family. A seamstress had been called in to tailor the gown to her, but several days on the rich food here had obviously put weight onto her. She would have to remember to watch herself and double her training if she wanted to keep her slender form.

A collective gasp went through the crowd as many of the women began to mutter about how beautiful she looked. It made her feel self-conscious in a way that made her question if she had been beautiful before. Maybe it was the addition of this makeup, or the tight gown which squeezed her rib cage so tightly she could barely take in air for the slight exertion of walking.

It comforted her to see her few relatives watching with smiles. Her aunt, her uncles, and a handful of scrawny cousins surrounded by several men and women who had protected Siva her whole life. A couple of the more loyal guards were stationed at the ends of the aisles wearing their full decoration of metals on their uniforms. It seemed so odd to see their full regalia, but it also filled her with pride for her people. They might be having challenges now, but they would prevail.

She made it to the second constructed archway at the base of the staircase which led to the palace where the sapere – this world's version of a priest – stood beside the king, the prince, and three of Henris' most loyal men.

This was it. This was the beginning of her new life.

The men standing beside the prince all wore full suits of armor, their helms removed and tucked in the corners of their arms. Their faces held no expression as they stared back at her. Prince Henris, dressed in a fancy gold and purple doublet, appeared freshly shaven, which was different from the last time she had seen him where he had a beard lightly squared off. She had thought him pleasing to the eye then, but he cleaned up very nicely and was handsome. Maybe her father was right. Maybe this wouldn't be so bad after all. One look into his blue eyes made her smile, which he easily returned.

King Rolant stood in all the accoutrements of his position. His purple doublet was fancier than the prince's and adorned with golden ropes and chains. A jeweled crown sat atop his head and each finger of his hand had a ring on it.

"Who gives this princess in marriage?" the sapere called out.

"I, Primieret Ozlem Candemir, give my daughter to be married."

Her father dropped her hand as if he were now relieved to have done his duty for this ceremony.

Siva stepped up onto the raised platform. The prince offered his hand, and she took it. Prince Henris had not been there at last night's rehearsal, but rather a stand-in who had not taken her hand.

They approached the sapere together as he unwrapped a golden cord from around his waist. "I am here to witness and sanctify this union." The sapere banded the cord around their wrists and tied the knot sharply around them. For a moment, Siva felt the cord bite into her skin. This also had not happened last night during the rehearsal. The man who had been standing in the sapere's place merely said a few words no different than marriage oaths on her planet.

Then the sapere moved aside and the king came forward, drawing his sword. This definitely had not happened in the rehearsal last night. Watching the king approach, weapon drawn on her, Siva suddenly understood why the bride of the older brother had started crying.

Not that she would do that now.

This was definitely a test.

It had to be.

The sapere began to speak in a weird tongue, and Siva had the sudden feeling now like he was cleansing her soul to be married to the prince.

Henris' grip tightened on her, the pressure on her fingers not nearly hard enough to make her want to cry out, but very secure.

Siva couldn't help her irritation, and she forced herself to smile to hide her glare at the king and the sword tip very close to her belly, yet she felt the rage spinning like a high angry ball in her chest, and she wanted to explode. But she couldn't. She was in their territory, not her own, and her father as well as her people depended upon her to do this. She squeezed Henris' hand back, trying also to not be hurtful, but definitely channeling her rage there.

The king began rattling off a series of names which held no meaning for her, but she was getting the sense it would matter to any children that the prince and she had. Still, it made her really pause and wonder if doing this was indeed the right thing to be doing. Her country needed it, and she was their servant. Not that she had chosen to be their leader, that was just how fate had worked out; she had never had her own choice. Because of the actions of her and her family, her people would get to live as they chose, but that was not a luxury afforded to her. Didn't she have a right to choose as well?

Siva tuned out as she allowed herself to feel her heartbreak. If she could just get through this moment, maybe the next would be better. After all, the prince was in the same circumstance as she was and barely knew her. Certainly, he would understand her feelings. They could get through this together, as it was meant to be.

For as hopeful as she was about this new thought, she also realized that apples never fell far from their trees. She stood a good chance that the prince would be just like his father.

She felt as if she might as well be rotting in a prison.

With that, a new resolve overtook her. While the treaties depended upon her marrying Prince Henris, they never said she had to be happy in this arranged marriage. She would give the prince one night to sway her, to convince her that he was worthy. If she could see some glimmer of hope within him, she would give him a second night. Alone was preferable to being with someone who did not love her and whom she despised. She wouldn't live like that, even if she had to forge her own life here on this planet.

She looked up and found the prince looking at her, assessing her. She wondered if he was thinking the same thing that she was. Or, maybe, his thoughts were darker. She didn't want to go there. She'd heard enough about brides being strangled in their sleep – or poisoned. She found herself raising just a little higher. If he had thoughts of that, then she would be dead by morning either way. One night.

The king had stopped his recitation of names of untold generations and began declaring himself as Lord on High above all as if he had to convince everybody around him that he was worthy of standing here and marrying them. She wished he would just get on with that already.

A trumpet blared in the direction of the palace, and the king stopped to listen. A stiffness entered the knights who stood by the prince's side. They glanced at the king, as did Henris. Was bloodshed about to begin?

Siva was about to open her mouth and inform the king that neither she nor her father had done anything against them when the king nodded to his son and turned away from them with his sword raising higher.

Another trumpet blared.

The ground beneath them began to shake.

Siva wanted to raise a protest, and was relieved when the prince quickly unknotted the gold cord from around their wrists and started to pull her away from the palace. The sapere tried to assist, but the prince motioned him back.

"Marcus, Kaelin, get everyone to safety. Stanton, go with my father," Prince Henris said.

The knights moved into position around them. "Your

sword, my prince," the knight said, handing Henris his weapon.

It seemed as if everyone on the prince's side of the aisle knew exactly what was going on and had been prepared for it, while the few guests who had been sitting on her side looked around questioning if they should be worried or not.

"It can't be over already," her aunt said.

The man sitting beside her aunt was already on his feet and trying to squeeze out of the aisle. "Oh, believe me, it's over."

Siva didn't recognize the man and wondered why he had been sitting on her side of the aisle. She noticed that once he reached the aisle, he started to follow her and the prince.

4

R ake had taken the first empty seat he could find, one he realized too late was on the bride's side which had significantly fewer people. The chair he had zoned in on was next to an older woman with a brown fur cap. When she smiled at him, every wrinkle on her face deepened. Fortunately, she said nothing to him, allowing him to lean forward with his elbows over his knees and start to keep watch.

He'd returned to his quarters to quickly wash and change for the ceremony, exchanging one tailored shirt for another. As he leaned forward, he could feel air against the exposed section of his back, but knew that no one would ever notice the hole in the back of his shirt beneath the short, black capelet he wore over it. The look wasn't as formal as most of the people here, but he wanted the ability to take every advantage he'd been given if it were needed.

The Humline sang of approaching danger. Rake couldn't

believe it. No ravagers had been near the quieted city. King Rolant had declared that today would be a peaceful celebration and encouraged his citizens to remain home, resting for the day.

To Rake, that sounded like the perfect opportunity for the ravagers to attack. Yet even they had seemed subdued and hadn't dared to cross the swathed barrier he'd spent weeks establishing in preparation for today. He'd really believed it might be quiet.

Except for on the Humline.

The trumpets blared as Henris' bride arrived, and he had a startled moment of wanting to slam his hands over his ears. He guessed he should have been expecting the fanfare.

Rake rose as everyone else did and turned to see the woman coming down the aisle. He heard the strong, steady beats of her heart which were a little quick, but, given the circumstances, perfectly normal. She tried to look confident. She even smiled his way, or he thought so at first until he realized she had to be looking at the woman in the brown fur cap beside him.

"Can't believe she's going to do this," one of the younger boys behind them whispered. "Something's not right about this world. It seems too perfect."

The boy was correct. Myeller did have a polished appearance, but once someone looked beneath the surface, they quickly saw the reason why Rake had been assigned to this world and why he'd called in several others of his kind, the novihomidraks, to aid him. This world was far from perfect.

Rake wondered if the youth was one of a rare few who could sense the Humline of worlds without first being reborn from a dragon. It was often said that dragons looked for those who were sensitive in that way, exhibiting signs of it early in their lives as toddlers, to incubate as novihomidraks, ones who were champions of the Onesong. But not everyone who was sensitive would become a novihomidrak. A lot of people then, especially the young, could sense the ripples before they happened.

As the happy couple stepped up before Sapere Hig, who wrapped the golden cord of bonding around their wrists to unite them in the eyes of the Dragon Council, King Rolant drew his sword and began to spout off the names of his ancestors. The bride's heartbeat sped up and Rake hoped she wasn't getting pushed to a breaking point. King Rolant enjoyed testing people, pushing them to their limits.

Rolant, in his arrogance, sincerely believed that the ravagers wouldn't attack today. Rake hoped that every name Rolant shouted was not as much of a fool as the man currently reigning. At least Prince Henris, the new heir to the throne since his brother's fateful death, seemed a bit more intelligent.

Rake hoped that Henris' bride, being from a planet with its own dire situations, could help guide Henris from letting this planet go in the same direction. It would be spectacular if this world no longer needed the aid of a novihomidrak — or several, as it currently stood — and he could accept reassignment.

The bride's heartbeat was getting faster. Rake felt his own doing the same. It had to be the Humline making him nervous. Could she feel it too? Was it possible that the people of her world were sensitive to the Humline? Maybe after the last disaster of a wedding, King Rolant had discovered a taste for blood, and Henris' bride was in real danger from the king. Rake hadn't considered that. The war with the ravagers might have gone on so long that it had driven Rolant toward insanity.

Trumpets sounded from the watchtowers around the palace as Rake felt the marble walkway start to roll beneath his feet. He suddenly knew why the ravagers around the city had been so quiet as the Humline unfolded the truth in his mind. The ravagers had planned to come at the wedding from beneath the ground.

Trumpets blurted a second warning. King Rolant and several of his guards rushed away. Prince Henris began shouting orders. Rake listened for his name. He was not one of them, which meant the prince wanted Rake with him.

Rake stood.

"It can't be over already?" the woman in the brown fur cap asked.

Rake squeezed out from between the chairs, assuring the woman that it was indeed over, at least for the moment. Before he could tell those around him to seek shelter, the bride's father began gathering his family close. Rake had to trust him to lead his people to safety. Right now, Rake's prime concern was Henris and his bride.

Her smile flashed through his memory and he tried to chase it away, but it remained firmly locked. The thought of something happening to her at the hands of the ravagers made his heart suddenly beat as quickly as hers had been. He raced to catch up with Henris.

Snaps and bangs filled the air from the direction of the palace.

"My father and I had nothing to do with this, whatever is

going on," the bride shouted over the commotion at Henris. Rake tried to recall what her name was; Henris had said it, but Rake couldn't pull it to memory. He reached out to the Humline for it. Siva – yes, that was what Henris had called her – obviously felt the need to defend her family. Somehow, she'd heard the tale of the last wedding held on the palace grounds. She glanced around, probably searching for her father, but already the commotion would've swallowed him and the rest of her family.

"I know," Henris said over his shoulder as he pulled her along harder. "It's the enemy. We had hoped to finish the ceremony before they attacked, but obviously luck was not on our side today."

"Enemy?" she asked, clearly not having been informed of this world's troubles.

A dark shadow whizzing overhead slammed into the ground in front of them, sending dirt and grass scattering and churning into the air. The metallic clanks drew closer and louder to them.

The prince looked back over his shoulder and abruptly came to a stop. Siva slammed into his chest, glancing first up at Henris, then also turning to see what he was staring at. It was her gasp that made Rake hesitate.

Behind them, the palace stood half demolished. The grass looked as if it had been gulped up by a hungry animal, chewed, and then spit out. Two great bulls of iron rolled across the landscape on metal wheels with huge spikes that bit into the earth. And bodies looked as if they had already been ripped in two, blood churning the earth into a dark brown mass.

"Don't look," the prince commanded, appearing as if he

wanted to turn his bride's face away from the devastation and hold her head against his chest. But his sword was in his free hand, and he couldn't manage the action. It was with desperation that he saw Rake coming up to them. "Take her."

Henris handed his bride off to Rake, even as she issued protest.

"No, wait, what's going on? I've got to find my father. What if he's back there?"

"Keep her safe," Henris said, his gaze locked with Rake's.

"Yes, Henris." Rake knew he couldn't manage to say any more than that.

The woman landed against Rake. Her body felt so warm against his, and yet Rake could tell that she could scarcely breathe and that was part of the reason she was overheated already.

Beyond that, it was a simple decision: the first thing that needed to go as soon as they were safe was her dress.

5

The air turned brown around her, and Siva tasted moist dirt. The noise echoed like the battle zones of her world. Wedding guests screamed and ran, but they all moved like dark ghosts through the haze. Faces and clothing were soiled in the mayhem. Flying objects whizzed through the air and landed with deep thuds. She swore she could feel the impacts vibrating along the rolling, churning ground.

Looking behind her, the devastation stretched out over the once beautiful lawn. Mounds of dirt were frosted with bodies and blood. The marble walkway no longer lay flat, with each slab of stone now looking like a jagged mountain peak. Chairs lay scattered, many now twisted. One of the constructed archways was skewed, the other tumbled and broken. Worse, half of the palace had sunk and the other side lie in crumbles.

Iron tanks had erupted from the ground, churning and spitting the earth, and currently rolled toward them.

This was not the world she had thought it was. Had truth of their own battles been kept from her? Siva suddenly found herself in the midst of strangers, even in the arms of the man who was supposed to be her husband by now. She didn't know any of this planet's people, what they had endured, or why they fought.

Henris turned her toward the alluring stranger who approached them rapidly from behind. He was the man who had been sitting next to Siva's aunt. Oh, and this man was heaven to look at, his well-formed appearance both thrilling and scaring her simultaneously. She was used to good-looking, strong warrior men. There were plenty of them on her planet.

But this man was different, and she couldn't even tell why.

Henris spoke quickly to the man and pushed her toward this stranger. Siva wanted to turn around and dig her nails into Henris. The demon you knew was always preferable to the "heaven" that you didn't know. She didn't want to leave Henris, but he was turning her over.

"Yes, Henris," she heard the prince's man confidently say.

Siva's eyes narrowed on the stranger as he reached out and took her from the prince. Was he a brother, or maybe King Rolant's bastard child? What other explanation allowed for him to speak the prince's name without any acknowledgment of title or rulership?

"This way, my lady." He pointed in the direction off to the right which still seemed vacant of battle.

It also seemed void of anything that could help them. The grassy yard went off for nearly half a mile before going into an evergreen forest. Did he really think that they could make it across that expanse and hide away in the pine trees?

Her dress caught under her feet, and she stumbled. Even wearing the comfortable flats beneath, there was no way she could move very fast in the dress. The man growled as he picked a bunch of the material up in his hands. Long talons extended from the tips of his fingers, seeming to grow right out from beneath his fingernails. Siva nearly cried out at the sight of it. She tried to draw in a breath to scream as she looked toward Henris who was already running back to the palace, but the material felt too tight around her chest. Her head swam with dizziness, both from the shocking sight and being unable to breathe in this dress. She felt like she might pass out.

The man made to slash the dress with his talons.

"You'll ruin it," she said. "Henris …"

"Your life or this dress. Which is more important?"

She acquiesced. "Do it."

With a quick slash, he tore off the front section of her ruffled skirt. He tried to drop the material, but she fetched it from him. As he gave her a look which she interpreted as him thinking she was stupid for being sentimental over the material and risking her life for it, she did feel quite silly and embarrassed. It wasn't like it was hers.

She almost let the material drop, but she couldn't. The dress had belonged to Henris' mother, and now Siva was afraid that it hung in tatters like her life. Henris and his father would never forgive her for this. She had to do her best to try to keep everything together. Her family and her people depended upon her. So, along with the sentimental value, the dress now became a symbol as well.

She began to move off in the direction that he pointed, her movements still impaired but much easier now without all the extra material.

The stranger's arms wrapped around her waist and Siva felt herself lifted off the ground. Did he not realize that she could run on her own? Carrying her would only exhaust him faster. Didn't he know this? She turned to tell him and caught sight of huge wings in her peripheral vision.

She stretched, pushing around to see if she'd really seen what she'd seen. There were wings. How had he gotten them so suddenly? That question zoomed into her head nearly as fast as the realization that he wasn't human. Humans didn't have wings.

The prince had handed her off to a demon.

Her feet came fully off the ground.

"For the love of the Onesong, quit squirming!" he growled in her ear. "Once we get higher, above their artillery, I'll change your position. But – until then – I want to be able to wrap my wings around you if I need to."

Wrap his wings? The thought seemed to enter her brain, echo, and stop like a cement barrier standing across a once open road.

She stretched out her toes, feeling her shoe come away from her foot and the cool air touching her skin. It wasn't her imagination. They were flying.

He raised one wing very rapidly, which tilted their flight. She grabbed onto his arms which circled about her waist as he threw his wings against her. In the sudden darkness stealing away her sight, she felt the slamming impact of an incoming shell that hit them and exploded. The noise boomed around them and the force of the blast knocked them askew, sending them spiraling.

They plummeted fast, and Siva wondered how long until they hit the ground. She had no idea how high they were. After that hit, his wing – what was this man who had wings? – had to be shattered. There was no way he could fly.

The wing that took the hit gave a shattering flap as he stretched it out. Air caught beneath it, boosting them up and thrusting them higher into the sky.

Grateful as she was, she didn't understand how they were still alive when the hit had been so direct. This demon was more like an angel who had saved her life. Who was this man? For as desperately as she wanted to know, she feared what the answer might be. Getting to know him better might just be dangerous.

More shots came at them, but only twice more did he actually have to wrap his wings around her to protect her. She heard the shots pinging off his resilient wings like rocks pelting off tight leather.

Soon, the sounds of battle fell away. She tried to look down, but their height and the remains of her billowing skirt made it hard to see what was actually going on down there. All she knew was that a huge chunk of the landscape had been turned from green to brown and the thick dust of battle made an anxious cloud over the scene.

"I'm going to change your position now." From the moment he informed her of his next actions to when she suddenly found herself being carried in his arms like a bride across the threshold, she barely had a chance to think and process what he had said.

"What are you?" she asked.

She knew he heard the question for he gave a low chuckle, but he ignored it as he looked around to make sure they were safe before pressing onward toward the clouds.

Carrying her like this, he rose swiftly and higher into the air. His wings carried her weight as though he did this often. Her dress, however, didn't provide much protection from the cooling air as she felt herself shiver.

"I'm sorry that you're cold. I'll take us down lower as soon as I'm sure that we're far enough away. I'll leave you with the saperes at the temple. They'll make sure you get warm and fed."

"Leave me?" she asked.

"The king will want me to put a swift end to this. I'm sorry that your wedding day was ruined."

What was this man who cared about her safety, comfort, and the fact that her wedding had been wrecked? Siva longed to find out more about him, even if it was the wrong thing to do.

6

The flight didn't take long. Even carrying Henris' bride barely hampered him at all, save for the dips in altitude they endured while he sheltered them from bombarding ammunition. To her credit, she never once squealed or panicked, even when they came disastrously close to the ground.

He didn't dare take them down to the shrine in the city of Myeller, but carried her further than that. If the ravagers found out she escaped, they would be looking for her in Myeller. By the time they realized that she'd been taken from the palace and city, the saperes would have her either secured or moved even further away.

He would never admit it to anyone, but he wished that he could take her to the remotest place on the planet, if not off it entirely.

She was Prince Henris' bride.

With himself being a novihomidrak, Rake knew he had no purpose in changing or meddling with the course of one human's life, no matter how much he might like to. His focus needed to be on the concerns on the larger world.

This was just a reaction to her, to a body so slender in his arms that he could feel the strength of her muscles. She was built well, for a starving waif from Nungh Two. A simple touch to the Humline and he could figure out how to make her body sing for him.

Henris' bride!

Needing distraction and to rid himself of her as soon as possible, he flew toward Plashia with due haste.

The town was small, and all roads seemed to converge toward one building at the center as if it were a glowing radius extending shining rays.

They flew low enough to glide between buildings, remaining high enough to avoid the wagon traffic on the road.

Strange animals which looked similar enough to horses pulled the carts. Had she been here long enough to learn that these animals were called parnors? Did the patrol officers walking in pairs up and down the street, occasionally tipping their hats to passersby, look anything like the officers on her planet?

He should do more than wonder about questions he had no right or time to get answers to. He should be paying attention and doing his duty.

Recognizing the patrol men, Rake flew up to turn, then dove back toward them. "Bernard, Elwyn, the palace is under attack. Secure the city."

Both men saluted Rake, then took off running in different directions. As Rake continued ahead, he heard more patrols being alerted by shouts between the men. Satisfied the town would soon be protected, Rake flew on.

Domed buildings throughout the town rose high above the tall stone wall that surrounded the building in the center of town – the shrine to those who held the ways of the Nefterru dragons. Rake swooped over the tall pillars which stood on each side of the open gateway, taking in the smell of the courtyard's freshly cut grass between each of the shrine's outbuildings used as lodgings for the saperes and other guests.

Beside the shrine's carefully tended garden with stones and waterfalls, rosebushes, vine-covered lattices, and arched walkways, Rake landed gently on his feet, and then settled her down upon hers. "We must hurry."

She looked around as she gave a hasty, but quavering huff. He tried to imagine what she was thinking about right now, and he took his own breath to see if he could smell the blood of an injury. He didn't, but that didn't mean she wasn't encountering some soreness. Even with his wings taking most of the hits, the blunt force of artillery strikes would hurt. But that didn't seem to be it. She was assessing the area around them, probably trying to figure out where they were. Add to that the tranquil calm as opposed to the noisy battlefield they'd left, and she might be feeling a bit heady from that alone.

He heard Siva gasp.

"It's more beautiful than the palace was before it was destroyed," she whispered. Then she looked sidelong as if checking to determine if he'd noticed her speak, her cheeks growing red as she realized he had.

A sapere rushed down the short wooden stairway of the center building toward them.

Siva gathered the remains of the shredded gown to her as if covering herself. It wasn't as if he'd left her indecent. The gesture stung his emotions more than Rake wanted to admit. At least with the sapere here, Rake could turn her over to him and be gone to dutifully occupy his mind and body with taking care of the ravagers.

Brown lines which appeared to be sparkling tattoos ran along the sapere's shaven head and face. Rake knew they weren't tattoos, but rather the glittering markings from the dragon who had bestowed the blessing of dragon language magic upon the sapere.

"Rake, what's going on?" the sapere asked, his tone frantic.

Rake reached out a hand toward the sapere and drew him closer to the woman, passing her off to him. "Sapere Falin, this is Princess Siva of Nungh Two, bride to Prince Henris. War has broken out at the palace. I must return."

"The ravagers? At the palace?" the sapere asked, taking a hold of Siva's arm, but it almost seemed as if she were the one giving support to the sapere rather than the other way around. "How is Sapere Hig?"

"I don't know his fate. I believe it is the ravagers, but it was hard to tell. If it is, they've gotten some technological help. Prince Henris asked me to take his bride out of danger, but I must go back. I will look for Sapere Hig." Rake took a step back away from them. "There's a chance the attackers saw me take her. If word comes the ravagers are headed this way, please continue her along the trail to safety. Henris' orders."

Rake opened his wings with a sturdy stretch and a solid

snap as he lifted into the air and began the flight back to the palace.

Now, if he could only leave his thoughts of this woman behind as well.

7

In the shrine's grassy courtyard, Siva felt the wind from the outstretched wings as the demon – Rake, for she now knew his name – began to rise. He gave her one last reassuring look, and Siva found her breath leaving her. Then, he glanced skyward and rose swiftly toward it as though he were a creature that belonged there. Siva found herself staring, her mouth open, as she watched him go.

The sapere at her side patted her hand and brought her back to this moment. "Let's take you inside and get you a warm cup of tea. You've had quite an ordeal. We must get you settled and feeling secure again."

She wasn't sure she would feel safe again until the winged demon came back. Though she would feel better if she had the nascent pistol at her side, her father had said that it was not appropriate for wearing beneath the wedding dress. She wondered, now that the palace had been destroyed and become a battleground, if she would be able to retrieve any of her belongings from within the tent where she had left most of her things. She figured everything she had left at the palace was now gone. It made her thankful that she hadn't packed more thoroughly for this trip. But she honestly hadn't known what a bride would need when she had packed. Additional weaponry was one thing she had never counted on needing when she'd been told that the world was peaceful.

Lies. She now knew those tales had been lies. Was the whole treaty her father had forged with this planet corrupted with omissions? It was no secret that Nungh Two had pollution and famine causing never-ending strife. People who were struggling to survive couldn't spare thought to solving problems. Was Myeller, at its heart, no different in being so embedded in conflict?

"This way, Princess Siva," Sapere Falin said, drawing her from her thoughts. They walked up the short marble steps, and Siva found this temple to be more beautiful than the palace.

The inside of the temple amazed her. It seemed to be a blend of antiquity and contemporary design. She could feel the air moving through the building from the soft whirl of fans. While this world didn't seem to have much technology, the saperes here were certainly more advanced than anything she'd seen at the palace.

There were columns of what looked like green marble ringed with gold that reached from floor to ceiling. White and black tiles covered the floors, and the walls were white and green. Everything looked smooth and glossy. Siva longed to walk over and touch it.

Much like the rest of the planet, the air here smelled fresh and clean, carrying with it the scent of the flowers from outside.

The sapere led her into a room containing green and gold sitting pillows and low tables, as well as larger chairs and coffee tables. And though she would've never imagined the two fitting well together, it did in this room. A low fire burned in the fireplace as if it had been burning since morning to chase away the early chill. The green marble hearth broke up the monotony of the black and white tile on the floor.

"Seat yourself however is most comfortable." Falin gestured around the room with his hand. "If you will just give me a moment, I will bring back some tea. I will also see if I can find some clothes for you to change into."

Bells began to toll in the distance. Then several more began to echo its chime.

The sapere once again touched her hand. "Do not fret, my child. The city itself is well fortified and prepared for invaders. The shrine is nearly impenetrable. You have nothing to worry about here. There is nothing that can harm you while you are here."

She didn't want to say so, but the sapere's words did not bring her relief. Usually when someone said that everything was okay, it was the quickest way to make sure that nothing went as planned. Besides, the palace had seemed fortified and long-standing, yet she'd glimpsed half of it reduced to rubble.

Falin left her and turned down the hallway. Siva waited for a moment, then went and popped her head out the door to look into the hallway. She couldn't believe how quiet the corridors were.

Turning, she returned to the room and began to examine

the tapestries on the wall. She first noted that they were old, showing ancient traditions which carried on to this day. This had become such a strange world, one that had some technology, but still held to doing things as they had been done in the past. Like Henris with his sword to fight an enemy which had crude versions of tanks.

Nothing had prepared her for this juxtaposition of their technology with their antiquated ways.

Her father, in trying to transition her to be a bride, had made her learn this planet's calendar system, highlights of its history, important ceremonies and holidays, and things that would be culturally significant. None of it had mentioned a current war. Her wedding, which had been a month in the planning since the treaty was signed, had ended in bloodlust and death. How was that for a great start?

She pulled her thoughts away from that, reminding herself that the ceremony hadn't been completed. It'd been nothing more than another trial run for her wedding. As soon as everything was settled, they would pick up where they had left off. Since the prince would come for her at the shrine, maybe they should immediately be wed in the garden. The grounds of the palace would not be fit for the ceremony now, and that would only cause delays.

So, the shrine garden it was.

She took to appreciating the tapestries and their age. Even at a slight distance, she could smell the dust caught in the old weaving. She reached out to touch the yarn, even though she knew it would be stiff beneath her fingers when she noticed the dates at the bottom. They weren't in alignment with this planet's calendar, not unless they changed their system at some point, as many planets did as science evolved.

But she wasn't certain that science had evolved even that far on this planet for them to realize that maybe their rotation calculation was different than actuality. They didn't even have space travel yet. It had been an emissary from her planet who came to this one to begin negotiations.

She hesitated, wondering what made her so nervous. She couldn't define it, only that something didn't feel right.

The next tapestry showed a swirling galaxy with a bright yellow sun at the center ,and was also dated strangely. She was familiar with all the planets in the system, at least the basics of it. Her position required that of her. Just because a planet hadn't achieved space travel didn't mean they didn't have an understanding of basic astronomy. While she couldn't claim complete knowledge of every era of every planet, she was pretty certain that these dates listed on the tapestries were not of any of the planets in the surrounding solar systems.

Siva chuckled to herself. Maybe she was just making wild assumptions that they were dates. Maybe they were really the name of the artists. But why would they have numerals? Unless, of course, Ipson had thirty-nine predecessors.

Confused by the tapestries, Siva moved over to the fireplace where several little carved statues rested on the gold-topped wooden mantel. Each beautiful figurine was different and had striking details. Some had great wings, many had claws or talons extending on their hands. All of them had extremely misshapen but darkly beautiful faces. Each one reminded her of the winged demon that had carried her here.

In the center was a dragon statue. The beast sat upright with long wings extended and tipped its head slightly to the side as though looking at one of the figurines which stood beside it.

Behind her, Sapere Falin cleared his throat as he entered the room and set a tray with a large round pot and two cups on the low table. "Do you take anything in your tea?"

"I don't know. What is this *tea* you speak of?" She came closer to see what was on the tray besides the larger dishes. There appeared to be two small and flatter bowls each with different substances inside. One was a yellow-brown liquid that didn't move like water, and the other looked like white crystals. A small pitcher beside the larger round pot appeared to have milk or cream in it.

Falin's eyebrows raised as his lips pulled down and elongated his face. "You've never had tea?"

"Never, not to my knowledge. Though I find the words on your planet are just slightly different than words on my planet, so it is possible we call it something else."

He flipped over both of the delicate looking cups and began to pour from the pot a dark colored liquid with a woody scent.

"I do apologize that we've not yet found clothes for you to change into," he said. "We don't normally keep extra clothing here, so this is a bit of an unusual situation we've found ourselves in."

"I'm fine," Siva said, knowing that her predicament of a tattered dress could be much worse. Even in such a state, at least she felt safe here.

Falin rose and offered her one of the cups. "This is one of our finest black teas. You may find it a little strong, and maybe a little bitter. We can sweeten it up with some sugar if you'd like. I have also brought honey. I actually prefer to have a little of both in mine." He pointed them out as he said their names.

Siva was glad he did, for honey and sugar were not foods she knew on her planet. She longed to try them individually just to see what they tasted like, and in the back of her thoughts she could hear her father yelling at her that she was a proper woman and not a child. She had to keep her fingers out of other people's food.

"There is also milk here. Sometimes I like to add a splash of that too." The way he said it held a certain amusement, and made her wonder if he had often been mocked for his choice of tea additives. Had people considered him a glutton? Were these delicacies and it was improper to take too much? Maybe there was something more, a cultural significance maybe, that she did not understand.

She accepted the cup from him and nodded her thanks. She smelled of the warm tea, and it seemed to awaken her senses.

He knelt down beside the table and began adding some of the honey and sugar to his cup as he'd said. With a shrug, he decided to add a splash of milk as well. Lastly, he stirred with a slender, long-handled spoon, which he clinked against the side before setting it upside-down on a spare plate. Cup raised, he swallowed and smiled warmly with his eyes closed, obviously savoring the taste.

Siva took a small sip of the tea and decided it wasn't bad, though it was a little bitter. She made a motion toward her cup. "Would you please fix my tea as you have done to yours?"

"Of course," he said cheerfully. "Set your cup down."

She placed her cup back down on the silver tray and watched as he added sugar, honey, and milk, then stirred it with the little spoon. Even in this action, there was a certain peaceful calm to the sapere as if he were performing a gentle ceremony. She would have to tell her father about this tea and maybe have some of it imported to her planet. Maybe this peace was something that her planet needed more than anything else.

Falin handed the cup back to her. "Try this. I can always add more if you'd like."

She took a sip of the sweetened tea and found it much more to her liking. She nodded. "This is very good. Thank you."

"Please have a seat and rest. You've had a harrowing experience, and your body probably needs a chance to relax from it."

"I feel too jittery to sit," she explained. Almost as if to back up her statement, she stepped over toward the fireplace mantle, holding the warming teacup in both hands. "These are beautiful. Can you give me some explanation? Are they like the man who brought me here?"

She knew that was really the question she wanted the answer to.

Even though she didn't sit, Falin did. He crossed his legs, putting one calf over his knee and, in the gap between the opening of his robes, she could see that he had loose cotton pants on underneath. "They are some of the honored novihomidraks from our liege dragon, who was their dragon mother."

"Novihomidraks?" She stared at the figurines on the

mantle. Such a strange name for such strange creatures. "I do not think I understand that word either."

He shifted in his chair, sitting more on one hip and bending an arm over the top of the chair so he could watch her as he sipped his tea. "Maybe I should start simpler then. Does your world have magic?"

Siva didn't understand what the relevance was. What did magic and novihomidraks have to do with each other? "No, I've heard of magic, but my world does not possess it."

Falin looked momentarily taken aback. "It was my understanding that you came from a planet not far outside our solar system. Is your world having great catastrophes?"

She returned to the coffee table and took a seat opposite the sapere. "Yes, I'm marrying the prince as part of an alliance to open trade between our two planets and bring in supplies my planet so desperately needs. The air is polluted and we cannot grow enough food to sustain ourselves. Millions are starving."

"Then your planet is one of the locked."

She shook her head. "I don't understand."

"Suddenly, explaining novihomidraks seems a simpler conversation. All I can say, my child, is that novihomidraks are humans that were incubated in a dragon egg and reborn with special powers in order to save worlds like yours. If you don't know the novihomidraks, then that means the Dragon Council has locked your world as a planet that is lost and beyond hope. The true danger comes if your planet has been sealed by the dragons themselves. That is a death sentence for any world. If the dragons cut you off completely from the Onesong, your world will slowly die. Since you can travel between solar systems and find planets that still access the

Onesong, such as this world, then your planet has not been sealed and there may still be hope."

Siva realized in this moment, with a sense of urgent anticipation touching her stomach, that a marriage and treaty was not what her world needed. What it needed was a novihomidrak.

8

From the sky, Rake saw the devastation of the palace and the signs of the ravagers having tunneled below it. With annoyance and disappointment, he'd followed the obvious trail zigzagging along the countryside and cutting under roadways. The tunnel had collapsed, leaving a snakelike pattern in the ground, and explained why the palace had suffered its fate since the ravagers had dug their way beneath it too.

This was a new technique for the ravagers, digging through the earth and coming from below, using equipment far more technologically advanced than he'd ever seen used by the ravagers before. They had to be getting mechanical help, which also meant someone had to be funding them, even helping them. It was a chilling thought to realize someone might hate Myeller's ruling family enough to do that.

Rake blinked his dragon lids down to sharpen his vision and quickly assess the whole situation below.

The west side of the palace had collapsed from the ravagers tunneling beneath it in their machines. The building walls lay crumpled, looking deflated, and several large stones rolled out over the grass.

Three machines had surfaced and, since only one had a drill on the front, it had been in the lead while the other two followed behind. Rake suspected they had been chained together like one machine, digging, grinding, and discarding the dirt in their wake while underground and only broke apart once they had surfaced.

These gunmetal grey machines looked like large oil barrels turned on their side, and pressed forward on huge metal wheels with spikes nearly the length of his wrist to his elbow which allowed the wheels to impact deeply into the ground for leverage. Each spike left a scar behind as it tore free from the earth. Once they cleared out of their self-made tunnel, slits opened on the sides for weapons ports and the attack began.

The palace guards tried to attack the slow-moving machines, but the ravagers seemed to have no fear of catching another quasi-tank in friendly fire just to destroy the humans banging on the sides. Those standing in the ravagers' way had little chance against the machines, and the would-be protectors either fled or died. Strange how the ravagers, who typically enjoyed hand-to-hand combat, were refusing to leave the safety of their digging apparatuses.

Several of the guardsmen had called off the direct attack in lieu of just trying to get survivors away from the scene. They joined the servants scouring through the debris looking for survivors, but became easy targets for ravagers who had turned their weapons to firing upon the would-be rescuers.

Additional help hadn't arrived on the scene. Rake would feel the other novihomidraks if they had. Whenever novihomidraks approached one another, each had a sensation of foreboding – an instinctual reaction bred into the novies so that others would know when one of their kind was near. Clearly, the other novihomidraks hadn't felt the disruption through the Humline, or something else required their presence more than this situation.

That made Rake's skin itch, almost as much as the thought of taking on the ravagers by himself. One question kept running through his mind: with the sudden increase in their technology, had the ravagers obtained novihomidrak-forged weapons too? That would be a real threat. But chances were slim unless the ravagers had taken their case to the Ch'bauldi dragons. Rake hoped that if that were the case, then the Dragon Council would step in. The last thing this galaxy needed was more clan wars between the dragons themselves over a situation some Ch'bauldi novihomidrak believed was a noble cause.

Rake took a sharp descent toward the ground. He needed to focus on battle. Later, he could worry about how this situation had come to be. No matter how fast his dive, he'd never reach the combat soon enough. So much damage had already been done.

The machines rolled over the dead and injured sprawled on the marble walkway and the lawn without a care. With a regretful pang, Rake saw a brown fur cap amid the grass a short distance away from an unrecognizable body. Reflecting now on the moment where he wished he'd disregarded the prince's orders and stayed to fight, he was glad he'd taken Princess Siva to safety. Prince Henris had made the correct call to assure that his bride got away.

Two-thirds of the royal family were dead.

Was the king one of them? Prince Henris?

Rake was too close to the ground now to see across the whole trashed landscape, even without his dragon lids down. He pulled out of his dive and swooped along the yard as he listened for the sounds of battle which would tell him where the king might be.

All he heard was the grinding of the machines' gears as they pressed onward and the pings of shots off stone. The ravagers didn't seem to be firing bullets, but rather round pellets, as evident from the noise of the ricochets. Still lethal if they struck someone from right – like in the eye – or later from an infected wound if they survived long enough for the shot to be removed.

There were no ravagers outside of the quasi-tanks, no one storming the palace either from flooding through the gates or out the tunnel made by the machines. Rake had issues believing that such a small number of ravagers had had this much success in their mission. It was even harder to believe that others weren't rushing in to begin the looting.

Which made Rake wonder if these were ravagers at all. He'd seen no faces, so it was hard to tell.

No matter who was in power on any planet, there always seemed to be opposing factions who wanted to bring the ruling party down. Myeller had the ravagers as the largest antagonists, but there were others. Still, the digging, rolling tanks were a crude clue that pointed to the ravagers. Who else would have the kind of connections to acquire modernized technology? Even someone helping the ravagers would have had difficulty without funding, yet people with money were typically targets of the ravagers. None of this made sense.

Until he knew for certain otherwise, he had to work on the assumption that these were the ravagers.

Rake landed on one of the cylindrical tanks rolling toward the castle. From up here, he couldn't be hit by the pellets being fired from barrels poking out of slits in the machine. He held on with one hand while trying to figure how to access the hatch, but no matter which direction he turned the mechanism, it didn't want to open. Chances were that it also locked from inside.

He wondered how long they could stand being in an oven.

Inhaling deeply, Rake blew out hot fire on the metal. It forced him back to the air, not because he would be injured by the flames, but his clothes would be. Besides, from above, he could make sure to toast all sides of the makeshift tank.

It didn't take long until it stopped rolling, the hatch popped open, and five men – if the ravagers could be called men – spilled out from inside. They screamed as they touched the heated metal. The soles of their shoes burned away as they jumped from the tank to the grass. Clothes caught on fire, forcing them to roll where they landed. The air filled with the scent of burning cloth and flesh.

Rake came down on them. Those that saw him swoop in had to believe he was an angel of death coming for their lives. They shrieked, making the others look. More screams. Several pleaded for their lives. But Rake wasn't here to take their lives. There were questions that needed answers, and only living men could talk. Instead, Rake's talons sliced along their legs or ankles, severing tendons and making it harder for any of them to easily flee the scene. Any that tried to drag themselves away would leave a rich trail of blood to follow.

With that tank taken out of commission, Rake started for the second. He still hadn't seen the prince or the king, and that made him worry.

Knowing how to take out the first tank, Rake didn't even bother landing on the second. He got in front of its rolling path and began to breathe fire at it. Round pellets fired out of the long barrels and struck him, but they didn't even sting. One even landed very close to his eye, but he didn't flinch. The tank slowed as he drew in air for his second breath. Before he could exhale, the occupants began bailing out. Rake ran after them, dispatching them on the grass as easily as he had the first.

Now, he needed to find the third tank he'd seen. From the destruction of the grass and the spread of rocks that had been pushed apart by something moving through the area, he suspected it had already made it back to the fallen palace. He started to run. The sounds of fighting which had been muted by the rubble now came to his ears.

There were still people trying to extricate survivors from the rubble. Rake didn't have time to stop for them now. He had to move on. Later, once the ravagers had been stopped, he'd be much more useful to the search. He took flight – swooping over the palace – and came down right behind the tank. Several of the king's men were trying to get inside or battle it from the sides.

"Get back," Rake shouted in a tone low and deep which would not brook any disobedience.

Soldiers jumped and rushed away from the machine. Shots were fired after them. Those in armor had little to worry about, but those without, who had been dressed for the wedding, fell. Their injuries would have to be determined later.

Rake heated the third machine until the ravagers tried to flee. He didn't even have to catch all of them himself this time. The armored soldiers detained a couple while Rake took down the remaining three before telling the guardsmen about the wounded ravagers on the other side of the rubble.

Then he found the commander. "Where's Prince Henris?" Rake asked.

The man pointed toward the castle. "This way, sir. I'll take you to him."

With the commander in the lead, Rake followed and surveyed the damage. The loss of the historic palace, or at least a good section of it if the rest remained structurally sound, was a tragedy for this world. The ravagers had dealt an echoing blow. But he'd leave that to Keystone to determine, as archeology and history had become a passion for the novihomidrak. Rake suspected there were reasons for Keystone's interest in the past, not that they were liable to make him heal. Keeping busy, however, would help Keystone's mental state.

Thinking of the other novihomidrak, he reached out with his senses, but felt none of the others nearby. That wasn't good. At least one of the novihomidraks should have broken away and come to see if Rake needed assistance. If they couldn't, then they were in more trouble than him.

A swirl of dread formed in his stomach. Rake sought the Humline for information and came away with nothing. His chills doubled. There should be some information there with the Humline.

The knight-in-command turned, having noticed Rake fall behind, and Rake doubled his steps to catch up.

The coppery stench of blood and dirt nearly knocked Rake backward while the human carried on as if he didn't notice it. At least not for a few more steps. But the commander carried on anyway. The reek hanging in the air spoke of death, but, without the sounds of battle, Rake didn't give in to his instincts to prepare for an enemy.

The odor grew stronger as they reached the side entrance to the kitchens. The door stood open. Rake saw a few of the staff standing back, looking scared.

The commander pushed his way through the door and moved aside for Rake.

Prince Henris stood over his father's prone body as he held the king's hand. The king had been rushed into the kitchens and set out on one of the tables. Vegetables, knives, a spoon, and a broken pitcher of milk lay scattered on the floor near one of the table ends as if someone had swept their arm over it to clear the surface. The king's physician stood solemnly near King Rolant's feet, while his tools and several blood-soaked towels rested on Rolant's chest.

"He just passed," Henris said.

Which meant Henris was now king, a title to be made official within short order. His marriage – would he postpone it now, or hurry to have it finalized as well? The disruptive emotions which went through Rake didn't even have time to settle before Henris asked, "Why aren't you with my bride? Is she safe?"

Rake bowed, hoping to hide the struggle going on in his mind. "She is with the saperes at the shrine in Plashia."

"Plashia?" he asked, looking down as if he didn't recognize

the town's name and had to think on it for a moment. "Very well. Why are you not still with her?"

Rake had known this question would come. He straightened his shoulders to stand up a little taller and raised his head. "With her safe, I thought it best to return and serve you as is my duty assigned by the Dragon Council."

For a moment, Henris' eyes narrowed and flickered with something akin to resentment. "You shouldn't have left her."

Rake didn't want to stand here and discuss this with someone he'd come to consider a friend, not when his friend's bride stirred Rake's emotions in a way that was unacceptable. "There is much to be done here. I suggest we get to it. Then, we can bring your bride home to you."

Rake wished he could mean his words.

9

Air drifted through the many windows of the shrine, making it feel fresh and cool in the room where Siva knelt at the small table on the floor. She tried to feel grateful for the delicate bone china cup in her hands, but the liquid was too sweet, and she didn't find it very refreshing.

Sapere Falin had drifted into telling stories of the shrine. He spoke of so many historical people that she lost track of who everyone was; his tales blurred together. She merely nodded her head every so often as if she was following along and hanging on his every word. Nothing could be further from the truth.

Siva glanced at the tea and set the cup aside. "I'm sorry. This is good, but may I ask if you have some water? I am very parched right now."

Falin jumped to his feet, looking appalled. "Yes, I'm sorry. I should have considered that you'd like water as well after the experience. I'll be right back."

The experience. Since when was a metal tank surfacing from where it had been digging underground to send wedding guests sprawling and running for their lives an experience? Maybe this kind of attack had become so common for these people that it all blurred together like one of the sapere's stories.

He returned shortly with a glass already filled with ice water and a pitcher for refills. He handed her the glass and set the pitcher down on the table.

She drank deeply. "Thank you," she said when she finally lowered it away from her lips. "I find myself in near constant thirst on your world even though my belly is full."

His head tilted so that he gave her a quizzical look as he sat down. "I'm afraid I don't understand."

Siva smiled lightly, feeling emotions trying to push tears into her eyes. "On Nungh Two, we've perfected water filtration to make sure that everyone has water. A stomach that is full of water doesn't feel nearly as hungry."

"Oh," Falin murmured.

"I'm sorry. I shouldn't have said anything." Siva felt guilty for her words. She should be glad, relieved that the circumstances her people knew now would soon come to an end. "How long do you think it will be before they have cleaned up those ravagers and Prince Henris will come?"

Falin still looked pale. "I don't know, Princess Siva. Come, let me invite you for a tour of our shrine and its grounds. That will help to pass the time."

She nodded as she stood. At least she'd be walking as he

told his stories. Plus, there would be interesting things to look at.

Falin asked her many questions about her home world as they walked through the shrine which was dedicated to the noble Nefterru dragons. She'd have to take his word for it as she'd never met a dragon, let alone a Nefterru dragon, to know if they were noble or not.

Afterward, he took her for a tour around the temple grounds.

"Do you have any dragons here now?" Siva asked.

"It's not often that a dragon likes to land on a planet inhabited by humans. Generally, the only time they do is when they are looking for a child to take as a novihomidrak.

"Do people just offer up their children willingly to the dragons?"

Falin gave her a gentle smile. "Not so much. Most people have no idea about the existence of dragons, and the dragons like to keep it that way. They usually hide out until the child is alone, then they snatch off with the child."

Siva found herself shaking with nerves. "Snatch off?"

"Yes, they take the child to be incubated."

"I'm sorry. How exactly does the child get inside of the dragon egg to be incubated?" Siva tried to imagine this happening to Rake and wondered what his experience had been like. How could a child not be scared of the large dragon standing before them?

Now the sapere chuckled. "Do you really want the details, or would you be better off not knowing them?"

She had come too far not to know now. Especially with her curiosity about Rake being so strong. "I want to know."

"They are swallowed."

"Swallowed?" Siva nearly choked on the word and couldn't imagine how Falin could say it without hesitation at all.

"Yes. The toddler is scooped up in the mouth and swallowed whole." Falin must have noticed her discomfort at that moment for he added, "It's not like the child is eaten. Dragons can eat, but they have no need to. In a female dragon, the toddler is sent down the throat but is diverted away from the stomach. It lands in a specially lined, nutrient-rich pouch where it is then incubated."

Thinking about it made it hard for Siva to breathe. There would be no food, no air, no light. "I think it would be terrifying. How long until the child is released? It comes out in a dragon egg?"

"Technically, it's not a dragon egg, but that's generally the easiest way to explain it to outsiders. True dragon eggs are for birthing of dragons. What happens to a child is more like what happens to sand inside an oyster, and therefore we call it a pearl."

"The toddler is like an irritant to the dragon and a shell forms around it? How can this not be seen as barbaric? I can't believe such a thing is allowed to continue. The horrors a child must endure. I'm surprised they don't have nightmares."

Falin folded his hands together, taking them inside the sleeves of his sapere robe as he nodded slowly. She could tell that he was unaccustomed to having this conversation with someone who had no knowledge of novihomidraks. Was it just that everyone who knew about novihomidraks automatically knew how they came into being? He lifted his head as he began to speak, "This is why a child must be young in order to be taken. Usually they are four years old or younger. Many novihomidraks do not remember being taken;

a few do possess early childhood memories, generally of their real parents, but they do not remember actually being taken by the dragon. There is a myth that if the novihomidrak remembers being taken by the dragon the novihomidrak will go crazy. I personally have talked to enough novies now to know that that is not always the case, though I'm sure some do go crazy."

"Novies?"

"It's short for novihomidraks. Novihomidrak is quite the mouthful, so many of us that have to deal with them on a regular basis have abbreviated their species."

Species? It wasn't that Rake was a demon, but he was a completely different species from her. Of course he was; he had wings. How did that not make him different than her? In feeling attraction toward him, what did that make her. She couldn't think on that. "How long are they in this pearl?"

"Generally, around a decade."

This just got harder for Siva to understand. "And when they come out, how are they birthed?"

The sapere gave a little chuckle and Siva didn't know if it was her ignorance or her morbid curiosity which amused him more. "They are born through the birth canal, like any other dragon egg. From that, the novihomidrak emerges. As the pearl dissolves, it absorbs into the novihomidrak's skin and gives them a sort of dragon armor."

"Since they begin as humans, the addition of dragon wings must happen while they are inside the pearl?"

"Not all novihomidraks end up acquiring wings. Those that do may only grow small wings that are not built for flight, or not at least for long-distance carrying weight. It takes a full set of dragon wings to be able to do that, which requires the novi to go through special ceremonies and some very painful rites."

"As if they haven't already endured enough," Siva muttered under her breath. "What other abilities do the novihomidraks have?"

"Oh, child, you could spend a lifetime studying the powers of the novihomidrak and still only begin to scratch the surface of their powers," he said and it nearly made her laugh. He wasn't that many more years older than her even though he kept calling her *child*.

He continued, "So many of them do things so innately that they may not even themselves realize that it is an ability. Others, like mimicking, are obviously powers the novihomidrak will realize that he has. But not all novies have the ability to mimic. The powers can range drastically between individuals even with the same dragon mother, so, to date, no biological reason has been found. Even when we find out that the dragon is carrying a child, we do not know what abilities it will have when it is born as a novihomidrak."

"The statues on the mantle all have strange faces. Why does that happen?"

"The changes in the facial structure come from the dragon teeth. There is no good or easy way to explain the metamorphosis they undergo when their dragon teeth appear other than to say it is very similar to their wings. We think it has something to do with – and this is a bad way to phrase it, mind you – advanced magic that they get while inside the pearl. Some novies have only small dragon teeth and sometimes not even a complete set. Others have full teeth but again only a partial set. It is very rare for a novi to have a complete set of full-length dragon teeth."

"Rake's face seemed normal," she said, feeling a blush hit her cheeks at remembering his handsome features. "Does he not have any dragon teeth then?"

"Now you understand why this is so difficult to explain. Rake has dragon teeth. All novies are born with them. It's only when the dragon teeth – what we call a dragon aspect – come down that the face undergoes that metamorphosis. You see, when dragon aspects are not strongly presented, they shrink down to a minuscule size. Fun fact though: if you touch the back of a novi with a full set of dragon wings when they are not protruded, you will feel only the slightest bump, almost as if they have a pebble beneath their skin, but that is all."

"Is that the same for the talons?" she asked.

"Yes. Some novies have talons and others have claws. Those with wings have talons. The rest, claws."

"Maybe things like this are based in the human gene structure."

"That may be." Falin stopped before the door and slid open the thin white paneling. "Here is your room while you are staying here with us. I hope you'll forgive the simple accommodations."

"Right now, simple is good."

"Please, take the rest of the day and relax and enjoy yourself here. You know where my office is, and any of the other saperes would be glad to help you if you need anything. Feel free to enjoy the gardens if you'd like."

Before the sapere could turn away, Siva stopped him. "I'm sorry. Please indulge one more question."

"Of course. As many as you like. What is it?"

"Do you have any more novihomidraks serving on this planet?"

"We currently have five on our planet, though they are spread out at all different locations."

She felt her stomach in a moment of worry. Five novihomidraks on the planet. That seemed like a high number, considering how rare they were supposed to be. Now that she knew their functions, was this planet in more dire condition than she had seen so far?

He must've seen the worry on her face because he began to laugh. "You need not worry. You are safe here. A member of the Dragon Council is here, currently on the other side of the planet, doing an inspection. She and her soulmate have requested two more novihomidraks to negotiate a couple different peace treaties in areas that have recently seen some unrest, but nothing major. Keystone was to be assisting the final details of the treaty between this world and yours, so you can see that this happens every day. But, as a shrine, we serve many novihomidraks traveling on their various missions."

She'd never heard the name Keystone before, but from the context she understood it to be another novihomidrak. "These ravagers? Will they not negotiate a peace treaty? Why is it that they attack?"

Falin looked uncomfortable once more. "The ravagers only know how to fight. It is all they have done for centuries. Because they used the same techniques of their ancestors, it was easy to squash their cells before they did any real damage. Then they began to adopt the technologies that were coming to our world from others." He hesitated. "That was when we had to call in additional novihomidraks."

"And how do these novihomidraks get their missions?"

"The dragons watch the Wells. When a world is in danger, they inform the nearest sapere. Those serving on the Dragon Council can also recommend missions that need to be completed as they see so much on the Humlines of various worlds."

"So essentially a mission has to come either from the Dragon Council or saperes like yourself, correct?"

"That's right."

Siva bowed her head toward the sapere. "Thank you, Sapere. I shall let you get back to attending your other business. Thank you for your courtesy."

He lifted up her hand and patted the back of it. "It has been a pleasure, Princess Siva."

He waited for a moment while she stepped inside her room, then he turned and she watched him leave down the hallway. She slid the door closed, figuring she would take a moment to familiarize herself with her room. She really hoped she wouldn't be here long, but she knew she had no control over her stay. How long would it be before she saw Prince Henris or her father? She knew she had to wait until everybody's fate could be assessed. Only then could she make another plan.

Her thoughts turned to the additional options she'd discovered, options that wouldn't require her to marry the prince. If a member of the Dragon Council was here on the planet, could Siva request an audience? Was it possible that she only had to ask for a novihomidrak to come and save her world?

10

Ravagers were called such because they acted like a plague upon the planet. They had thick, extended foreheads and massive jaws. The overall size of their heads made their bodies look prematurely small as if they were overgrown children. If they weren't so destructive, one might believe that they were merely stunted and immature versions of the adults they were to have become.

Worse, they were intelligent and wrathful.

Until recently, on this planet they had been nothing more than raging barbarians, but their numbers were held in small, often isolated clusters so it had been hard to tell how many there really were.

When they'd appeared on the surface of the palace grounds with their digging machines, Rake knew it had changed. The ravagers had come together and someone had brought technology to them.

Rake walked into the windowless room where one of the

ravagers sat chained to a chair. Whoever had wrangled the ravager in here had tied his arms up high behind his back and crossed one of his legs over the other knee. The chain then wrapped around his waist and went under the chair before looping tightly around his ankle, making it so only the toes on the ravager's one foot touched the ground. They had even used rope thrown over the exposed rafters to hold the chair upright and keep the ravager from tipping it over in an attempt to escape.

Closing the door behind him, Rake leaned against the wood and watched the ravager, who stared back at him through dark, narrowed eyes.

They remained in this state and silent for several minutes. Rake wanted the ravager to have a good long look at him as he did the same to the ravager. Every time Rake encountered one which had been captured alive for questioning, he discovered more about them. Keystone had told Rake that the ravagers were a race of their own, one discovered long ago by someone seeking to make them slaves. They'd been spread across the Onesong to other planets. Some called them cavemen, shruggers, wild ones, animals. Someone had brought them to this planet too only a few generations ago. At first, they'd been called men of the mountains, for that was where they'd been found, and had been hailed as a lost culture. Then the men of the mountains had become destructive beasts and taken on the name ravagers. Attempts to stop them met with cries of opposition screaming genocide. And while those were not wrong, the considerable intervening time filled with debates about how to handle the ravagers had given them time to multiply.

Rake had been sent here by the Dragon Council to find

out more about the ravagers and see if negotiations were possible. He'd long ago determined that relocation was the best option, but too much time had gone by and the ravagers' population had superseded containment.

The last report Rake had made to the Dragon Council had contained words like unable to rehabilitate, irrational, unwilling to negotiate, and a danger to all life on this planet. His next one would have to include escalating warfare with technology above their means; outside assistance indicates they are pawns in a larger plan. He would hate to write those words, but the Humline trembled with fear of where this battle was going. He felt tendrils of it spreading out into the Onesong. Someone wanted to make the ravagers a plague, not only on this world but throughout the universe.

He also couldn't help the thoughts that the attacks on this planet were merely an experiment. Drop the ravagers in a remote location and let their population spread naturally. Eventually they'd be discovered. Then watch how both the inhabitants of the planet and the ravagers interacted, because all across the Onesong humans were the same and would be identical in their reactions, and watch the fighting to see who wins. Experiments like this could be running all over with injections of different technologies to see what precisely gives the ravagers a winning edge.

But why would someone do this?

Someone under the influence of chaos energy.

His job was merely to report the events. Those on the Dragon Council had far more experience. He didn't need to find who was doing this and should leave it to those wiser than him, those further away from the situation. Rake had personally come to know too many people on this planet and had lost objectivity. He could tell that by the way his hands heated when he felt rage firing his blood. He wanted to wrap his fingers around the ravager's throat and watch the life drain from the misshapen body.

The ravager chuckled, having smelled the emotions coming off Rake.

Rake pushed away from the wall and took a calming breath while gazing at the floor. "Tell me what you find so funny," Rake said when he thought he could hold his voice steady.

The ravager replied by glancing at the wall where a picture of King Rolant hung.

"You believe the king is funny?" Rake asked.

The ravager resumed his stony gaze at Rake.

Rake moved closer. "Why did you attack the palace today? What was your intent?"

Still, no answer came.

"All right. We can do this the hard way." Rake squatted down in front of the ravager. The man had been staring at Rake the whole time, and now Rake had him right where he wanted him – looking him directly in the eyes. "Tell me everything you know about the attack. Don't leave out any details."

The ravager jerked, and Rake felt the familiar snap in the Humline which brought the two of them together.

"Rolant isn't who you think he is." The ravager swayed and saliva gathered in his mouth as he spoke.

"Doesn't matter. He's dead," Rake said.

He'd been hoping for a reaction from the ravager, but none came. Neither did any further details, so Rake prodded, "The attack. What was the ravagers' intentions?"

"Can't be everywhere."

The tremble he'd been sensing in the Humline seemed to quicken, doubling the vibration of it. As a novihomidrak, there was little that could make him afraid, but this sent fear tingling into the back of his neck.

"What does that mean?" Rake asked.

"Weak people follow weak king. Should follow someone strong. You are stronger than weak king. You make people follow you."

"Henris is now king."

"Not Henris." Drool started to flow over the ravager's lip and down his chin.

"What do you mean by can't be everywhere?"

"Novies can't be everywhere."

There was that wiggling sensation along his spine again. His hair started to rise. "Are the other novihomidraks in danger?"

The ravager rocked back against the chair and the ropes creaked as they continued to hold him upright. He wasn't trying to knock the chair over, only trying to break from Rake's mental restraint. "Everyone's in danger. We will destroy everyone. Make it unable to leave."

"What is this 'it' you refer to?"

"Rolant. Wrongful king."

"Rolant's dead. Do you understand that?"

"Novies dead."

There was so much spittle in the last two words the ravager spoke that Rake wasn't certain he'd heard him correctly.

With startling suddenness, Rake felt a different sensation go through the Humline, one that held a mixture of irritation and power. The novihomidraks weren't dead, at least not all of them. One approached quickly.

Rake turned toward the advancing sensation just as the door opened. A familiar novihomidrak with short dark brown hair entered. Ruckus wore a tan tunic with dark green trim around the collar. Holes for the laces ran halfway down his chest, and he hadn't bothered to tighten the laces. The tethers hung untied and the tan beads at the ends swung as he rushed into the room. A dark brown belt with a sheathed knife surrounded his waist atop the tunic. His hazel eyes were wide and quick to assess the situation.

"We need to go," Ruckus said with a broad wave of his hand. "Now."

Rake broke the hypnotic connection to the ravager and started to follow Ruckus from the room. He signaled to the guard to do with the ravager whatever he'd been ordered to do. There'd be no more information to be gathered from the prisoner, especially not now that Ruckus pulled him away.

"Where are we going?" Rake asked as he caught up.

"One of the negotiators is dead, Cal has been taken prisoner, and ravagers are attacking every major city."

"Holy –" Rake hadn't imagined such news. Even with all the ramifications that threatened to pile on top of him, his mind stopped at one thing. "Plashia?"

Ruckus' hazel eyes flashed at him. "We have word the shrine is destroyed."

Rake had been trying so hard not to think about her, but now her name sped into his mind. Siva.

Behind him, the ravager started to laugh, a sound that followed him down the hall until the guard's blade cut it short.

11

As soon as Sapere Falin wished her a good nap and she closed the door to her room, Siva knew that she wouldn't be able to sleep. Not armed with all the new knowledge she had now.

Glancing around the room, she took it in to assess her resources. There was a bed which looked very comfortable if she did actually have the time to sleep. After she made her plans, she would allow herself rest, but right now her people had to come first. These novihomidraks seemed like exactly what her world needed.

Along with the bed in the room, there was a small, wooden writing desk and chair. The side of the desk had drawers which went from small to large.

Knowing that she would have to make some plea to the Dragon Council member here on this world right now and that it would need to be organized, she began to search the desk drawers for pen and paper, grateful to find some immediately tucked inside the top right-hand drawer. Wondering what else she might have, she pulled out the other drawers. Most were empty, though their size indicated they were meant to hold clothes, which most guests probably brought with them.

She pulled the chair out and took a seat. She wished she thought to ask what novihomidraks usually received as compensation for completing a mission. She quickly scribbled a note to herself to ask that question the next time she saw Sapere Falin. She could write around that for now and fill in the blank later.

She had written down several beginning thoughts several lines below her question when a rapid knocking came to her door. It startled her and she jumped, making her drop her pen and send an odd scrawl all across the page. She sat there with her hand against her chest, feeling her heartbeat flutter beneath her palm, when another hurried knock sounded.

"I'm coming," she said, rising from the chair.

She hadn't even lifted herself all the way out when the door slid open with a bang. Sapere Falin stumbled into her room.

"We need to hurry and get out of here."

"I thought you said we were safe here," she said, feeling really scared suddenly.

"I know." There was a touch of guilt and sadness in his voice. "The ravagers have planned their attack well. Our novihomidraks have failed, and we have at least one dead."

She couldn't say what really scared her about that, considering that she'd only found out about the novihomidraks and their abilities, but to know that they had fallen brought forth many questions. How many? Were they all dead? Or was it just the negotiators? Was Rake dead? He had taken the artillery shells against his wings as if they were pebbles being thrown at him. What could possibly harm him? She had no idea if novihomidraks could even be killed.

Falin rushed forward and grabbed her hand. He didn't wait to see if she started moving on her own, but just started dragging her forward. "Come on," he insisted. "I've got to get you through the tunnels before the ravagers cave them in."

She had not a clue about what he spoke about but did sense his urgency. She ran with him, realizing that she hadn't even changed her clothes. She still wore the tattered wedding dress belonging to Henris' late mother. "I can fight. Do you have a pistol?"

"This is a place of sanctuary, my lady. We have no weapons here."

"Not even for novihomidraks?"

"Novihomidraks have their own weapons. They have no need for us to keep any at our shrines."

Feeling helpless as Falin dragged her along, she began to wonder if she'd ever feel like herself again. This was certainly not how she imagined herself to be, hiding and cowering away while others fought battles for her.

Falin led her through a door which had been covered by a false wall at the end of the hallway she'd been down during his tour. Inside the hidden room, two saperes stood near a hatchway in the floor. A green and gold rug had been rolled up and placed off to the side. Each sapere carried an unlit electric lantern in hand and one of them had a backpack over his shoulder that hadn't been zipped fully closed in his haste. They motioned for Falin and Siva to hurry.

Falin held onto Siva's hand while he helped her onto the

ladder which dropped into the tunnel below. Siva hurried down and took a quick assessment for danger. The way was lit for a short distance with two overhead fluorescent lights. The air was stale, but not entirely stagnant which meant there had to be ventilation along the way. There was a leftover odor of heat down here, much like the scent of a wildfire drifting hundreds of miles from its origin. The walls here were metal. Perhaps they had been welded, and that explained what Siva now smelled.

Falin entered behind her, followed shortly by the other two saperes. The last one lowered the trapdoor over their heads.

The long fluorescent light tubes in the tunnel didn't go on for long, ending at the spot where it turned to a tunnel of dirt. The two saperes holding the lanterns turned them on and one took the lead, the other following behind. The lanterns provided just barely enough light to see the gently sloping floor. Siva couldn't tell what powered the lanterns, but clearly they figured two was enough for wherever they were going.

The study of the maps Siva had done of this world hadn't prepared her for being below ground. If her direction sense was good, she figured they were heading out toward the forests which existed between Plashia and Reba.

They hadn't dropped too far down when Siva noticed the tunnel changing yet again. The walls and floor now looked as if they were made of glass. Hesitant reflections of herself stretched and shrank in the glossy sheen of the odd curves. She wasn't the only one. The images of the saperes did the same, but they seemed not to notice the wavy distortions moving along the walls with them. Siva wanted to reach out and touch the wall to see what it felt like.

Thunder shook the ground from above them. Everyone halted to stare up. As the rumbling increased, grit began to fall from the ceilings, first like a snowfall, then like a hailstorm.

Falin gripped onto Siva's hand. "Run!"

As they dashed forward, the sapere behind them grabbed Siva's other hand and began to haul her along. Siva felt like she was caught in a tidal wave, and the sensation mounted as the ceiling behind them began to collapse. She feared they wouldn't make it.

"Go, go, go!"

She wasn't sure which sapere shouted. Maybe all of them.

A clatter followed by the sound of something shattering and the sudden pitch toward darkness indicated one of their lanterns had been dropped and lost.

The stupid wedding dress kept catching around the legs of the sapere behind her. She wished she didn't have it on anymore.

The scent of freshly turned dirt filled the tunnel, reaching from behind to choke them and slow their progress. The single lantern remaining between them swayed and Siva felt a bit seasick without being out on the ocean. Their reflections mocked them with a macabre game of hide and seek in the light and shadows as they raced along.

More of the tunnel gave way, collapsing behind them. Also lost were the chunking and clanking sounds of machines working.

Siva didn't want to slow, but the saperes were. She couldn't believe they were all tiring at the same time.

The remaining lantern flickered and the sapere smacked

the side a couple of times to keep it working. It wasn't helping. The light seemed determined to go out.

Falin continued to pull Siva along. They only had the way forward, now that the way they'd left behind was collapsed. Would they be going along blindly as well?

Right as she was about to ask Falin where the tunnel ended, a door opened ahead of them and bright light shone into the darkness along with the portly silhouette of a man.

"I figured I'd be seeing you soon," the man said.

They arrived at the end wall and Siva realized that the bottom of this doorway stood at about her navel as if someone had misjudged the level they were at and missed the floor of the adjoining shrine. If it was a shrine beyond. At the moment, she couldn't be sure.

Falin sighed, his shoulders falling with the relief that went through him. "I'm glad you sent word when you did, Sapere Iphen. Rake has left us with Princess Siva in our charge."

The more she heard that honorary title, the more she hated it. She wasn't some delicate, royal creature who needed protection, yet that was exactly how others reacted to the title. This man was no exception.

"Princess Siva? This certainly is an honor to meet you, though the circumstances poor." Iphen extended his hand to help her up the short distance from the tunnels to the doorway as there was no staircase here.

Siva wasn't sure about accepting his help, but she knew better than to delay. She grasped his hand firmly in both of hers. While the portly man didn't seem capable of hauling her up, he did so easily. Once out of the tunnels and into the light, he looked her over while she blinked and tried to get her eyes to adjust quickly.

"Well, lookee here. I never expected anything to come out of that hole that was pretty as this. Gosh, look at them eyes. I always expected I'd only see drunk saperes come out of the tunnels." He gave her a wide, friendly grin, then went to help the saperes out while Siva moved to the side.

Iphen didn't look like the other saperes. He was dressed in denim jeans, a white button-up tunic, and brown suspenders to hold up his pants. The room where Siva stood in wait was a cellar with wooden slats for walls. Several tree roots were trying to make their way inside this makeshift room. Several kegs were stacked against one wall and shelves of preserved food on another.

Sapere Falin brushed himself off as he walked over to Siva. "Everything okay? You all right?"

She nodded.

Sapere Iphen's eyes widened. "I thought the ceremony was today. I take it the event didn't go as planned."

"The ravagers attacked during the ceremony. Rake got her out and brought her to us, thinking it would be safe."

Along with a disgusted sound, Iphen shook his head as he turned. "Hadn't expected them to be working with the ravagers. I still can't believe they turned. Do you think they are fully broken?" He started to lead the way along this bright hallway painted in a pale yellow.

Falin shrugged as he shook his head. "Can't say. But since they attacked Plashia, I'd say it doesn't look good."

Siva wanted to know who Sapere Iphen was referring to, but figured she might learn if she kept quiet and let the saperes forget that she was among them.

"Well, the ravagers took out half of my inn. You're lucky

they didn't decimate this part of my tavern. I waited just in case you'd be coming along. I'd almost given up hope."

Siva thought that saperes lived at the shrine, possibly more than one. But Iphen had spoken of a tavern and inn. And what had he meant by someone being broken? The more she listened, the less she seemed to understand.

"There was almost reason to give up hope," one of the saperes with them said. "The tunnels are gone, collapsed behind us."

Iphen glanced back with his eyes going wide. "Ravagers took out the novi forged tunnels?" He seemed thoroughly shocked by the idea.

"Yeah," the sapere said as though voicing the thought everyone else in the room had to be having, "meaning the novihomidrak-forged their digging blades. Who knows what else they have."

They stopped at the doorway, and the saperes huddled close. Siva remained near their ring, but tried to stay invisible.

"Do you think something like that would be enough for a dragon to come to our planet? Would we be locked away?" Iphen seemed highly nervous about this thought.

Falin shook his head. "At this point, I don't know what this all means. What I do know is that there is probably a dragon mother out there right now who is very pissed off. We can't do anything about that, but we should prepare for two things. First, we may have novihomidraks coming in with injuries. Second, they may want to get off-world. We should decide on how much resistance we want to push back with. They are still our only hope."

"Sorry. If a novihomidrak comes to me and says he wants off-world, I'm gonna let him," one of the other saperes said.

"The convergence is still open, isn't it?" the other asked.

"I don't know that either. We fled pretty fast and I have no idea of the fate of the shrine."

Iphen opened the door and started up a short staircase. "Then we best figure out a way to find out, but let me say that, if the ravagers hit it like they did my town, I'm not sure there's going to be much left."

At the top, he threw open a hatch and climbed out. As Siva and the saperes followed, she saw that the rest of the building, whatever it had once been, was nearly demolished and hanging in tatters. Debris had been cleared for Iphen to get to the hatch. Falin, Siva, and the other two saperes had been very lucky indeed. From the looks of it, Iphen had worked hard to get down to the hatch. If he hadn't, they would've been trapped in the tunnels below.

Worse still, as her gaze looked out over the rest of the area around them, every building looked flattened. Several were caved in places too as if they'd collapsed in upon themselves. Everywhere, there were people crying, looking for survivors – or doing both at the same time.

Siva quickly realized she and the saperes all owed their lives to Iphen's dedication to getting down to the tunnels.

12

Rake stood in silent anger at the edge of what had once been the shrine of the Nefterru dragons. He stared at the ground beneath his feet to keep from looking at the mass of fallen and splintered wood mixed with broken green marble.

At least he couldn't smell blood, not close by anyway. People from Plashia had gathered a short distance away from him, each hoping to find sanctuary at the shrine. Instead, they now wept quietly at its loss. A few spoke questions about the novihomidrak standing nearby, wondering how he could have let this happen, wondering if his mind was now broken. They feared to approach and ask how he was doing.

He wished he hadn't left Siva here. If someone had approached to inquire about his mental and physical state, that's what he would have told them. Henris had been right; Rake shouldn't have left her alone.

She wasn't alone. She'd had the saperes. They were

nowhere near as invulnerable as a novihomidrak was, but they did have certain skills, ones that even he didn't possess. Plus, they had the tunnels. Certainly, that was how the saperes had gotten Siva out safely.

Rake circled around the remains of the building where one of the ravagers tanks sat dead in the middle. They'd abandoned it after it broke down, leaving the top hatch open as they fled. Surely they expected an angry novihomidrak to swoop down on them every moment until they'd managed to get far enough away.

Once he got to the area where the gardens had once been, he stepped inside the perimeter. This was one of the moments when he wished novihomidraks were permitted the strength of the dragons in addition to their other abilities. It seemed like a fatal flaw that they were missing such a power. He'd love to be able to push the tank away from where it had made its final stop. Or flip it over and make it roll a few times. He could punch it without risking injury to himself, and he'd probably leave a dent, but he wasn't certain it would make him feel any better.

Instead, he lay down on his stomach and crawled beneath. The tight space barely accommodated him to raise his head, and he had to keep it turned sideways as he progressed. Clumps of overturned landscaping filled his nose with the rich scent of earth and plants. Roots clustered in tight webs. Disturbed worms were trying to slither to safety, one that wouldn't be found as he shoved boards and rocks aside. He pushed dirt with his hands, gliding the cool ground aside. It left a fine powder on his skin.

It took a moment, but he soon found the soft blue-white glow of the umbilical cord which linked this world to the

Onesong. He closed his eyes and rested his head against his arm while he whispered a silent gratitude. As highly unlikely as it seemed for the ravagers to be able to destroy the convergence, they'd surprised him much already today, and he didn't want this to be another.

Rake slid out from beneath the tank and dusted off his clothes as best as he could. He tried to spit the sensation of grit from his mouth. Feeling the zing of another novihomidrak approaching, he glanced up to see Ruckus jogging toward him.

Ruckus stopped and bent over, panting. "There's good news and there's bad news. Which do you want first?"

"The bad." Rake touched the erratic Humline, hoping that Ruckus wasn't about to tell him that Siva was dead. Anything else, no matter what it was, would be good news.

Ruckus held up his bleeding index finger. "The tunnels are collapsed. The shovels and blades on the tank that did it, novihomidrak-forged. I don't see how one alone could do this."

Well, that wasn't good news. Still, it didn't shock Rake too much. They'd already come to figure as much. What Rake did know was that they hadn't come through the Wells to this world. The saperes only had record of the novihomidraks he knew about, those who had come to help him. Which meant the novihomidrak they faced had come to this world from another on a spacecraft.

Or, he'd been here a very, very long time.

"Worst part about this," Ruckus said, "is that now I need a sapere to heal this."

"Aren't you glad you're not a Ch'bauldi novihomidrak?"

Rake said with a chuckle. "Can't go around seeing if things will cut you then."

"True that."

Rake felt his mood go serious once again. "The saperes got out of the tunnels though, right?"

"They did. There's no scent of blood or noises inside the tunnel that I could hear," Ruckus said.

"Which means we should go check on Sapere Iphen. He may know which direction Sapere Falin went."

"Why's it so important? What even makes you think he isn't with Iphen?"

Siva. The answer was so simple, yet he feared speaking her name aloud, as if it might hook in his heart and he'd never be rid of it. "After the attack at the palace, I brought Henris' bride to the shrine thinking that she'd be safe and out of harm's way."

"Ah," Ruckus said with a nod.

Rake wondered if Ruckus suspected more. If the other novihomidrak did, he didn't show it.

"I guess they would've kept moving," Ruckus finished. "They might not know that nowhere is safe at the moment. Still, I think we need to forget the human and go get Cal. Henris can find another bride."

In all of the Onesong, Rake knew he should agree with Ruckus. Novihomidraks were necessary, prized, and important compared to humans. It took a long time for a novi to be born. They couldn't risk Cal's life, especially knowing there was another novihomidrak on the planet who would see them dead. If the tanks had been equipped with novihomidrak-forged shovels and blades for digging, then they had to presume that weapons had also been made, and that didn't even include the two weapons a novihomidrak was gifted by their dragon mother at birth. Cal might already be dead. One novihomidrak already was. In every way, Ruckus was correct about them rescuing Cal first.

"Let's at least talk to Iphen first," Rake said. "We might find that catching up to Henris' bride and saving Cal aren't mutually exclusive."

Ruckus nodded, but there was a hint of begrudgement in it. "I'll go back to the ship and move it a little closer to Iphen's tavern. I don't want a long walk back. Not all of us were graced with wings, you know."

Rake considered extending his wings and flying for Iphen's tavern as he watched Ruckus start the hike back to the ship, but he decided against it. Someone may have offered to help Sapere Falin and his charge, and Rake would only have a clue about it were he to catch scent of it along the way. He took to jogging instead.

There were ravagers out on the streets who continued to make mayhem. People shrieked and ran away. A few gun blasts sounded throughout Plashia. But whenever a ravager spotted Rake, they ran to hide themselves. Rake hadn't yet figured out how the ravagers identified novihomidraks. Unless a novi had morphed to bring out his dragon abilities, be it teeth, claws, or wings, there was no external difference between novies and humans. The only thing that Rake could figure was that maybe novihomidraks had a little different smell or put off different pheromones which the ravagers could pick up on. Whatever the small – nearly imperceivable – difference was, ravagers clued in on it like no other species Rake had ever encountered.

The area of town where Rake expected to see Iphen's

tavern was heavily demolished. Iphen's tavern was gone, as was half of his inn. What remained had rooms exposed, and the building leaned precariously as if it would fall at any moment.

Here, there was the stench of blood along with the other odors that came with death. Nothing fetid yet, but bodies emptied of bowels and bladders would be found here.

Rake blinked down his dragon lids and looked around for signs of Iphen. There were so many people standing around in shock and grief, and they all looked so identical. If Sapere Iphen still lived, his livelihood was gone. At least temporarily if he decided to rebuild. Iphen was one of the people who took the title of sapere so they could be educated, but had never received a dragon blessing. It was a hard road to go, as many were shunned by those children who had received the breath of a dragon on their skin which imbued them with dragon magic, but those that pulled through had friends for life. They were not usually accepted into positions at the shrines, though it did happen. Instead, they often returned to run a family business or make their own, which in turn helped to support the saperes and shrines. Iphen was one of the men capable of the necessary long-term vision to see that pilgrims to the shrine, both on-world and off, would need food, drink, and a place to rest.

Except now he'd have the hard road of reclaiming that vision. Yet, Rake knew the saperes would rally for the citizens of Plashia to help with that. Aid would come to Iphen, just like he had donned the mantle of sapere to go out and help his city now if he had lived through the destruction.

Rake shook his head to focus. He had to carry on if Iphen wasn't here. Ruckus would be along shortly and could follow

Rake if he wished by following the Humline as well as Rake's scent.

He'd made it a couple blocks further, trying to find any sign of Iphen, the other saperes from the shrine, or Siva. Especially Siva.

That was when he saw a flash of white material in the hands of a ravager. With the dragon lids still down, he identified the remains of Siva's wedding dress.

13

ooden beams lay scattered about like a child's kicked toys. Boards and other pieces of wood which had once been furniture lay in broken splinters. Glass fragments covered the ground, mixed with splattered food. Dark spots indicated where liquid had been spilled and soaked in. Everything smelled like fire. The saperes tried to go first and clear a steady path for Siva, but she finally gave up pretending to let them help her and made her own way through the rubble.

Part of a two-story building remained, but a large section of wall was missing which exposed three of four of the rooms. That must be the inn which Iphen had spoken of. The hatch was close to the inn. If the ravagers had decided to bring down all of the building, then it would've been impossible for Iphen to reach the hatchway below without heavy machinery to shove the debris away.

As Siva stepped further out and began to look around

more than just the immediate vicinity, she couldn't believe that this was the town she had just flown over – in Rake's arms – not too long ago. Buildings were crushed and fires burned. People, mostly women and children, stood shellshocked and crying in the streets.

A hand came to her elbow as Falin drew her attention. "Princess, we need to get you to safety."

She turned toward Falin, intending on telling him that she wasn't a princess, and as she did so she saw the other saperes staring agape. Following their gazes, she let her gaze look to the distance and saw the saperes' shrine, or what remained of it. It was hard to assess the damage that had been done to the buildings, but some of it rested at a tilt where the underground tunnels had been collapsed by the ravagers.

"Princess, it's really not safe here. There might still be ravagers about. We should go," Falin said.

Siva met his gaze and saw tears gathered there. He knew his shrine was gone. He'd probably looked in that direction the moment they'd surfaced. And she knew that he needed to get moving to distract himself from the vengeful thoughts that wanted to invade. He needed something to do. Right now, it was his duty to keep the princess safe. As much as she knew she was not royalty, it motivated him. She nodded.

"I'm staying here," Iphen said. "I have people to help still and I'll see if I can keep the ravagers off your trail."

Falin seemed too tired to fight – or even give the weak smile – so he nodded. He began to lead, but Siva wondered if he even had an idea of anywhere to go. At the moment, nowhere seemed safe. The other two saperes followed, their heads down.

They hurried through the chewed-up streets and tried to

stick as close as they could to some of the war-torn buildings which remained standing. It seemed as if half the town stood out in the middle of the streets waiting to become targets. Of course, most of these people had probably gone running from their homes and places of business believing themselves to now be safe, especially since some of the structures were still in the process of collapsing and were just taking their time about it.

With the exception of the shrine, the heart of the city seemed in better condition than the outskirts. Some of the ravagers' machines had died before getting to the center. It looked as if they were just trying to make circles around and around through the streets, destroying everything in a spiral pattern, working their way to the temple. When they'd lost several of their tanks, the remaining ravagers had turned their destruction toward the shrine.

The machines left behind didn't look too different from the ones that had come out near the palace, except some had big blades on the front and other battering rams.

People ran about in the streets. Siva didn't even know what the enemy looked like, which made everyone a threat.

"They began looting," Falin said. Turning to the other saperes, he instructed, "Stay here with her. I'm going to see if there's anything left. We're going to need supplies."

Falin took off at a run, heading toward a building which appeared to have been sideswiped by a tank that barely made it much further after that. The sapere stepped over a rock wall, the toothy remains of the front edge of what appeared to be a mercantile. Surprisingly, part of the roof was still standing, and Falin vanished within the darkness of the shadow it cast.

Siva couldn't watch. What if Falin never came back?

She distracted herself by turning to the other saperes who had fled with her and Falin. "I'm sorry. I never got your names."

They both smiled and gave her embarrassed looks. "We're sorry, Princess Siva," one of them said. "I guess we figured Sapere Falin had told you already. I'm Sapere Andaris and this is Sapere Celain."

"It is a pleasure to meet you both, though I'm sure we all wish circumstances were different." Anything further she might have said vanished when a crying whimper drew her attention. Siva looked across the street and saw a woman with two children clinging to her legs while she wept over a body bent over backward on top of a pile of rocks. Blood ran over the blue surface of the stones. How terrible that the children should have to see their own father dead so gruesomely. For all the horror she'd seen on her own world this was like nothing she had ever encountered. Why had the novihomidraks, five champions, failed this world? Would they let hers, which wasn't in much better state, also fail?

She thought about her own father and wondered if he'd made it away alive, or if his body lay somewhere broken and battered. She remembered when her mother had passed away after a sudden illness and how her father had wept until she thought he would never stop. Until then, she had never seen a man cry.

She had a thought to go across the street and offer her condolences and see if there was anything she could do to help, but Sapere Andaris stepped in her path and shook his head. "We must all handle our own grief at the moment,

Princess. It is obviously the will of the Onesong that all this be done. We need to take care of ourselves, of you, right now."

"I'm not a princess. I'm in this damn wedding dress, and I have no way to defend myself. The least I can do is comfort someone in pain."

Andaris continued to block her way, but he also took ahold of her arm. "We have no idea if she's a ravager. She might not be on our side. They go to some pretty sick lengths to ensure aftermath damage too."

She hadn't contemplated that, but she had promised her father she would get away and remain alive no matter what. As she thought about it now, she wondered if telling her father to meet her under the oak tree if something were to happen was a strange premonition. Had she known in her gut that this was going to happen?

Right now, getting back to her father seemed to be her long-term mission. "What do you think we're going to do now? It doesn't seem as if there's anywhere safe from these ravagers."

Both saperes shook their heads. She had the thought that maybe they didn't know what to do either. Even with their world at war, this might be as new to them as it was to her. Except, they had most likely known the novihomidraks who had been lost. "Which of the novihomidraks was killed? Am I correct in hearing that one of them turned against the others?"

Andaris answered, though he was watching the mercantile for Falin's return. "The one we lost was the Dragon Council member negotiating treaties for us."

Siva remembered Falin saying that she and her soul mate

had requested assistance. "The husband of the Dragon Council member, is he all right?"

"Novihomidraks don't often marry because of what they do," Celain softly explained. "They were soul mates, which means they had a bond naturally stronger than any bond that could be spoken in words. He will never be the same again."

"I see." Siva believed this novihomidrak had been the one who was to oversee the final negotiations on the treaty with her planet. If he was devastated from personal loss, he'd be in no shape for the work to be done. Right now, it sounded like he'd be in no condition to serve as a novihomidrak.

"As for the novihomidrak helping the ravagers, we aren't sure who it is yet," Celain said.

Siva looked down in dismay at her dress. She really needed to do something about this. It certainly wasn't doing her any good right now. "What do they sell here at the store?"

"All sorts of things Food, clothing, household stuff."

At the word clothing, she was already moving forward and stepping over the wall.

"Sapere Falin told us to stay here," Celain said.

"If I stay in this dress any longer, it's going to get us all killed. Not only is it cumbersome, but it stands out. We need to be able to blend in." She glanced at them and shouted back, "If you guys were smart, you'd ditch your white robes as well."

Andaris and Celain exchanged looks, then followed her into the mercantile.

Sapere Falin looked up from where he was filling a knapsack with food cans from a toppled endcap spilled over the floor. "We've gotten really lucky."

Siva knew they didn't have time for congratulatory conversation. "Which way to the clothes?"

Sapere Falin pointed in a direction, and Siva moved off in the way that he pointed. She found the racks easily enough toward the back but the light was awfully dim – the electricity had been lost to the mercantile at some point, for even the shredded wires hanging near the demolished opening weren't sparking – and she couldn't read the sizes. She ended up holding clothes up to her to see if they were close to her size or not.

She pulled a pair of pants she thought might work up beneath the wedding dress. They hung a little loose, but not so loose they'd fall off her hips, and that would serve her well. The shirt, a neutral brown tee shirt, was much easier to find.

"Sapere Celain, could you come help me for a moment?" She knew she'd never be able to undo all the lacings and catches on this dress by herself. When he came over, she presented her back to him. "Do you have a knife to cut the lacings?"

"Excuse me? Do what?"

"Cut the lacings. Please don't tell me that you saperes do something stupid like take a vow of celibacy or something. Certainly you've seen what a woman looks like naked before?"

"Uh, no ... neither," he stammered.

"For the record, I am not naked under this dress, but I do need to get out of it."

Celain nodded and called for Andaris to help. It took a moment, but the saperes found a pair of scissors and, with Andaris' help, began to snip away the lacings right down the center. Andaris muttered something but she couldn't understand what he said.

"What did you say?" she asked sharply.

"I said it's a shame that your dress is ruined. None of this should've happened."

She almost regretted snapping at the sapere as he did sound genuinely sorry. "It's not your fault. No one could have predicted today's events to turn out like this."

His fingers worked quickly to undo the catches and, once released, Siva felt comforting relief of her chest expanding again. She felt so amazed that she hadn't passed out from lack of oxygen, especially when they'd been running through the tunnels.

Barely noticing that the saperes had turned away, she pulled the material from her shoulders and let the dress hit the floor. Then she dragged the tee shirt over her arms and head. For the first time in days, she was beginning to feel normal again. Now, if only she had her pistol at her side.

"Do they carry pistols here in the store?" she asked.

"Pistols?"

She was really beginning to wonder if any of the saperes had no clue about weapons whatsoever. "Guns?"

Andaris raised his shoulders. "I don't know."

With a shake of her head, Siva went off to search the area for pistols and ammunition. She didn't find pistols, but she did find a couple crossbows. Granted, the arrows she found to stick inside them were nonlethal, but, if she put some effort into it, she could change that. She took a couple packages of arrows and a quiver, then she tucked a multifunction knife into her pocket. Lastly, she grabbed a backpack from the shelf. With the crossbow hanging at her side, a knife in her pocket, and a plan, she felt a little bit better.

For a brief moment, she considered stuffing the remains of the wedding dress into the backpack as well to take back to

Henris, but she thought against it. The dress was ruined beyond repair, and he didn't need to see that. It would only break his heart.

Besides, now that she had seen the fighting on Henris' world, she knew that this planet was no more capable of helping hers. She needed a novihomidrak first.

Siva returned to the other saperes and began stuffing food items into the backpack.

Her planet needed supplies, like all these spilled all over the floor. A novihomidrak, though, to help deliver them and stop the fighting came first to her mind. Once things were settled, then they could start rebuilding.

In her mind, she saw Rake standing triumphantly by her side as they saved her world.

"What are you doing?" Celain asked, giving her a questioning look.

"Packing extra supplies."

"You really don't need to do that. We've got you covered."

"We are all in this together if we want to survive. I'm good to carry my own weight." She looked around at the others to see if they would broach an argument. None did. "Good. I'm glad that's settled. Now, what other supplies do we need?"

14

The sight of the white material in the ravager's nubby hands as he pressed it to his face and took the scent off of it along with the gritty stench of the destroyed town raised Rake's hackles. His face extended as his long dragon teeth slid out from in front of his normal teeth. Talons ripped from his fingertips and his wings stretched toward the sky.

The ravager took notice even at this distance. His eyes widened as he tossed down the cloth and began to lope away.

Rake began to run, letting the air catch beneath his wings and lift him easily off the ground. Flying straight, he snatched up the material, swerved to avoid hitting a wall, then glanced the cloth over. It was definitely Siva's wedding dress. Her scent was all over it. The laces were slashed down the back and slowly dropping away.

Pressing his wings, he redirected toward the running ravager who tried to make an escape. The air pumped beneath Rake's wings like a solid cushion. He didn't go too high, but enough so that he had a view of the vicinity in case this was a trap. Once there, he heard sounds of fighting which had been muffled by the few structurally sound buildings.

The purr of an engine approaching signaled that Ruckus had arrived and had adjusted course to match Rake. Ruckus had to fly his craft a bit higher and he held back some to give Rake room to maneuver.

Which he needed.

As he topped the mercantile, an arrow whizzed toward him. Rake did a wingover to avoid the wooden missile. His dragon vision instantly had sight of the one who'd fired it: a barbarianish-looking novihomidrak with long blond hair. He wore no shirt, and his leggings looked freshly made compared to the worn belt around his waist which held an iron sword. Rake's leg jerked as he felt the presence of the novihomidrak. The barbarian who had fired upon Rake was not only a ravager, but a novihomidrak as well.

In the debris-cluttered streets, a small group of humans fought against ravagers trying to overtake them. Among them, he saw Siva.

Before taking off running, the ravager novihomidrak fired another arrow at Rake, who tucked his wings in and dove beneath it. Rake somersaulted as he hit the ground and came up on his feet. Sprinting, he chased after the escaping barbarian.

Ruckus tried to stop the novihomidrak by bringing the ship down in front of him, but he changed his escape path. Ravagers were now trailing along behind.

Rake's wings caused drag and slowed him down. Since he didn't have enough distance to fly either, he pulled them away as he kept racing after the novihomidrak. If he could catch the barbarian, he sensed he could end a lot of their troubles now.

The Humline rang out, like a guitar string played under tension.

The barbarian novihomidrak turned and drew his sword.

Ruckus had swung the ship and now sat off to Rake's left.

Ravagers were coming up behind. A good chance they had novihomidrak-forged weapons in their hands.

Rake realized too late that he was trapped.

The barbarian screamed, held the sword over his head, and rushed for Rake.

Lowering himself and keeping his knees soft, Rake let the barbarian rush him. The need to finish this once and for all flowed through him like fire in his veins, yet there was a part of his mind that tried to rationalize a ravager novihomidrak as the leader. It didn't add up. The barbarian was a barbarian for a reason, and Rake doubted the man had the skillset needed to plan this massive of an attack, even being a novihomidrak with access to the Humline. If they wanted to find the mastermind behind this, the barbarian would need to be captured rather than killed.

The barbarian slashed downward with his sword. Rake pounced, coming up beneath the sword strike, and tackled the barbarian. A risky move, but one that worked. The barbarian staggered backward, toppled, and slammed hard into the ground. The sword fell onto Rake, but it didn't have enough force on the edge to even cut his clothes.

Rake scurried up over the barbarian, trying to gain control of the other novihomidrak's arms. The sword rolled off Rake and clattered onto the ground. Rake ignored it. But the barbarian realized regaining the sword might be his only chance and fought against Rake to grab it. His hand got by Rake.

Raising himself up, Rake made to punch the novihomidrak. He felt the barbarian's hand close around the sword's hilt. Rake swung.

He struck nothing as his fist swished the air. Then Rake dropped down on his arm against the ground.

The next moment, the ravagers were upon him. They hit and kicked. Something clubbed him against the back, then in the head.

Rake rose up with a roar. His wings extended, scattering those closest to him. They began to pummel at his wings and, for a moment, he worried about them being cut. He flapped, scaring back some of the ravagers. Those still near him continued to batter him with whatever they had in their hands. Those who were pushed away now began to toss rocks, cement stones, and debris at him. Other than being a nuisance, none of it could harm Rake.

A few of the ravagers broke off and scurried back toward Siva and the saperes who were making their way toward where Ruckus was trying to land the ship – trying because the ravagers were now attacking it too. The ship was more likely to take damage than a novihomidrak, and Ruckus wanted to keep it space-worthy without repairs, which became evident in his indecision to land. That had led to the ravagers noticing the humans trying to escape.

Rake knew he needed to put an end to this.

"Everyone stop," he said. His voice boomed much deeper than normal. Humans and ravagers alike halted. "Siva, saperes, continue to the ship and get aboard."

He knew his next move was risky, but he had to take it

anyway. "Ravagers, gather close." Rake gave them a moment to slink forward a few steps. When not attacking, ravagers moved very slowly, almost cautiously.

"One of you is brave enough to answer my questions. Which one of you is it?" He gave them a few seconds to glance around at each other. This let the seed be planted in each of their minds that he might be the one, as well as giving Siva and the saperes time to rush by.

Meanwhile, he tucked his wings away and let his face transform back to normal. He wanted to look less like a scary novihomidrak and more like a human, but he also didn't want to do it fast and let someone realize what he was doing and break the hypnotic spell. Especially if he'd already held one of these ravagers before.

Siva had slowed down, trailing further behind the saperes now as they started to hurry up the ramp and onto Ruckus' ship. Rake wished she would just go. His hold over a group such as these ravagers was tenuous at best. He couldn't afford the distraction.

Which was exactly what his mind wanted to give him as he watched her stride confidently forward in her tee shirt and loose pants while her eyes, those enchanting eyes, remained on him. All seemed to get lost for a moment as he imagined himself against her, his mouth exploring every inch of her face, even caressing over her eyelids and down along her cheek.

Yes, she needed to move much quicker. He could command it, but what it would do to his hold on the ravagers he wasn't certain. If he didn't have complete hold on each of them, then any who weren't fully under his enthrall might be able to break away and attack, which could spur others to fall out.

So he held quiet.

Until he felt it was time to speak to the ravagers again. "Who will talk with me?"

"Rake, look out," Siva hollered.

The arrow struck his back just above his shoulder blade and sunk in. With a howl of rage and pain, Rake spun around to see the barbarian setting another arrow against the bow string.

She was running toward him.

Henris' bride.

Rake's concentration snapped back to his surroundings as the ravagers around him closed in and resumed their attacks. She had to get aboard that ship where she was safer than being out here. Didn't she realize that? Why was she coming this way?

The flurry of thoughts didn't help Rake's rising panic that he couldn't do much with her so close. He couldn't protect her against the barbarian novihomidrak whose arrows would be deadly to both of them unless he spread his wings and faced the barbarian, allowing any arrows to strike him. Not only would that be lethal to him, but it would leave the ravagers around him, especially those who would then be behind him, able to attack her.

But with his hypnosis broken on the others, he had nothing left to lose. "Siva, go get on the ship." He packed as much power into his low tones as he could muster. Much of it got lost between the grunts of pain as thumping blows landed against his face and back. An extremely successful whack shattered the arrow, driving splinters, head, and shaft further into the muscles. Diamonds of light glimmered around the edges of his vision. He nearly passed out.

Blood slicked his back and shirt. Air coming through the custom slit for his wings made the moisture feel cold.

Another arrow dropped early and caught him in the leg. His knees buckled. The only reason he fell was another well-placed blow by a ravager fell across his lower back.

"Rake, no!" he heard Siva scream.

Not surprisingly, his deep command hadn't worked on her. Every step brought her closer to danger.

He had no choice.

Rake spread his wings. The broken arrow twisted, further embedding itself. He'd successfully split the surrounding ravagers in two. But the greatest danger was those behind him and the barbarian. Standing, he shook his wings as he started for Siva.

An arrow struck him in the middle of the back, but the trembling of his wings had probably knocked the arrow from its path. Or the tip might have been partially dulled. Whatever the cause, it didn't penetrate and fell with a rickety sound behind him. Death might not be for him today.

Or he might be counting his luck too soon.

Then Siva was in his arms. He wanted to pick her up and carry her. It wasn't possible. But there she was in his arms, and he closed his wings around her, surrounding her like a fortress. She murmured his name against him and held him close while he protected her as the blows came.

He had to get them back to the ship.

She was crying. Why in the name of the Onesong was she in tears?

Rake tried to tell Siva to walk backward. It was the only

way. The words wouldn't come. He wanted to stay here and protect her from the world.

It was only a matter of time before the barbarian fired another arrow for a fatal strike.

A novihomidrak roared, and Rake felt something go by him. Then, a familiar sound echoed an accompanying warning from the Onesong.

"Get down," he said to Siva as he dragged her down to the ground. "Tuck in really tightly." He put his head over hers and circled his arm around his head as another layer of protection.

Bullets started to fly, pinging out at rapid fire from the barrels on the spaceship. When not on a planet, they were useless, but they worked in times like this. Not being novihomidraks, the ammunition struck the ravagers. Rake heard them screaming as they went down. A few collapsed against them while the slugs ricochetted off him. He held as still as he could.

He expected to have Siva fight in terror to get free or at least to scream, but she didn't even tremble. She stayed down perfectly as he had told her.

The novihomidraks fought for a moment on the other side of them. Those noises were the first to quiet. It didn't last long. Suddenly, there were more novihomidraks in the vicinity. Other than shielding Siva, the only reason Rake didn't look up was because he hoped these novies were on their side.

More screams came from around them as well as the call of ravagers to retreat. Then he became aware of panting as novihomidraks circled around Rake.

"You're good to come out now," Ruckus said with a pat on

Rake's uninjured shoulder.

Rake stood and unfolded his wings from around Siva. At first, she looked up, blinking as she took in the small group huddled around them, then she straightened. "It's over?"

"For the moment," Rake said.

A novihomidrak with long blond hair came over and held out his hand toward Rake. "Why didn't you invite us to the party sooner?" Keystone said with a grin.

Rake reached around Siva and embraced Keystone's forearm as he felt the novihomidrak grip his arm. "I heard you had your own going on."

"Yeah," Keystone said, growing somber now. He looked back over toward the female novihomidrak who had moved slightly away from the others. "Don't ask. It's been hard."

Rake nodded slowly. "For both of you, I'd imagine."

Even though it caused him pain, Rake put his arm around Siva just to hold her closer to him for a moment. "Keystone, Ruckus, Maylene, this is King Henris' bride, Princess Siva Candemir of Nungh Two."

"King?" she asked, twisting to look up at Rake.

At nearly the same time, Keystone raised one of his perfectly shaped eyebrows and asked, "Henris' bride?"

Rake dropped his arm from around Siva, though it caused pain to flare through him. Ruckus came around and lifted the custom slit in Rake's shirt. It drew a hiss of pain from Rake.

"Good thing we're not Ch'bauldi novies," Ruckus muttered. "Let's get you in to see a sapere."

15

The ship – a spaceship, Siva had been told – wasn't very large, especially compared to one Siva and her family had come to this planet on. As she climbed aboard, and one of the saperes grabbed her arm to usher her the rest of the way inside, she saw that there were few walls. Nothing separated the front of the craft where the pilot would sit from the main bay. Here, there were bench-style seats with harnesses hanging on the walls. Apparently, passengers were meant to sit down, strap in, and shut up.

Further back were two closed doors. Siva seemed to get pushed that way as everyone else climbed aboard.

"Take him to the quarters," Ruckus shouted as the novihomidraks hauled Rake on board.

Just a moment ago, Rake had seemed fine. Now he staggered and looked pale. His eyes rolled around.

Maylene pushed to the front and grabbed Sapere Falin.

"Novihomidrak arrow in his shoulder. From the looks of him, I'd say it was poisoned as well."

"Poison?" Siva asked as the two men dragged Rake toward the back of the ship, nudging her aside as they came.

Falin nodded. He took Ruckus' position as they reached the left side door which Ruckus had just opened. "Go fly us out of here."

Ruckus hurried toward the front. "Where are we going?"

"Considering Rake's condition," Falin grunted under Rake's weight, "it'd be nice to find Sapere Hig. He's got far more experience with this."

Pausing in his steps, Ruckus stopped to look at Siva. "Let's not forget we have a civilian aboard." Then he continued until he reached the pilot's chair and dropped down into it.

Siva started to follow where they were taking Rake. She saw that it was a cabin with an unmade bed and the stale odor of sleep. No wonder the door had been closed.

The female novihomidrak reached out for Siva's wrist. "Let's go sit and strap ourselves in. Knowing Ruckus, this won't be a gentle flight even if no one's firing on us."

Siva felt herself being drawn toward the bench seats. She gave a weak protest to follow the others. "But Rake ..."

"Is in the saperes' hands now. That is where he needs to be. There's nothing you or I can do to help him. We should go sit." This last sentence came out a bit lower and deeper than the rest and Siva felt compelled by the words to move with Maylene.

The ship lurched as it began to rise into the air, bumping Siva into the seat. She'd taken to the left side so she could look through the door. They had Rake face down on the bed now. The blond novihomidrak, Keystone, sliced Rake's shirt off with just his claws. While the action seemed easy, Siva shivered at the sound of the rending cloth.

"I suggest you buckle in," Maylene said. She reached over and grabbed one of the harnesses to jangle beside Siva.

"Right," Siva muttered, starting the motions of figuring out how to get the harness buckled up around her. It wouldn't have been too difficult if her attention hadn't kept wandering back to what they were doing around Rake. "What's happening? I thought novihomidraks couldn't be hurt. Wait, you're the one whose mate died. They killed him too."

As soon as the words were out of her mouth, she slapped her hands over her face. "I'm sorry," she said after a moment, long enough for her to see tears welling up in Maylene's eyes. "I didn't mean it so callously. I just don't understand what's happening. Are you up to explaining? If you aren't, I understand."

Maylene's face softened, and a smile emerged. "Thank you for your consideration. It is appreciated. I will do my best to explain, but I hope you understand if I am overcome with emotions as we speak. The ravagers are being led by a novihomidrak, Thralic. It was one of his arrows that struck Rake. Chances are good that he will be fine if the saperes can get the arrow out and heal it up."

"But you said poison."

"Yes, that is how my mate died. We hadn't yet realized there was a novi on the ravagers' side. We sat down with the ravagers one day expecting to meet with their leader. Thralic teleported in, stabbed Talon. Fortunately, there was a sapere from the local shrine there, having joined us to act as a scribe and record the peace talks, who was able to heal Talon's wounds. But he didn't get better."

Siva glanced back over her shoulder toward Rake, then faced Maylene once more. Feeling Maylene's need for comfort, Siva took the novihomidrak's hands. "What happened?"

"There was poison on the blade, and it had been sealed inside Talon."

"It couldn't be countered? There wasn't an antidote?"

"Not in time, not without knowing what type of poison it was." Maylene squeezed Siva's hands. "But this time the saperes know about it and can check. They will be able to pull it out of his blood."

A loud moan came from the room, and Siva whipped around at the sound. Her fingers pulled free from Maylene's.

"How's Henris? Have you had any word?"

"Who?" Siva had turned halfway back to Maylene before she understood Maylene's questions. "Um, no. I haven't heard."

"But you're ready to go back and marry him, right? I imagine it'll get done quickly this time."

"Um …" She hated saying that, but it seemed like all she was capable of. "I don't know. Right now, I think we should focus on getting through this. There's been a lot of devastation and destruction. I think we should just … um … wait."

Now came a pity smile from Maylene. "I know we novihomidraks seem like fascinating creatures. At first, exotic and new. It seems like it would be a really great thing, almost like getting to know a god. But mortals just aren't ready to deal with the truth of what we are."

"I'm sorry. I don't understand what you're getting at."

"Rake. You've fallen for Rake," Maylene said.

Have not, Siva wanted to protest. But Maylene continued, "You must know you've fallen for him because he's protected you. It's perfectly natural to have those feelings for someone who saves your life. We novihomidraks have to deal with it all the time."

"Wait, what? No." Siva tried to inject some indignation into her voice, but her true feelings were right there, telling her that Maylene was correct.

"Try not to look at him for the rest of the flight then."

Siva turned back toward Maylene and crossed her arms. All right then, if that was what she needed to do, then she would do it.

The saperes broke into a melodic chant. Beneath their tones was another long moan from Rake.

She couldn't help it. She looked. Her hands went to the buckles.

Maylene placed a hand on Siva's knee. "When a novi is physically injured, it takes a sapere to heal them. Very few things can harm a novi, but, when something does, a sapere blessed with dragon magic has to chant over the novi to heal the wound." Maylene's grip tightened a fraction as she grew somber, almost as if it were by subconscious connection. "When a novi is emotionally injured, nothing heals that. We feel death through the whole Onesong, especially when it's someone close to us. This is why novies rarely take human mates."

Her speech was a warning.

"Should I not be concerned for him then?" Siva asked.

"Quite frankly, it is unnecessary. As soon as the saperes finish their blessings over him, he will be restored to new. If the pain is bad enough, he may be unconscious for a while.

But when he wakes he will be completely healed and without a scar." Maylene removed her hand from Siva's knee. "I suggest you keep your feelings toward your intended groom. That will serve you much better."

Siva placed her hands on her thighs and forced her harsh thoughts away. The novihomidrak had lost her mate. If what Maylene said was true, then she felt that loss throughout the Onesong, whatever that meant. Add to that the fact that her peace talks had failed. Commanders didn't like losing. From the first words she'd spoken to Siva, the woman was clearly a capable diplomat. She'd suffered a double blow. Siva understood how one could get cruel under such conditions. But Siva also realized she had an opportunity here, and she didn't want to waste it.

"I am truly sorry about your loss, and on the day in which I was to be married," Siva said. "But I wasn't going to marry for love. Prince Henris and I, as I'm sure you know, were arranged to seal a bargain between our two planets. Now, I am not certain that Myeller is in any better condition than Nungh Two is to help itself. We, my planet, need something else, a different plan. We need a novihomidrak."

Maylene closed her eyes and breathed deeply. For a moment, Siva wondered if the member of the Dragon Council had fallen asleep. It might have been her first chance at peace in days. But then Maylene spoke without opening her eyes. "Your planet is polluted and your people have nearly killed the bubble in which they live, poisoning air, land, and water. It became a pit of chaos long ago and has been spun off from the Onesong. The only reason you might have a chance is that you are within space travel distance of another inhabitable world. I suggest you get the people off your planet and let it die. You don't need a novihomidrak for that."

"But—"

Maylene's eyes opened wide as she turned to glare at Siva. "You don't get it, do you? Your planet has been removed from the Onesong. For all practical purposes, it's dead. Consider yourself fortunate that your people can get off-world to relocate. Many civilizations aren't lucky enough to be able to evacuate. I suggest you explain this to your people so they don't destroy their next home as they did their first."

Siva wished Maylene had remained in diplomatic mode, as Siva flushed between embarrassment and heated anger. It helped to remind herself that Maylene had just suffered a deep loss, one that Siva couldn't imagine. After all, even though Siva found herself attracted to Rake, it might just be that: an initial attraction. She hadn't spent any great deal of time with Rake. Maylene had lost someone she'd spent significant time with, years and maybe even lifetimes.

"I understand and agree with you, but I don't want my people coming to this world either. This planet has a large population already, plus they shouldn't be thrown into another war. We need peace and time to heal, a period to reflect so that we can do differently. Can the novihomidraks and the Dragon Council help us find a new place in this Onesong, a planet where we can start over, and help to guide us along?"

Maylene softened. "Even if we can bring Myeller to peace, you are right that it has population enough. It is also at a time when it needs guidance to prevent a future like your planet is currently seeing. I will recommend that your population be evacuated to Myeller and moved. It will not be easy, and I suggest you offer your people a choice because they will endure hardships – and survival is not guaranteed – but we will do what we can."

Siva nodded as the warm feeling of gratitude brightened in her chest. She had saved her people, or at least anyone who wished to start over, and she'd done it without the promise of marriage and involving them in the war with the ravagers.

16

Rake climbed back to consciousness by following the sounds of voices in the room. When their words started to make sense to him, he found he could blink his eyes.

Ruckus' room on his ship came into view with the grey walls and the scent of the novihomidrak. There was the coppery reek of blood too. Rake nearly retched at knowing it was his.

Two people came into view, Saperes Falin and Celain. Falin sat in a chair by Ruckus' table, while Celain busily studied the portrait of a nude woman hanging on the wall.

"Ah, there you are," Sapere Falin said.

"Siva?" he asked, her name coming out mangled due to his pasty tongue sticking to the roof of his mouth.

Sapere Celain handed Rake a cup of water and held his head up while he drank.

Falin had understood enough that he answered, "She's fine, completely unhurt. We've also picked up Sapere Hig."

Rake drank his fill, then pushed Celain's arm away from him as he tried to sit up. He couldn't hear the engines, which meant they had to be landed. Being in one spot meant they were a stationary target for the ravagers. "See her."

"I think she's sleeping right now," Celain said with a glance back over his shoulder toward the door.

Falin placed a hand on Rake's shoulder. "You're not stable enough to walk just yet. The arrow tip was poisoned, and it's taken a lot of you, as well as Sapere Hig, to heal you. He's sleeping now too. You'd fumble your way about and wake both of them up.

Rake saw the reasoning in that and lay back down. "But she's okay?"

"Completely," Falin said as he straightened the blankets up over Rake.

He wished the sapere wouldn't. The sheets were scented like Ruckus and unsettled him. But Rake knew the saperes couldn't smell it as well as Rake could. Ruckus wasn't a bad novihomidrak, but, if Rake had his preference, he wished they would've taken him into Cal's room on the ship instead. Ruckus and Cal, short for Callous, often worked together. Not surprising since they had the same dragon mother, and it made it easier for the two of them to cohabitate without the awkward sensations novies usually felt around one another.

"You fired on us," Rake said, trying to keep a hint of humor in his voice.

"Yes," Falin said with an equal amount of amusement, "but I knew that they weren't novihomidrak-forged bullets.

Besides, I had to do something. You were surrounded by ravagers."

Rake recalled his wings wrapped around Siva, protecting her as the sapere fired the guns to get the ravagers off of them. She had remained perfectly calm. Or had she been frozen to the spot?

"You said that Siva is okay, but what about her mental state?" Rake asked. "She's not in shock or traumatized by that experience, is she?"

"She's fine, Rake."

He couldn't help the feeling that the saperes weren't telling him something. "Did she try to see me?"

"Rake …" Celain started, but he turned away.

"What?" Rake glanced at Falin. "What is it you're not saying?"

"Maylene told us there's a protective bond forming between you two." Falin looked uncomfortable as he said this. "Once Princess Siva learned you were out of danger and going to be okay, she started to insist that she be here when you woke up. Maylene put her to sleep so we'd be here instead."

"She is Henris' bride, and I was charged with keeping her safe," Rake said. "It's not surprising that there is a slight protective bond between us."

"That's just it," Celain said in his soft tones. "Princess Siva and Maylene worked out an arrangement to help Siva's planet. Siva no longer plans to marry King Henris."

Rake felt his heart leap at the news, and he did his best to hide the reaction from showing on the outside.

But Falin must have noticed something, a twinkle in Rake's eye or the flush of his skin, for he said, "How do you believe King Henris is going to take the news, especially considering that Siva's plan still involves bringing her people to Myeller to get them to safety? Not to mention that, after this highly publicized wedding, if people believe he's been jilted, it won't help to stabilize his rule."

They had a point, and Henris could easily stand in opposition to Siva's newly formulated plans.

"So, you see, Rake, that it would be even worse for his citizens to believe that she left King Henris for you, a champion helping to rescue them from the ravagers. You would be seen as the hero, not him, and they would never accept him as their ruler."

Rake shoved the blankets away and sat up. Swinging his legs over the side of the bed, he made to stand. "She's a mere human, and I am charged with protecting her. If she bonds with me, I cannot control that any more than I can dictate the rest of her emotions. But do not overlay what you see in her reactions onto me."

He was going to add that he could control his energy, but he evidently couldn't, since he couldn't hold the anger from his voice right now.

All he knew was that he had to see her.

"Rake, you should lie back down, rest," Falin said.

"I'm healed, right?" Rake asked. "You know as well as I that once a novihomidrak's injuries are healed, we are able to return to our mission. We don't have need for rest."

"Yes, if you had just taken an arrow. But you were also poisoned. For that, you'll need some time to recover."

Rake stood, trying not to show that he was testing his feet beneath him. But he was. "Callous could be out there somewhere, bleeding, dying. I'm sure Ruckus is trying to come up with a plan now, and I should be there for that. Besides, the sooner I get moving, the faster my body can flush the remaining traces of the poison from me. Another fact you both know well."

Rake turned and walked out the door. Behind him, he heard the saperes step closer to each other. "I hate it when novihomidraks tell us how to do our job," Celain whispered.

"Anytime a novi gives someone a dressing-down, it's a sign they are feeling better. I've never known one to take being injured lightly. It's stomps on their emotions and pride. Rake will be fine," Falin said.

In the cargo and passenger area of the ship, saperes Andaris and Hig were stretched out on the opposing bench seats trying to get some sleep. Andaris was lightly snoring, meaning he was out. But Hig just lay still, and his heart beat fast, showing that he had yet to tip over the edge and into his dreams. Rake thought about touching Hig's shoulder and telling the sapere a quick thank you, but Hig didn't need disturbing. He needed sleep for the days that would come.

"Sleep well," Rake said, his voice in that deep, commanding tone. By the time he made it to the open door of the ship, he heard Hig snoring too.

The dark forest and the scent of burning pine awaited Rake as he stepped out into the night air. A short distance away, a fire burned low and Rake made out the silhouettes of several novihomidraks sitting around it. They each turned as they sensed his presence.

"Rake, join us," Keystone offered.

Coming down the stairs, Rake glanced around for Siva. He found her prone form sleeping on a blanket a short distance from the fire.

"Yeah, don't worry. We're keeping good watch on her," Ruckus said.

Rake nodded his thanks, not trusting himself to actually say anything which might betray a hint of emotion. He knew they were all watching him now to see if he was bonding with this human. The saperes were right that she needed to remain Henris' bride, whether she realized it yet or not.

Keystone held a folding pocketknife in one hand and a piece of wood in the other. He never looked away from his whittling as he slid over on the fallen log.

"Anything from Cal on the Humline?" Rake asked right before he sat down next to Keystone.

Maylene shook her head and gazed down into the fire. But Ruckus said, "We know he's alive."

It might not be much, but it was a start.

"Rake, tell us about the novihomidrak who attacked you," Keystone said. "It might give us insight into what's going on with Cal."

Rake expected this question from the moment he'd been struck with the arrow. There were many of his own he wanted answers to as well. But he had to start with the one that had been raging around in his mind since the start. "I keep trying to figure out why a dragon would take a ravager to incubate into a novi. They aren't human. It doesn't make sense. Maylene, have you heard of anything like this? Is anyone getting information from the Humline?"

"He may have been an experiment," Maylene said. It wasn't unheard of for dragons to occasionally attempt to create a bigger, stronger novi, especially if the dragon hoarded emotions like pride, strength, or fear.

"It failed. Why wasn't he institutionalized?"

"Rake – " She shook her head slowly back and forth as she rolled her eyes. "The Dragon Council is far from perfect. Now that we know about his existence, we can—"

Her words were interrupted by Keystone standing up. He held the knife in one hand and a piece of wood in another, both down at his side. "It's too late. A lot of damage has been done. The ravagers now possess novi forged items and we have no idea how much. He could have been working here in secret for centuries, hiding among the other ravagers. Who knows, maybe he was their protector. But none of that matters now. We can't just try to bring him into our fold. 'Hey, you're one of us. Come play nicely.' It's not going to work. We have to destroy him, as much of the ravager's weapons and tools as we can find, and –"

Now Maylene stood up. "To do that, we'd have to eradicate most of the ravagers too. Are you talking about genocide?"

"They are not a productive species," Keystone shouted back. "I don't suggest genocide, but a significant portion of them will be killed as they get in our way. That's inevitable, even if we weren't here. But their population does need thinned."

"Cull the herd," Ruckus said.

"I can't believe I'm listening to this." Tears flooded Maylene's eyes. As Keystone opened his mouth to continue, Maylene shoved her index finger toward him. "No! I understand your anger, Keystone, and where it comes from. I get it. But I did lose my mate to the ravagers' hands. I should be vengeful and want them dead. I cannot succumb to that kind of thinking right now."

"We also need to find out who his novimather is and get a

full record of her novies. If any others are dangerous, we need to know."

Though Ruckus' words were spoken softly, Maylene whipped around to face him, her finger still pointing and tears flying from her face. "No. We can't just go around starting to accuse dragons of ill-deeds either. I can't believe what I'm hearing. This will be dealt with in the way that we've always dealt with broken novihomidraks."

"Don't you see we're beyond that? The circumstances here have become dangerous, not only for the population of this planet but for novies and dragons too," Keystone said.

Rake looked over to where Siva slept peacefully even while the novihomidraks were shouting. He would give anything to be able to go and lie down beside her, let these arguments fall away, and find peace with her in his arms.

Except that she wasn't at total peace either. Her arms and legs twitched as if she were entangled in uneasy dreams. What memories haunted her?

"Hey, guys?" A lump of dread circled like armor around the question Rake knew he had to ask. He waited for silence to come. "What if Princess Siva is the reason for the ravagers' attacks?"

17

The passenger section of the ship felt cold this morning. Siva sat with her arms around herself trying not to shiver. The smell of the fire outside and what the saperes were trying to cook for breakfast from their cobbled supplies drifted through the open door.

Siva had woken up on a bed with Maylene watching over her and soon discovered that it was the room opposite of the one Rake had been taken to last night for healing. He was up walking around. She'd seen him. He didn't appear to be weak or in any residual pain. She'd tried to talk to him, but he barely looked at her and certainly didn't speak beyond what was necessary. Siva had the feeling that this had to do with Maylene more than any of the other novihomidraks.

Maylene had informed her that they would be gathering at breakfast for an important discussion. At first, Siva thought they meant to discuss Cal and what they intended to do to rescue the novihomidrak, but, when she overhead harsh whispers between some of them and the saperes, she realized it had to do with her. As Siva sat on the bench seat awaiting whatever discussion they wanted to have with her, she wished she could go home now. She thought about telling them she only wished to get her father and fly away from this planet. Now that she knew evacuation was the only option, she wanted to get started. She just hoped that the Dragon Council would still aid her and she could count on the saperes.

But she'd wait until they had said their peace today. Whatever it was, it was so bad that even Rake didn't want to look at her.

The first plates of food began to arrive. Sapere Andaris handed her what appeared to be pears, scrambled eggs, and toast, but the last two were nearly burnt beyond recognition. He flashed an apologetic smile. "These were the best I could do for you. I tried to tell Falin not to let Hig cook, but Hig always insists that he's got this."

Siva accepted the plate. "I've eaten worse. I'm grateful that there is food."

Andaris looked like he might say something else, but changed his mind. He headed back outside. Maylene took a seat across from Siva and looked down at the plate she'd been given. She might have refrained from speaking her comments aloud based on what Siva had said just now and in their prior conversation about Siva's planet. Siva suspected Maylene knew more about the conditions Siva endured than any of the others did. If Maylene thought that Siva wouldn't continue seeking help for her people, then Maylene had a surprise coming.

Celain and Keystone returned with plates, Celain sat by Maylene, but Keystone sat by Siva. The action brought her a measure of comfort and made her feel not quite like the evil step-child.

The others were beginning to eat, so Siva did as well. She was a couple bites in when Andaris, Rake, Ruckus, and Hig came in with their plates. Rake, never meeting Siva's eyes, went to sit by Maylene.

"Am I good to sit by you?" Andaris asked.

"Yes," Siva said, looking up at the sapere and wondering why he would bother to ask when Keystone hadn't. Whatever was going on, she felt more and more uncomfortable because of how they were treating her.

Ruckus sat on the other side of Andaris, with Hig going over to sit beside Rake.

Keystone was the first to finish, and he set his plate and fork down on the floor. Then he pulled a small knife and a piece of wood from his pocket and began to work at the wood.

"You're going to clean up your shavings, right?" Ruckus asked, thumbing in the direction of the flaky mess growing on Keystone's lap.

"Yes, don't worry about it. It's only wood."

After Siva finished, she continued to hold onto her plate, not knowing what else to do with her hands. She watched Keystone work at the wood. It looked like a swan. "It's pretty," she whispered, leaning over into him a little.

He held it up, blew some shavings off of it, and then inspected it. "I make a new one on every planet I visit."

"You must have quite a collection then."

"He doesn't," Ruckus said. "He leaves them behind."

Siva sensed tension going through Keystone, and it kept her from asking why he would do such a thing. It didn't matter though because he answered her anyway. "White Swan was my mate. I lost her in what feels like an eternity ago. I carve these, regardless of how silly some may think they are, and leave them on the worlds I visit. Wherever I've gone in the Onesong, she's joined me, at least in my thoughts, and been a part of my journey. It makes eternity a bit more bearable."

"I think it's sweet," Siva said.

Keystone smiled and gave a grateful nod.

As soon as they were finished, Sapere Hig stood up and collected all the plates and utensils with Celain's help. "Not bad if I do say so myself," he said, chuckling and patting his round belly. "Now, I hear there is something that needs to be discussed. Maylene, I believe you are presenting this."

Sapere Hig sat back down while Maylene sat up straight and leaned forward. "Saperes, we were having a discussion last night and realized that we hit an unforeseen wall in dealing with the ravagers. This has become so important that we decided delaying Cal's rescue to discover the truth here is vital."

"We did have to take a vote on it though," Ruckus said.

"Yes," Maylene said, "but most of us felt leaving Cal in jeopardy a little longer is worth the risk."

"Well, that would be quite the discussion you novies had last night then," Hig said.

Siva realized that they had kept Sapere Hig in the dark as much as they had her. She hadn't seen any of the whispers going on with Hig.

"So, what is this discussion?" Hig asked.

Maylene turned her head to look down the line. "Rake, you're the one who asked the pertinent question, and you have served on this planet for a few years. Maybe you should begin."

Rake nodded and sat up a little straighter. "This was the ravagers' first massive, coordinated attack, and they've never tried to get into the palace before. It's usually small attacks based on getting what they need to survive. I always felt they had a leader, but never found out who that was. That's why I invited Maylene and Talon to come negotiate. I had been hoping they would discover who was behind it."

So far, Siva didn't see why there should be harsh whispers or why they would ignore her. Not unless they thought she was involved with the novihomidrak. It made it hard to sit and listen when she wanted to tell Rake that she knew nothing.

"Something made this attack different," Rake said. "I believe it was the wedding of Prince Henris to Princess Siva."

"No," Siva interrupted, unable to contain herself any longer. "I don't like the accusation that I was a party to this."

Keystone reached over and took her hand. "No one is accusing you. Listen to what Rake has to say."

Siva tried to clamp her mouth shut and sit back, but she felt like she'd already been judged for something she hadn't done. Slowly, once Keystone had seen that she'd calmed down, he slid his hand away from hers and cast a glance over to Rake.

He continued, "The marriage brought up a lot of opposition. For, as unalike as they are, there are people who sympathize with the ravagers. I routed out a lot of ravagers from around the palace because we'd heard rumors of a planned attack. We assumed they'd attack directly and not from below ground like they did. Someone is assisting with their level of technology."

"It's not my people. I didn't know anything about these ravagers until after they attacked. I surely didn't want my people being thrust into your war," Siva said.

Rake finally met her gaze directly. "Whether you knew it or not, using your people for fodder was always Henris' plan."

Siva slapped her hands over her mouth.

"I know you had no direct involvement with this," he said, "but something about your wedding to Henris frightened whoever is aiding the ravagers."

"Princess Siva," Ruckus said, "you must realize that this person was so afraid of it happening that his lieutenant, for lack of a better term, was sent out to destroy every novihomidrak on the planet. This lieutenant is the barbarian novihomidrak."

"Okay," she muttered, placing her hands back down in her lap.

Now it was Maylene who spoke up, "Novihomidraks come to planets in one of two ways. Firstly, they can get through the Wells. All one must do is walk through the convergence, which is different on every planet depending on its connection to the Onesong. Secondly, a novi may travel through space in a craft just as any other mortal capable of the technology." She held up her hands here to indicate the craft around them.

"I see where you're going," Sapere Hig said.

"I don't," Siva spoke up quickly.

"Novihomidraks, when they come through the convergence, are logged by the saperes as being on-world. When they leave, we make note of that too. If they come on a ship, they are supposed to visit a shrine so the saperes know about their mission. But, if a novi didn't want to be recorded, they could only land by ship and keep their presence from the saperes," Falin said.

"Which is what you are saying the barbarian novihomidrak did, correct?" Hig asked.

All of the novihomidraks nodded slowly and nearly in unison.

"And we suspect it was a long, long time ago," Keystone said.

"Siva came to me to plea for help to save the population of her planet, and I reached out to the Onesong to see if there was an answer," Maylene said. "It came back that the only way was to use a spaceship to go from Nungh Two to Myeller because the world had been spun off from the Onesong. From here, we could continue to evacuate her people."

"How?" Andaris asked. "Humans can't go through the Wells. It would be deadly."

Maylene swung an index finger toward him. "That was a question I didn't think to ask myself when the Onesong first answered me."

Siva felt completely deflated. "So, are you telling me that, if we brought my people here, we couldn't go anywhere else, that we'd be trapped here … with the ravagers?" It felt as if all hope was lost.

Maylene averted her gaze toward Rake, and Siva knew it was to avoid an answer. "It was when Rake started raising questions about the barbarian that I realized the same thing Andaris just did. I had to excuse myself and go start a meditation. While I was under, I realized that the Onesong had repeated to me exactly what the barbarian had originally planned to do. The dragon had incubated and birthed him on Nungh Two hoping to save that world. Because at birth ravagers look similar to humans, perhaps the novimather didn't realize her mistake until it was too late. She tried to contain him by spinning off Nungh Two."

"But how did he get here?" Siva asked. "You said he'd been on Myeller for a long time."

"We believe the first inhabitants of Myeller came from Nungh Two. Chances are he stowed away and came here aboard the ship that brought the others. Only he didn't realize at the time that he was returning home. Because saperes are quick to protect convergences, he found it already guarded, and knew he couldn't get through. So, he stayed with his people. "

"I suspect that his penchant for being a champion kept him trying to help people. It's probably those people or relatives of them who became supporters of the ravagers. It makes sense with what I've been able to learn about them." Rake looked at Maylene. "I also believe the ravagers were here first. The dragon probably took him from this world and flew to Nungh Two."

Sapere Hig's cheeks grew big and round as he smiled. "A speculative history lesson is nice, but you still haven't mentioned this so-called wall you've run into."

Siva noticed that the novihomidraks all looked to each other as if wondering which one of them would say it.

Keystone broke the silence. "Now that the shrine is destroyed, the barbarian has easy access to the convergence. Someone has to go back with the saperes to protect it. It may even take two of us."

"But that leaves us down to three novies to go in for Cal,

and not a sapere among us," Ruckus said. "We don't know how many novihomidrak weapons they have, only that the barbarian seems to have forged some. How long he's been at this is another unknown. One thing is clear though. They have them, and they like them to contain poison."

Falin turned to Sapere Hig. "We don't all need to go. We can call in some of the unblessed saperes to help protect the convergence. I'll go with the novies going after Callous."

"I'll go to protect Falin," Siva said. When she started to see the alarm rising in their faces over the possibility of her being injured or killed, she added, "I have weapons and defense training. You've seen me stand up to the ravagers. Novies might be injured in the rescue, and it doesn't do any of you any good if you lose the sapere meant to heal them. It will be best if he has someone there to help him if he runs into trouble."

That seemed to settle the argument.

Rake stared at her with a stony gaze. "I'm charged with protecting Siva. I will be one of those going to rescue Cal."

18

After dropping the saperes and Maylene off at the remains of the shrine, Falin and the others flew to Callous' last known location. Ruckus flew while Keystone, Falin, Rake, and Siva sat in back. Harnessed in, the clips holding them against the walls clicked as Ruckus flew through storm clouds to keep them from being seen by ravagers. Turbulence knocked the passengers around.

Rake still had some soreness going on around where the arrow had penetrated his shoulder. Being jostled about wasn't helping, but he wasn't about to complain. If the other novies didn't believe him completely healed, they'd bench him. The last thing he wanted was to sit on the sidelines, even if it would be better … meaning he'd remain behind with Siva and Falin, but mostly Siva.

He sat across from her now as he had during their meeting earlier so that he could watch her. It seemed like her beautiful brown eyes were always moving, always checking out the surroundings. Except that right now she was doing anything but looking at him. Her gaze followed this invisible boundary that stopped just at the edge of his seat. It would then either go up to the ceiling or down to the floor before taking in the rest of the craft. Was she doing this consciously? It didn't really matter because he got to watch her without having to look away himself. If in her peripheral vision she caught him staring at her, she didn't show it. If she had, her gaze would flicker and lock right with his eyes.

But if Siva hadn't noticed him, Keystone did. Rake noted that Keystone had waited until Rake took his seat and harnessed up before deciding where he would sit, which was next to Siva. Now, Keystone kept making head movements toward her while giving nudging glances that Rake should talk to her. He kept these in line with the rocking of the turbulence, and, because his own movements were sporadic, Keystone was probably also watching to make sure Falin wasn't watching.

Rake tried to ignore Keystone. Until he couldn't anymore.

Keystone shifted his knees toward Siva. "So, that was pretty impressive when Rake had his wings around you and Falin was shooting to get the ravagers away from you. You didn't make a sound. Weren't you scared?"

Siva's anxiously darting gaze zipped to Keystone. "We were shot at as we flew from the palace to the shrine. When Rake put his wings around me, I knew we were protected."

"That's adorable. Don't you think so, Rake?" Keystone asked.

Siva flushed, which was adorable, and she looked back toward the two ship cabins as if wishing she could escape. Falin, however, knowing the novihomidraks had incredible hearing, whispered to Keystone without any movement of his lips, "Knock it off."

Keystone chuckled low. "I think you're being modest. You did say you had training. Tell us how you got that."

Siva's look said she was testing Keystone to see if he was being serious or if he wanted to mock her again. Deciding he must really be curious, she said, "My world is a flat-out mess. Everyone needs to know how to protect themselves, and we start learning young. Families hire masters to come in and train their children in defense. My master provided protection for my family, since my father is primieret, so we didn't need to hire anyone since he already lived with us."

"Things must be really bad."

"They are. You've heard Maylene say that my world is spun off from the Onesong, whatever that means, so I'm sure you know how bad it is."

"It's sad to think that it wasn't even your own people's fault," Keystone said. "But your world has technology which allows for space travel, so you must have a good educational system."

"I was fortunate enough that my mother went to one of the last schools to remain open before the education system completely broke down, so she taught me at home how to read and write. She said it would be important for some people to retain the skills for the time when we'd manage to correct the mistakes of the past. Except now I know that doesn't even matter, not with my world fated to die."

Rake felt himself shift into wishing he could do something to help Siva. It wasn't fair that her world fell to chaos and destruction because some novimather realized too late that her novihomidrak was broken. Why hadn't she contacted the

Dragon Council and told them about her novi? Experienced novihomidraks could be sent to capture him, and he could have been institutionalized while he was still harmless.

The true story of what happened didn't much matter now because irrevocable harm had already been done, and Siva's world was in the final throes of its death.

"You have been very lucky to know your family," Keystone said. "We're taken at such a young age by our novimathers that we probably wouldn't even remember our families anyway. I believe that one of the reasons we have no memories is so that, with every world we are sent to, we have to wonder if that is where we came from. That question alone instantly connects us to the people there."

"Is that part of the reason you carve a swan and leave it?" Siva asked.

Keystone smiled. "I hadn't thought of it that way, but I guess that, yes, perhaps it could be."

"Well," Ruckus said from the pilot seat, "let's see what they've got. Hang on, in case that includes surface-to-air missiles."

Rake heard Siva's heartbeat quicken, and he was fairly certain her body heated. If it had, Keystone had picked it up. Now, as Keystone gave him another solid glance, Rake wished he'd had the nerve to speak with Siva.

Keystone made a show of tightening his harness around him. While he had his head lowered, he whispered in a tone only Rake and Ruckus would have been able to hear, "You'd be a fool to let her go."

Rake knew Keystone was right. As Rake sat here, feeling their flight starting to descend, and watching Siva as her gaze continued to dart about except for at him, he couldn't help but feel the rhythm of his own heart match to hers as if they were entrained.

"Holy –" Ruckus muttered, and it drew everyone's gaze to the front of the craft, then out the view screen which emulated a window.

"Is that real?" Falin asked.

What lay in front of them was a massive military complex. There were platoons running in formation in several areas around the complex. Over to one side, little blue pinpoints of light showed where weapons were being welded.

"There's no way the ravagers built that by themselves," Rake said.

"Whoever is helping them then has war in mind. They're planning for a takeover," Keystone said.

"I was hoping I'd be able to land and demand they hand Cal back over to us," Ruckus said. "There goes that plan."

"As if you expected it to be that easy," Falin said. "You hoped you'd get to go in firing your weapons."

Ruckus lifted a shoulder in a shrug. "Yeah, you're right."

Rake began to laugh. "No, he fully wanted to demand they hand Cal over, then let the shooting start!"

"Novies!" Falin said, shaking his head.

Ruckus didn't take them down too low, but flew along until they found a grove of birch trees to land behind. Most of the land was open meadow overgrown with weeds, but at least the trees would provide some shelter for the ship.

Before Ruckus unbuckled, he turned toward Siva. "Do you know how to fly too?"

"No, not really," she said.

"Good. Neither do I, and I trust you more than Falin, so come here."

Rake watched Siva head toward the front of the ship. A line of tension ran up her back from the thought of having to pilot the ship, but she held confidence in every step anyway. Even if she was uncertain of herself and her abilities, she knew that she could learn. Fear of the unattempted wouldn't hold her back.

"If you have to, if you find yourself in a bad situation, get out of here," Ruckus said. It wasn't often that he was serious when he spoke, preferring to cause havoc as his name suggested. Then, his voice dropped much lower. "You will remember all my instructions and you will do whatever is necessary without fearing for us, including Rake who can fly away if need be. Understand?"

Siva nodded. Rake felt a shuddering breath leave him, knowing how grateful he was for Ruckus' suggestion to take hold. Rake saw Keystone giving him a look as if saying, "Glad we both know that is a good thing." Rake nodded back.

Ruckus gave instructions on how to fly the ship and Siva acknowledged each bit with affirmatives. Whether that was from Ruckus' suggestion or her own training at handling situations as they came, Rake wasn't certain. It might even be a little of both.

Then, when Ruckus finished, he unbuckled and joined the others.

Keystone opened the door, and the novies went quickly down the ramp. They closed the door to both Falin and Siva looking down at them.

"Good luck," Siva said.

Rake winced at the words. Nothing was more ill-fated than someone wishing a novihomidrak luck.

"Can't be perfect," Keystone said, leaning toward Rake and nudging him with his elbow.

"I'll explain," Falin said. "Go with blessings and abundant fortune."

Ruckus held up his hand with two fingers extended upward as if he were making rabbit ears. "Peace!"

The apprehension settled into Rake's stomach the moment he started to turn. Bad things always happened when he left Siva … which so far had been one time, he had to remind himself. He hoped it wouldn't be a second.

19

The craft felt small and cramped even though only she and Falin were in it. Every breath came to her with heavy tension. It felt like she and Falin were sitting around staring at each other while waiting for someone to die.

At first, she moved toward the front of the craft and reviewed the controls which Ruckus had told her about. Strange confidence told her she'd be able to fly this ship if she had to. She really hoped she didn't, but she could.

She wished that looking at the panel would have taken longer than it did. All too soon, she was back to staring at Falin.

"How long do you think it'll take?" she asked.

"Depends on how hard it is to pick up Cal's scent," Falin said. "I'm sure the Humline has already given them clues where to go, but who knows how much trouble they'll find along the way."

She couldn't believe she understood everything the sapere had just said. Two days ago, it would've sounded like gibberish. Now, she felt versed in a whole other language. Not to mention able to fly a spaceship. She hadn't expected this much of an adventure. She should be a married woman now. That was the role she'd prepared for. Not this.

"I need some air. I'm going to step outside for a minute," she said.

Sapere Falin stood up. "Do you mind if I join you?"

At first, she did. Then she realized he was probably just fulfilling his unnecessary mission to keep her safe while Rake was gone. But this might be a good time for her to find out more about Rake. "Sure."

Once outside, Siva reached her arms over her head and stretched as if she could touch the beautiful blue sky. What would it be like to have air like that all the time? She could scarcely imagine.

As Falin followed down the ramp behind her, he said, "Princess Siva, let's be mindful not to stay out here too long."

That was his way of saying that the ship was safe, outside meant danger.

She acknowledged him, but figured that he'd mellow out soon enough. He might even relax and enjoy the sunlight. She could only hope.

The small stand of birch trees was just that. It didn't have much depth to it, and once Siva had crossed to the other side, she could see the tops of the buildings in the complex they had flown over.

Falin made his way through the trees to come stand by her. He swatted at a couple of bugs flying in the air. He didn't seem to know how to deal with natural nature. She figured the sculpted and manicured landscape of the shrine felt more in his control. To him, this probably seemed like chaos. The more she learned about the saperes, the more they grew to irritate her.

"It's probably not a good idea to be out here. If they have sentries, they might spot us," Falin said.

Her mission was to protect the sapere. She'd rather be out there alongside Rake trying to rescue Cal. But Rake would have disagreed with her going any further. There was some measure of safety at her remaining here.

It was time to give-a-little to get-a-little. She nodded and started back through the stand of trees.

"What can you tell me about Rake?" Siva paused to look at the way the white bark of one of the birch trees curled away from the trunk.

"Princess Siva, I must tell you that Maylene instructed me not to allow interactions between you and Rake," Falin said.

"But I'm not interacting with him. I'm asking you the question."

A measure of irritation tightened his lips. "Rake's novimather is a Nefterru dragon named Nyla. She is extremely bad tempered and cunning, a trait that rubs off on many of her novies. Rake is her fifth novi. He is five hundred and sixty-nine years old, and the saperes estimate that his lifespan, assuming he doesn't take another poisoned arrow or something like that, will be eight hundred and seventy-five or somewhere about that."

Siva drew in a sharp breath and staggered backward a bit.

"Do you understand now why novies should not dally with humans?" he asked, his voice very matter-of-fact. But, if she hadn't gotten the point, he continued, "He may appear only a few years older than yourself, but, within your short lifespan, mine even, we will both be grey and wrinkled while he will be just getting his first grey hair. A normal relationship would be impossible with him. Do you understand?"

Siva nodded, even while her heart seemed to shatter. She ignored the pain, wishing it off into a far corner. Why did she feel so hurt? It wasn't like she really knew Rake. Before a couple days ago, she hadn't even known of the existence of novihomidraks, let alone Rake. She couldn't possibly have enough emotional entanglement to feel as crushed as she did.

"Oh, my," Falin said.

Siva glanced over at him, expecting that the sapere had seen something. Instead, he stared at her, his eyes getting wider. She bit back the words she wanted to ask about why he was staring at her and stomped back toward the ship.

Her foot struck something metal. Her shin clipped against something round and hard in the weeds and she nearly tripped. Falin caught her arm and steadied her while Siva hobbled to rub her leg.

"What was that?" she asked as she tentatively put her leg back down and tested her weight. It was sore, the bone probably bruised, but nothing was broken.

Falin pushed apart the weeds and uncovered a round hand wheel valve. "Looks like this is what you kicked."

He dug down further and found the metal plate Siva had stepped on. He knocked on it and a dull ring came back. "Sounds hollow," he said. "Could be tunnels beneath."

"Do you think it's a way into the compound?" she asked.

"I don't like what you're thinking. We're not going to find out."

"But we should know. If they come back saying that one of them has been hurt and left behind, this might be our only way in to rescue them."

Falin shook his head. "You don't know novihomidraks."

"I think I've seen enough. They are incredible until that moment they aren't." Siva reached for the hand valve. "Are you going to help me with this?"

"One peek to see if the tunnels even go in the direction of the complex," he said. "Then we close it back up. Ravagers could come pouring out of this just as well."

"Deal."

It took some effort, but between the two of them they got the valve turned under squeaking protest which left the scent of rust in the air. The hinges were a little more cooperative and they swung the hatch back easily until it came to a rest at a slight tilt. There was another hand valve, though smaller, on what would have been the underside of the hatch.

A metal ladder attached to the side of the opening quickly faded to darkness.

"You're going to tell me that we need to go down to check, aren't you?" Falin asked.

"I'll go down myself if you want."

"No, but let me go get a light first. It won't do us any good if we can't see anything once we get down there. Stay right here. I'll be right back."

Siva waited while Falin retrieved a flashlight from the ship. When he returned, she took it from him and descended the ladder first. Reaching the bottom, she swung the illuminating beam around to check for immediate danger. Seeing none, she looked up to see that Falin did indeed want to come down. She wasn't certain he would since they were just checking which direction the tunnels ran, but he might be afraid that she was going to run off. Or he might be as curious as she was.

Falin took the flashlight from her when she offered it to him. He pointed it around the tunnel as she had. The stone walls did run toward the complex and stopped just shortly beyond where they were standing.

Stepping closer to the walls, Falin ran his fingers over the stone as a frown came to him. "These tunnels were made by a novihomidrak."

Siva realized there had to be more that she didn't know about novies yet. "How can you tell?"

"See these flares?" he said, pointing to where part of the rock made an outward curve which left a sharp-looking ridge. "This is made from the edges of their dragon breath."

"You mean they can burn these tunnels out simply by breathing?"

"It's not exactly simple, but, yes, some can. Rake can. The tunnels we used to escape the shrine were tunnels he made."

"Rake made those tunnels? Do you think the barbarian made these?"

"Undoubtedly, but there is a slight difference." Falin turned the flashlight toward the ceiling where there were wooden beams. "Rake had no choice but to tunnel beneath the city of Plashia. The barbarian burned through the ground from above. They probably used those machines with the blades to scoop aside the top layer of dirt and clear a path. Then, after he burned the tunnels into the earth, they lay boards over the top and scooped the dirt back over. It would only take a year or two for the weeds to completely cover this and leave no trace of what had been done."

"This is something that definitely had some planning?"

"Oh, yes. It was a long process when Rake did it. This would've been faster, but it still would've taken awhile."

"Do you have any idea who could be behind this?"

Falin shook his head. "Let's go back to the ship. I think we can be fairly certain these tunnels go all the way to the complex, considering who made them."

Siva went up the ladder first. They closed the hatch together and went back to the ship. It wasn't until they climbed on board and pulled the ramp up to shut the door that they eyed their surroundings.

It was then they realized they weren't alone.

The barbarian novihomidrak sat in the pilot's seat.

20

One side of the compound stood against rough land and scrawny trees that had tried to dominate the land. There were remains of huts and foundations of older buildings now turned to ruins. This might have been the first efforts at making the military complex, especially when the buildings on this side of the compound were the oldest.

Something had changed – but what? – to bring the ravagers out of the rocks and trees.

Rake found himself frustrated that he'd always assumed the ravagers were a violent people. But what if they weren't? What if something had made them that way?

Weeds, very dry so early into the summer months, crackled with an occasional snap as they moved through. Each novihomidrak had their dragon lids down to search for approaching danger they might ordinarily miss. As they moved around, they looked for a spot not heavily guarded.

That, quite frankly, defined the whole complex and made them extra nervous. It seemed like all they did here was train and make weapons and, other than the chain link fence, they didn't care who saw them.

"You know," Ruckus said back over his shoulder, "there's a good possibility the fence is dragon forged. That's what I'd do if I wanted to keep people out without looking like I was keeping them out."

Keystone nodded. "I'll go try."

Crouching down, Keystone loped over to the fence and, with claws out, tried to slice the chain link. The metal shredded beneath his fingers with a clatter as the tension of the links broke.

"So much for that idea," Ruckus said.

"It was a good theory," Rake said, thinking that it had been a good idea, but either the barbarian novihomidrak didn't think like the rest of them or hadn't been expecting an attack from another one of his kind. The height of the fence would keep most inhabitants of this planet out.

Ruckus seemed pleased that Rake approved. Then they progressed over to where Keystone was in the same fashion. In another moment, all three of them were through the fence and inside the compound.

They'd discussed where they thought Cal was as they'd headed over from the ship, but they all knew that the Humline could guide them better once they got here. Now that they were inside, Rake connected to the Humline. It felt as if a small, fist-size portion of his chest relaxed near his heart and the information started to flow.

As if they were a flock of birds, they moved along the sides and backs of buildings as they wove their way through, toward where they felt they needed to go. Each one of them was trusting the Humline and going on instincts. Novies learned young to trust their internal compass as guided by the Onesong. Everything in the universe moved as a system. The connection of the universe, the Onesong, was tuned in through the Humline of each world. It all worked together, and novies sensed the mechanics of it all better than most.

The buildings appeared to be wooden at their core structure. Maybe the ravagers had cleaned the land of all but the slimmest of trees to create their complex. Then, against the slatted wood boards, there were mud bricks. Finally, a layer of pale yellow-green paint had been slathered on top. It made the walls thick and strong. They wouldn't be easy to topple.

"Are the ravagers capable of this kind of construction?" Keystone asked in a low tone.

"Not by themselves," Rake answered. "With an intelligent novihomidrak, like we must presume the barbarian is, then a bit more likely. With someone who understood military strategies, definitely."

The Humline zinged and the novihomidraks crouched down beside the building in the shadows while two ravagers thumped by in what must be a march for them. Someone was undoubtedly trying to get them disciplined.

Unfortunately, the Humline worked as a guide, not as an information file. They would only know where to go, not who was behind all this.

It was time for them to head into one of the buildings; however, that meant going around the exposed front where they might be seen. With his back against the wall, Rake silently signaled the others to follow him one at a time. This way, they could minimize the risk of all of them being spotted.

Rake went first. The wooden door, as expected, was locked. He couldn't imagine ravagers understanding about locks. They might bar a door to keep it secure, but not something like this. Rake thrust his weight against it. At first, it didn't want to give. It took two more hard presses against it to force the lock to break from the jam.

Inside was dark and smelled of blood and urine. Rake turned his head for a moment toward the door for one last gasp of clean air. Then, as he turned back, he realized why he couldn't see anything with his dragon lids. Several dark sheets, probably stained with blood to give it the dark color and reek, hung in a semi-circle around the door and closed off everything behind it. What a way to fool a novihomidrak's heightened senses by overloading them. Behind this makeshift curtain could be several men with novihomidrak-forged weapons just waiting to attack.

The one sensation that hadn't been removed was sound, and Rake couldn't hear the creaks which accompanied weapons being raised or the tiny clicks of arrows being notched against a bowstring. Only a faint heartbeat in the distant background.

Keystone came in the door behind Rake and stopped short. "Woah."

"Yeah," Rake muttered in reply. He wasn't sure there were any other words for this. While novies usually didn't like to work together, they also didn't actively plot against each other. This spoke of a novihomidrak who knew they'd be coming.

"Do you think he's become a Necronosti?" Keystone asked.

A Necronosti was a novihomidrak who'd become so broken and influenced by chaos that they dabbled in dark, forbidden magicks. Rake hadn't seen evidence of that so far. "No," Rake said. "None of this is magic. I've never seen him use magic, and there've been no traces of it ever having been used against us. I think he's just broken, and maybe misguided and unfortunate is really a better term. He might not know any differently. He's just doing what he's told."

"You're being generous considering he's already killed one of our own, and he's using Cal to lure us here so he can kill us too," Ruckus said, coming in the building next. He instantly winced and made a face.

Rake knew it was no use defending. Even if the barbarian hadn't been the one whose hand had killed Mayleen's partner, Talon, he had at least made the weapon that did it. At least with all their talking, they could be certain that no one was waiting behind the curtain.

"Which one of us is going to do the honors and see what mayhem awaits?" Ruckus asked, pointing toward the sheet darkened with dried blood.

"I checked the fence and made us a way in," Keystone said. "Rake went first into the building. I'd say that you're up."

Ruckus shrugged. "All right. Here we go."

He spent a moment inspecting the sheet, noting with a point to the others that it was hanging from a cord. In the end, he decided just to lift it up.

Behind the sheet were five rows of barrels stacked two high and two deep. A web of wires strung overhead led from the cord to the barrels.

"So glad you didn't just yank the sheet," Keystone said as he stepped closer to examine the barrels.

Rake felt anger rise through him. "Ravagers don't use explosives. This is all wrong."

Ruckus punched Rake's arm lightly. "Looks like they've stepped up their game a couple of times. Who knows what else they are capable of now?"

"These were definitely rigged to explode," Keystone said. "The barbarian must expect everyone to react like he would, which would be to tear the sheet out of the way."

"I think we have a more important question to ask," Rake said. "Why did the Humline lead us here to discover this? How does this get us closer to finding Cal?"

"The Humline wants us destroyed," Ruckus said, raising a hand into the air. "It betrays us."

"Knock it off," Keystone said with a shake of his head as Ruckus dramatically pulled this hand to his chest and clutched it as if he were mortally wounded. None of them really believed that the Humline was out to get them, but leave it to Ruckus to make a scene.

Still, Keystone's eyes held a heavy worry as Rake saw him trying to find an answer to the questions Rake had just asked. They were indeed good questions. "Then let's find out why the Humline needed us here," Keystone said finally.

"Keystone, why don't you do a deep connection and see if you can find anything," Rake said, knowing that he could trust Keystone to be serious with the task. "Meanwhile, Ruckus and I will carefully try to assess if there's anything relevant here."

Keystone nodded and headed back toward the door, closing it until he could lean safely braced against the wood. He shut his eyes and Rake nearly felt the heavy trance that came over the other novihomidrak. That left Rake and Ruckus to begin looking beyond and around the barrels.

"Oh, sheesh," Ruckus said.

At first, Rake thought Ruckus had also seen the nail ends sticking out of the sides of the barrels. They had been pounded through the wood from the inside. Chances were good that additional shrapnel had been placed inside the barrels, most likely some novihomidrak-forged metals. But then Rake noticed Ruckus leaning over the top of the barrels to look behind them. When Rake glanced down, he saw the same thing Ruckus was seeing: the corner of a trapdoor which had been purposefully left exposed.

"Oh, sheesh," Rake said back.

"What do you want to bet that some of these barrels have some sort of liquid or pressure triggers?" Ruckus said.

"Not taking that bet."

Ruckus glanced toward Keystone. "So, we got any other options?"

It was another few seconds before Keystone opened his blue eyes and pushed away from the door frame. "I'm afraid not … and it just got a whole lot worse."

21

The barbarian grinned at them as he rose from the pilot seat. Siva doubted the ravager knew how to fly, but he'd done a good job of tearing wires from the console. A few of the electronics still sparked, mixing the odor of smoke with that of musky sweat.

Siva instinctively reached for the knife at her side.

Sapere Falin grabbed her arm and stayed her hand. "Don't," he whispered solidly in her ear. "Remember he's a novihomidrak."

Siva dropped her hand.

The barbarian grunted at them with a motion for them to turn toward the wall.

Falin stepped around Siva and put a hand against his chest. "Sapere. I'm a sapere. Do you understand?"

The barbarian hissed like an angry cat.

"I don't think he likes saperes," Siva said, now being the one tugging Falin into being sensible.

The barbarian ravager slapped the ship's metal wall with his hands and gave another hard grunt. Siva and Falin both put their hands on the wall, leaning slightly over the bench seats.

Stepping closer, the novihomidrak leaned in to sniff Siva. Then he pulled a piece of fabric from beneath his brown tunic where it had been tucked into the waist of his leggings. He smelled it, then took another whiff of her. She recognized the material as having come from one of her shirts.

"He's been scenting me the whole time," she said.

He pulled a loop of rope from his pocket and began to tie Siva's hands behind her with it.

"Do you have a name?" Falin asked. "I'm Sapere Falin and this is Princess Siva."

The barbarian growled again, but that could be at the mention of the word sapere. Siva wasn't certain that was a good word to use again, but she understood that Falin was trying to get the hierarchy across.

The novihomidrak gave a final hard tug on the ropes which jerked Siva. She watched the material of her shirt, now tucked back in his waistband with only a little edge of it still visible, give a little jiggle. How had he gotten her clothing?

"Vochey, Smash," the novihomidrak said, his voice thick.

Siva jumped when an iron sword appeared in the barbarian's hands. He pointed with a grunt at the spot where she'd been standing and pulled her back. She wished she could now reach the knife, but the novihomidrak hadn't taken it from her either. He wasn't scared of her weapons. Given what she now knew about novies, she wasn't surprised either.

The barbarian turned toward Falin. "Sapere will walk. Run and die." He raised his hand, a claw extended on his index finger, and made a slashing motion near Falin's throat. The curve of the claw was against the skin. He followed this with another grunt.

"I've got it," Falin said.

Picking up the end of the rope dangling from Siva's tied arms, the novihomidrak pointed toward the door to the ship. "Open. Walk."

Falin hurried around and opened the ship. The ramp lowered to the ground and Siva and the novihomidrak went down first, waiting while Falin closed the craft back up. Siva couldn't understand why he was bothering. The spaceship wasn't going anywhere until the console could be repaired.

And yet, since Falin had spoken so assuredly about him being a sapere to the novihomidrak, maybe Falin had a way of secretly sending their novi friends a message by simply locking the door.

"Walk," the barbarian repeated, using his sword to thrust at Falin and swing in front of them to point at the compound.

Falin nodded and took the lead.

So many questions went through Siva's mind as she followed Falin. If she'd known he had a larger vocabulary beyond basic words, she might have started to ask. As it was, she remained silent. They all knew someone had to be helping the ravagers, yet it obviously wasn't this novihomidrak. With a little bit of patience now, she and Falin would soon learn who that person was. Did Falin realize this as well?

In the weeds across the open land, Siva saw the tracks where the three novihomidraks had moved toward the compound. They'd moved in a line, following a deer trail to hide their tracks. Only freshly snapped branches and a couple spots of overturned mud suggested someone had gone through here recently. That, and she knew the novihomidraks had. Did the barbarian know that as well? Had they all crossed paths?

What if no rescue was coming?

Sapere Falin had to be counting on the novihomidraks finding out that he and Siva had been captured and them coming to save the day.

What if the other novies had already fallen?

The barbarian glanced at her, his gaze narrowing, as she took a couple hard breaths. Just thinking about something happening to Rake made it difficult for her to breathe.

"Sorry," she said.

"Turn left," the barbarian commanded with another thrust of his sword in the direction he wanted them to go.

They weren't going to get to the compound. The novihomidrak was just taking them a short distance away before killing them, then he'd hide their bodies, and the others would waste a lot of time looking for them. The distraction would provide an excellent opportunity for the barbarian to dispatch the other novihomidraks one-by-one. Her fearful thoughts reflected in Falin's eyes as he glanced at her.

She took the opportunity to glance down to her side where her knife was. It wasn't much, but, if she could get free, she might be able to defend herself and him long enough for her to get her hands on the crude sword. She was trained for that.

Falin shook his head. "Are you sure you're all right?" he asked her. He used the question to let his gaze slide to the barbarian's sword.

Didn't he realize that was exactly what she wanted to do, but she couldn't take the weapon with her own hands tied? She tilted her head a bit and gave him a terse glare, "I'm fine, thank you." Once again, she looked down and gave a little motion of her shoulders.

"Walk," the barbarian ordered. He stepped forward slightly in order to point the sword at Falin.

Siva pounced, knocking into the barbarian. He staggered under the hit.

Falin swept out his leg and tripped the novihomidrak, who went down. Siva followed with a knee to his chest.

Knocking the wind from his chest also made the novihomidrak release his sword. Falin kicked the sword away.

"Quick, the ropes. Cut them with my knife."

Falin hesitated.

The barbarian tossed Siva off. As she rolled onto the ground, she kicked out with her legs, but he seized onto them and held them tight against his chest with one hand while the other reached to his sword.

Falin tried to grab it.

The barbarian latched onto his wrist and twisted. Bones snapped and Falin somersaulted over, crying out as he landed flat on his back.

Siva managed to use the moment to kick herself free. She scooted as far away as she could, then rolled to her knees. Bringing a foot beneath her, she stood. There was no way she could reach the sword now.

Falin held his arm up to his chest. His eyes were squeezed tightly shut. No way he was going to get the sword either.

Her best chance was to run.

Siva turned, but, before she'd completely about-faced, her head struck hard, flat metal. The force of the hit and the shock knocked her down.

The barbarian laughed at her while he picked up his sword. He took slow steps toward Falin and put the tip of the blade to Falin's chest.

"No," Siva shouted. "Don't."

He stared at her for a moment, then his hand once again pulled out her shirt. He held it up to his face and inhaled deeply while Falin lay quietly on the ground knowing how much danger he was in.

"Don't, please," Siva said. Her head still rung a bit from whatever she'd hit.

"Don't need him," the barbarian said.

"Yes, you do," she stated quickly. "You might not think much of saperes, but others … the other novihomidraks … do." She wasn't certain how much he understood, but he did look down at Falin who now had tears running down his cheeks. His skin had gone pale with shock.

"He's valuable as your prisoner," she said. "Alive. If you kill him, he's worthless to you."

"Where dragon blessing?" the barbarian asked, looking down at Falin.

The sapere grunted with pain, but moved to push his shirt aside. "Here."

Siva barely saw a brown curlicue on the front of his shoulder, only noticing that it seemed to sparkle just a little.

"Bad sapere," the barbarian said. He sliced the end of the sword against the marking. "Next time, kill you. Get up."

This last order was issued to both of them.

By the time they were on their feet, the barbarian had

removed a box from his pouch and pressed a button. A vehicle with flat sides very much like a cargo van on Siva's planet shimmered into view.

A cloaking device. People on her world used them to hide stores of food from those who would steal it. She'd never thought of them being put on a vehicle.

"Get in," the barbarian said.

Once they were inside, if he decided to cloak it and leave, she and Falin would never be found.

22

Rake's own touch of the Humline confirmed that Siva was in danger. Yet, if he went back to help her, their mission to find Cal would fail. Whatever lay ahead of them would take three novihomidraks to do.

His senses felt overwhelmed by the scent of blood and urine in the building, and beneath that he could smell the iron and other metals which filled the barrels of explosives.

"We all know Cal is unconscious in a hole beneath these barrels. We've got to move them. There's no other solution," Keystone said. "We should just move forward quickly."

"No," Ruckus said. "You and Rake should go back to the ship and help Siva."

"You can't do this without us," Rake said.

Ruckus gave a dismayed chortle as he shook his head. "Rake, you don't get it. Keystone is an amazing novihomidrak. For all he's lost, he still has hope in this whole stupid Onesong. You've gone through the ceremonies to transform yourself into the height of what a novihomidrak should be. That makes you the most valuable one among us. This mission can't afford to lose either of you. Me, I'm the troublemaker. The Onesong will probably celebrate if I blow myself to kingdom come."

Rake ignored him and turned to Keystone. "What are the chances my dragon breath can ignite these so fast they don't have time to explode?"

Keystone didn't even need to connect to the Humline for his answer. "You can put your palm on a flame and, for a moment, it isn't hot. Then it is. If the wood wasn't protecting all the explosives, it might be possible. As it is, we don't know what kind of explosives are in there. They might not even be triggered by fire. You've already suggested some might have liquid triggering mechanisms. Others might be sensitive to shockwaves. Burning the barrels isn't an option."

"No, but the two of you getting out of here is. Let me do this," Ruckus said.

"We're not going, and you know it. We're all aware that it's going to take three of us, and it will be faster that way, so let's just get this done," Keystone said.

As much as Rake agreed with Keystone, he wanted to run back to Siva. The sensation of her being in danger tore at him. Yet, as Keystone had said, they all knew it would take the three of them to free Cal. Siva would have to handle herself for a bit until he could get to her. He had confidence that she could handle herself. Just thinking about seeing how she'd handled every situation thrown at her so far filled him with pride for her.

Keystone and Ruckus had moved back to the barrels to come up with a plan.

Rake glanced up to the ceiling of the building. It was made of a few wood beams overlayed with metal. "I might not be able to ignite the barrels, but I think I could make a good-sized hole in the roof."

"Then what?" Ruckus asked, still clearly unhappy about them staying. "You going to fly them out? One little tip could be bad."

"Aside from the lead wires from the cord, there's no wires on any of these," Keystone said. "Each barrel is self-contained."

"Or only one of them is a bomb," Rake said. "The rest are shrapnel meant to break and go in every direction once the explosion hits."

"How do we tell which one is which then?"

Rake crouched to look at the barrels once more and examined the nails sticking out of each one. "The nails," he said finally. "They are meant to pick up the vibrations and help crack the wood during the explosion. All the ones on the outside are going to be shrapnel barrels. The bomb will be further back. If we assume these are pull cords going from the rope holding up the sheet, then they are also to remove lids on most of the barrels. Only one is going to the real bomb. That one won't have any nails but will have a lead wire attached. Whoever carried it in here wouldn't want the nails catching on anything."

"You've got a point," Ruckus said. "If I was setting up a trap like this, that's what I'd do. Maximum damage. Plenty of decoys. Plus, I'd set the bomb on the trap door. That way, if the novihomidrak woke up and tried to get out … boom!"

"Okay, then all we have to do is push these to the side," Keystone said.

"There's not enough room, and I think Rake's right. But, instead of flying them out the roof, where someone on the ground might see us, I think he should burn a hole in the wall and the fence. Then we just pass them through to each other."

Rake nodded, agreeing with the plan. "Let's do this."

In short order, he had a hole blazed through the wall and the fence behind it. Because of the barrels, Rake couldn't make it as low as he wished. Keystone had to slip out of the building and run around to the back. There, Keystone tossed dirt onto the wood which harbored embers to keep them from smoking. They didn't want the odor to draw attention. Then, while Keystone stood back, Rake melted a round hole in the fence with his dragon breath.

"You almost make me wish I'd gone through the ceremonies," Ruckus said as he watched Rake with awe. "Except for the pain. I'm just not a fan of it. Is it really as bad as they say?"

The Crossover ceremonies, sometimes known as the Crossing, were trials that Rake didn't often like to remember. But Ruckus had asked, and there was no reason not to be truthful to another novihomidrak. "You can't even begin to imagine. Having all these barrels explode and hit us with shrapnel would feel like a tickle compared to that."

"That makes my mind up," Ruckus said. "I'm going through the hole. I'll do the stacking on the other side of the fence."

With that, Ruckus climbed out, nodded to Keystone, and jumped through the hole melted in the chain link fence while Rake turned and sought out the first barrel containing nails. This one wasn't connected to one of the wires coming from the cord, so it made a good test to see if his theory might have any accuracy at all. With a deep breath, he hefted the barrel up and handed it through the hole to Keystone, who then gave it to Ruckus. When Rake discovered that all three of them were still in one piece, he looked for the next barrel, and then the next.

Soon, as he'd surmised, he came to a barrel with no nails but connected at the top with a wire.

"I think I found it," he said.

"Be careful. Don't bump it. Let's get the rest of the barrels out," Keystone advised.

"That's the plan," Rake said, handing Keystone another barrel.

Then it came time to start cutting the wires from the cord holding the sheet. Just in case these barrels were also rigged inside, Rake didn't want to use his talons and chance a hard pull on the wires. Instead, he let his dragon teeth come down and bit through the first wire. He'd been destined to have small dragon teeth, but he'd lost all of those in the Crossover ceremonies and larger ones took their place.

It wasn't uncommon for novihomidraks to want to be better, but few could suffer the ordeals of the Crossing, especially when it meant losing the deficient parts for the upgrade. He'd been meant to have small wings too. He could still remember the crack of the bones as they'd severed and fallen away.

In many ways, the thought of losing Siva was just as painful as that which he'd endured to become the strong novihomidrak he was today. Yet, it was experiencing those very ceremonies that enabled him to cut through the wires steadily and capably in order to get to her sooner. With every one he bit into, he sent a little energy prayer to the Humline as an offering to keep her safe. Just a little bit longer.

If the Onesong desired him to continue as the strong novihomidrak he'd made himself into, then –

Shouts went up around the complex and Rake heard a motor revving as an object came closer. He lifted his head –

-- let the Onesong keep her safe.

-- and the wire he held in mid-cut stretched against his jaw.

Sacrifices were to be made, the weak cut away to provide space for the strong. The ceremonies had taught him this.

So did the explosion that sounded right beneath him.

23

Falin lay fetal on the flat grey floor of the cargo truck while Siva had taken a spot to sit cross-legged with her arms and back against the dingy and chipped white wall. Her hands were still tied, and her knife was only a short distance away at her side. The novihomidrak hadn't taken it from her, only warned Falin that, if he cut Siva's bonds, the novi would cut his throat. Falin took it as a very real threat and lay down to hold his arm against his chest.

Two open vents in the roof of the truck let in not only air, but light and kept the interior dimly lit. There wasn't enough air flow to completely dilute the scent of the ravagers who had been packed in here for transport so they could carry out their missions. Siva knew the odor of packed-in bodies well.

Every time the truck hit a bump, she and Falin cringed with pain. The sway banged her head against the metal of the truck. She took her own jarring injury as compensation for her ever wanting to step outside Ruckus' ship. If she'd stayed put, none of this would've happened. How much more harm would be caused for her mistake?

The truck slowed. The rough shakes caused by the land beneath the tires seemed to elongate and roll rather than bring jerks and jolts of bouncing pain. Outside, Siva thought she heard the muffled shouts of others as they whooped with joy. Of course, the ravagers' novihomidrak had just returned.

Then there was an explosion.

Siva flattened down on the truck bed, her arms moving reflexively to cover her head, but they pulled against the bonds until the muscles pulled in strain. When she dared to open her eyes, she found herself looking directly into Falin's brown eyes. He'd dragged himself out of his agony to look and listen to what he could.

"That didn't sound near us," he said.

She wasn't certain if it was the bumpy ride or the deep worry that something had just happened to Rake, but some ill sensation moved through her.

"I hope none of the novies were caught in that," Falin added.

She wished he hadn't. Since the sound seemed far away, while the shouts had been closer, the knowledge that it had to be the novihomidraks on their rescue mission made more logical sense.

But now, the cheers of excitement turned to exclamations of surprise and calls for troops to amass. It couldn't be good. The noise had come as a shock to them as well.

Once again, the truck picked up speed, the engine revving hard. Siva heard the tires roll onto gravel with the crunch and pings of flying stones hitting the undercarriage. They jostled hard and a hard turn sent Siva sliding into Falin. He cried out, and she tried to push herself away, but another untimely sway rolled her right back into him.

The barbarian shouted in the cab, swerved, then brought the truck to a skidding halt. A moment later, the cab door opened and slammed shut.

Siva moved back and sat up with effort. "I'm sorry. Are you all right?"

Falin snorted. "I will be. It's almost ironic. I could've fixed a novihomidrak's broken arm in the time it took us to drive over here. The whole way, I was thinking about the healing prayers I'd use to keep my mind off the pain."

"So, you heal like a normal human?" she asked.

Another snort. "Yes."

She noted the blood on his shirt. It didn't look bad, as if the novihomidrak's cut hadn't been deep. "What was that marking on your shoulder? The novihomidrak called it some sort of blessing?"

"A dragon blessing. As a toddler, I was taken before a dragon who bestowed some of his magic upon me."

"Like a novihomidrak? Did you incubate like they do?"

"No, this is a much faster process." Falin shifted onto his back. "Very painful. The child gets a blast of the dragon's breath."

Siva gasped in shock. "Wait, doesn't that burn you? I mean, you showed me what a novihomidrak's breath can do to rock in the tunnels. How are you still alive?"

"It's not their full breath. It's more a breath of magic, but it feels like being out in a sandstorm." Falin raised his hand away from his injured arm and held it before him as if the memory of it had possessed him and he was trying to stop the air from hitting him. "When it's done, the child who will be raised as a true sapere has a blessing mark on them. Mine goes from my shoulder and down my chest. I just didn't want to expose my heart to the barbarian."

As he spoke, he gently tugged his shirt aside so that Siva could take a closer look. In the faint light, she saw the brown markings sparkle as if they were a tattoo that had been dusted with little bits of glitter.

"Do you know why I'm showing you this?" Falin asked as he pulled the shirt back over the marking.

She didn't, not really. She doubted it was merely because she'd asked about it. After a moment of pondering for an answer, Siva shook her head.

"The novihomidraks and saperes is a world that's very new to you. It seems exciting, but that's only because it's foreign," Falin said. "I stood as a four-year-old child before the dragon, and it was scary and agonizing. Then, I was removed from my parents and taken to the shrine. Not all saperes have to do that, but I did. They said it was better for my training. As the years passed, I saw my family less and less until I don't even know if I'd recognize them if I saw them today. I see you trying to avoid Rake, but I'm afraid that only pulls you toward him more. This life we live is filled with hurt and regrets and danger. You keep denying you're a princess. But it's a better life. You'd do well. It's your destiny. Not this life we lead."

"Shouldn't it be my choice?"

Falin looked pale. His long speech had worn him out. "No," he said harshly. "This life takes you young and doesn't let go until it's drained you to death."

Eyes stinging, Siva tried to shift away. The cargo van had suddenly gotten very small and suffocating. She looked up to the vents, not only to try to hold the tears she couldn't wipe away in her eyes, but as if she could somehow will more air to circulate inside. She listened to the sounds coming in.

The slow realization of what those exterior noises were settled heavily onto her chest. She started to hold her breath so that her own breathing wouldn't interfere with her hearing. She wished she could tell Falin to stop breathing as well.

She hadn't noticed it at first, but now she did. Smoke entering through the vents. A harsh fire put up black clouds, and it had dulled the light coming in. Only the thin metal walls of the cargo van separated them from the fighting going on outside.

"Falin," she said, trying to get to her feet. She called his name again as she braced against the wall, and pushed herself up with her legs. The wall let out a crack as it popped outward at her weight pressing against it.

He wasn't paying attention.

"Falin," she called a third time.

He licked his dry mouth, his breathing ragged and stressed. Falin's eyes were closed. He may have tried to mutter something to her, but it was lost in the sounds drawing closer to the van. He certainly looked like he was draining toward death as he'd said only moments ago.

They were sitting targets here, and Falin was growing weaker from pain. She couldn't get to her knife to free her hands. But she also knew that remaining here and doing nothing was very bad for them.

Without her arms for counterbalance, she couldn't kick down the doors. Even with her hands free, she doubted she could make that happen. She didn't recall getting a good look at the locking mechanism, but remembered that it sounded like a solid metal rod sliding down into place.

What else could she do? Siva looked around for an answer. If only she could make enough noise for Rake to hear. He'd come for her.

She recalled how the wall had popped when she stood up. They weren't thick metal. If they were pliable enough, she could make a lot of noise. Then, it wouldn't be hard for Rake to shred with his talons.

Heading to the side, Siva began kicking the walls. It wasn't creating enough noise; she started to slam her body against it. If she did that at the back and then the front, she could make the panel protrude at both ends in turn. It made almost a thunderous noise like someone waving a metal sheet, but much slower.

"Rake. Rake," she shouted, hoping that he could hear her. No, she knew he could. He'd come for her. "Rake!"

For several minutes, she kept on beating the sides of the van and calling for Rake.

The sounds of battle drew closer. He was coming, fighting his way toward her.

Emboldened by the progress, she pounded harder, screamed louder.

Outside the van, someone gave an enraged scream. Long, curved talons sliced into the walls. At first, the new light coming through startled Siva. Then, she realized she could see the battle a little better. Thick, dark smoke rose from the remains of a burning building. She saw Keystone's long blond hair flying as he fought hand-to-hand with someone right outside the van.

She couldn't see Rake or Ruckus, but she stayed back from

the sides of the van knowing that, at any moment, Rake would take another swipe at the wall and finish tearing an opening she could use to get Falin and herself out.

Any moment.

A javelin struck Keystone in the back. He pitched forward and fell to the ground.

A novihomidrak-forged weapon, Siva realized as she screamed Keystone's name. They probably had plenty of them here in the compound.

Why hadn't Rake come for her yet?

She threw herself against the sides of the van again. "Rake!"

The sounds of battle calmed. Siva watched as Keystone was picked up off the ground under his shoulders by two men and dragged out of her sight. Others were putting out the flames of the building on fire.

"Rake?"

All the noise settled. Siva watched what she could. Had Rake fallen to another novihomidrak-forged weapon? Was he now a prisoner too? She refused to believe that any of the novihomidraks were dead. Falin was here. Once his arm was set, he could heal the novies. Everyone would be fine.

Everyone.

Including Rake.

The back of the van opened and the silhouette of a man appeared. "Darling, I have been looking everywhere for you," Henris said.

24

Rake realized his mistake in lifting his head the moment he felt the wire press against his tongue and the metallic taste of it filled his mouth. That was the second before the explosion lifted him off his feet.

The force of it being so close slammed into his rib cage, not only knocking the air from his lungs, but cracking a couple ribs as well.

Behind him, he heard Keystone shouting his name. It sounded as if it were far off and through a tunnel as the roar of the detonation filled his ears. He became aware of the building raining down on him. Boards landed on his shoulders and chest. Mud bricks bludgeoned him. Some broke on impact, sending dirt and grit into the air. The metal sheeting of the roof clattered all around him.

He closed his eyes, wishing he could as easily cut off all his other heightened senses. Darkness swam around him – like fish swarming around a whale – until it finally overtook him.

When consciousness returned, Rake realized that he still lay beneath the debris of the building. Above him there were noises, the sounds of people walking. He felt the zing of a novihomidrak nearby but couldn't tell if it was one of his allies or the barbarian. He had to be prepared for the latter.

Moving slowly to get his hands near his head, Rake spread his palms out as flat as he could. He listened to the various sounds, the clinks, clunks, and clatters of metal, wood, and stone made by someone walking over the rubble. The approaching novihomidrak's heartbeat was steady though a little quicker than normal. Rake knew his was probably about the same.

"Hear you," the barbarian said. "Smell you too. Smell bad, like smoke."

A piece of sheet metal was lifted nearby and tossed to the side. It twanged with reverberating vibrations.

Rake decided to let the other novihomidrak do all the heavy lifting. He wouldn't move until necessary.

A board and a brick were both thrown aside.

The barbarian chuckled. "Ship no fly."

Rake tested himself by putting slight pressure on his hands. Pain went through his chest, as he'd expected, but otherwise he felt whole. There didn't appear to have been any novihomidrak-forged shards in the barrel with the explosives. An oversight on someone's part. Someone who had expected them to just rip the sheet aside to begin with and not approach with caution.

Rake heard something drop and couldn't identify what made the slight sound. But then he caught Siva's scent and his whole body went rigid.

"Heard that," the barbarian laughed. "You care. She's here. You won't find."

Then the barbarian turned and walked away. Rake damned the fact the barbarian knew how to roust him from his spot. Were his feelings for Siva so apparent?

Mindful that one of the barbarian's weapons was a bow, and the arrows for it could be fired from a distance, Rake cautiously pushed himself up. As he surfaced above the debris, he found the source of Siva's scent nearby. The shirt lay in a crumpled pile very close to where his head had been. He suspected the barbarian had known all along where he was and had merely been toying with him.

But why?

The barbarian climbed into the cab of a truck with a large cargo unit behind it and started the engine. A moment later, he was driving off. The barbarian waved as he headed down the road.

Rake climbed to his feet, shaking the dirt and wreckage off him. "Keystone? Ruckus?" he called out. Taking a deep sniff of the air, he smelled ravagers in the distance, but no novihomidraks. At least, not on the surface. His thoughts turned to Cal. He might still be trapped below.

The pile of barrels Ruckus had been stacking beyond the fence as Rake and Keystone lifted them out was still there. It looked as if the explosion had knocked a couple down, but none had broken open. Once again, Rake thanked the Onesong for letting them safely get the barrels out and doing so before the blast. He was very grateful his mistake hadn't cost him his life, or that of the other novihomidraks. He might not know their fate, but he hoped they had retreated to regroup. He expected to see them at any moment.

As he turned back to the spot where the explosion had occurred, he saw Siva's wadded-up shirt. He wanted to go after Siva. Every fiber of him shouted to give chase. He grabbed the material off the ground and raised it to his face. Then he fought the growl that rose from deep in his chest which threatened to make his dragon teeth extend from his gums. All over the top of Siva's scent was the barbarian novihomidrak's, as if he had already claimed her.

Rake tucked the material into his back pocket. It wouldn't be that easy to put her behind him, but right now he had to focus on Cal. The intent had always been to bury the novi beneath the rubble with the bodies of his brethren above him.

It took several moments to get down to the trap door, all the while the broken ribs in his chest flaring with pain. Many times, Rake reminded himself that it wouldn't kill him. He looked around often in case the ravagers approached with weapons. That he needed to watch. A novihomidrak weapon in their hands would be lethal.

But none came, to his surprise. He noticed them watching every so often, but it seemed as if they had been warned to stay back. It made him wary of other dangers, like another bomb set on the trapdoor.

When it came time to open it, he spread his wings and prepared to wrap them around himself like a shield.

The door in the floor had a metal pull ring. He placed two fingers inside.

What had happened to Keystone and Ruckus? Were they following Siva? Why hadn't they returned already?

With a tug, he pulled the door.

A series of detonations went off beneath his feet. He felt himself falling.

Then he was flying, watching as the floor gave way onto sharp metal pikes impaled into the stone of the underground level. Like a funnel, the center fell and pulled with it all the building's rubble. Boards struck the pikes and slid down the shafts. Metal sheets rippled with discordant tones as they fell and rang out against the pikes. Debris plopped as it splashed into something denser than water. Dust billowed and made a thick cloud below Rake.

If Keystone or Ruckus had pulled the ring, they would have fallen onto the spears, and, much like the wood, they would be skewered there. If those were novihomidrak-forged spears, they'd be dead. Even if they were normal pikes which didn't break the novihomidrak's skin, it would be quite painful. Rake had no desire to find out if those spears would cut him or not. If he hadn't had his wings out, he wasn't sure he would've had the time to extend them.

Rake steadied the thrust of his wings so that he could listen for the faint heartbeat he and the other novihomidraks had been following from the moment they entered this building. He could scarcely hear it now, but at least it was there and not muffled as it had been previously. Cal was there, but now covered in building debris and dust.

A part of Rake wished he could use his dragon breath to clear away the litter, but he knew that even the lightest touch could kill Cal in his wounded state. If Cal had been healthy, he would have been able to withstand it. The protection imbued by the pearl, the shell which incubated the novihomidrak, afforded not only the novi a toughened skin, but also gave resistance to heat and cold, as well as the dragon breath of another. Novies had even been known to survive on planets and moons with little gravity and even in the cold vacuum of space for short periods of time due to the pearl's armoring.

But even a novihomidrak had limits and, once they had been reached, injuries became severe. It appeared that the Onesong wanted its champions, but, once they fell, the weak would quickly be culled.

For as much strength as Cal had to last this long, even that was fading, and Rake heard it in the other novihomidrak's fluttering heartbeat. Rake hoped Cal wasn't ready to give up yet.

Somehow, Rake had to find Cal and safely get down there to get the novi out.

A few ravagers were peeking around the sides of other buildings in the complex, apparently checking to see if he had fallen to his death. When they saw him flying above the ruins, they quickly ducked away. He hissed at a couple who dallied to look too long and sent them scurrying back. Rake needed to be quick before they went to locate their novihomidrak-forged weapons and gained enough courage to formulate an attack.

He landed on a stable portion of the foundation, but he didn't tuck his wings away until he was completely sure it wouldn't crumble beneath his weight. Even then, he kept them at the ready as he knelt down and blinked down the dragon lids to sharpen his vision. The whole pit smelled like it had been a urinal, and perhaps the building above had been some sort of outhouse before they'd set it up as a trap. Something this rancid would definitely disrupt a novihomidrak's senses. Even the spikes were set up so evenly spaced that it reminded Rake of certain shrines that were used as gateways to longer jumps across the Onesong. On these planets, they had complicated dialing systems that required columns and a lot of magic.

It seemed so unlikely that the barbarian novihomidrak had ever been through one of those. How did he know, or was it instinctual? Either way, now it held such reminiscence for Rake that he barely could think of anything other than the columns and the last time he'd walked among some.

How nice it would be to go somewhere far, far away.

Except, Siva couldn't travel with him like that.

The thought shook Rake. He knew he had to stop thinking about her. The saperes had warned him.

Yet, Keystone had told him Rake would be a fool to let her get away. Had Keystone touched on something in the Humline, or perhaps even deeper in the Onesong? Or was Keystone saying that to make Rake just enjoy the moment. Human lives were so fleeting, especially compared to a novihomidrak.

He couldn't believe his thoughts were sweetly turning to Siva while he was here facing blood, urine, and rot. What had come over him?

Rake turned his face to the sky as if he could plead to the heavens to understand this situation.

Maybe chaos had gripped him. His thoughts decidedly weren't his own, and he questioned his every emotion. For the love of the Onesong, he was supposed to be on a mission here and all he could think about was a woman. What other explanation could there be other than chaos? Was it possible that the barbarian by his very birth had caused the disruptive energy which threatened the Onesong to be an ally to the novihomidrak? Often had he been told that, if any thought were allowed in the Onesong, then it could be a reality. If that were true, then, when the barbarian had lent his energy to devising this trap, chaos had been infused with it.

At least he was no longer thinking of Siva.

Not until then.

Shaking his head, Rake looked back down into the pit and tried to see Cal. The Humline still spoke of him being down there. But it no longer indicated three novies would be needed. They had gone beyond whatever had required the help of the other two. It was all up to him now.

Slowly, he slid feet first very carefully down into the pit. He sucked in his breath and held his chest tight. The feathers of his spread wings ruffled over the uneven rock and slime behind him. He hated doing it, but he had to keep his wings extended so he could remain flat against the wall and fit in the small space before the spikes started.

Broken boards and crumbling mud bricks shifted beneath his weight. He felt himself sink into the ooze with every step, and Rake quickly realized that the muck was deep enough to cover a man lying flat on his back. It would be filling every orifice -- mouth, nose, ears – and Rake choked at the thought. It wouldn't kill a novi, but it certainly wouldn't be pleasant. He gagged again at the thought of waking up like this.

Yeah, his thoughts weren't so pleasant now.

He wished the Onesong was telling him that Cal was dead, because Cal might not wish to be rescued after this. Would the saperes be able to do anything to ease Cal?

He might be broken after this.

Unsettled, Rake slipped wing first between two spikes and started to make his way toward the middle of the pit. If he were to make someone endure this either as a rescuer or as a victim, he'd make sure to place the victim in the middle of the pit to prolong the suffering for all involved.

What he wouldn't do to have Keystone's help, or even Ruckus' right about now. Rake couldn't stop thinking about that moment when Cal would wake up and discover what had happened to him. With luck, they'd be a long way from here and Cal would be cleaned up. Life rarely tidied up so nicely though.

The muck deepened even as the debris thickened. It had all been funneled toward the center as the building fell, yet it seemed like that too had been expected, or that whoever had created this cesspool wanted it to last a long time and fill to the center.

Unfortunately, that put Cal even deeper.

Rake held onto the spikes as he moved through. They didn't hold as firmly as they did at the edge where he'd entered. This seemed to be another sign that there wasn't enough dirt to hold the poles in place. Whatever lay beneath the surface of the black goo was very soft.

A sharp tip of a submerged spear pierced his shoe and drove all the way through his foot. At the unbearable pain, Rake drew his foot up, watching blood darkened by the muck splatter onto the dark, glossy ooze. Holding his foot with one hand, he didn't dare give up the spike he held in the other.

He was in trouble, and he knew it.

The spike wobbled, threatening to send him toppling over.

Rake seized another one and regained his balance even while this second one also teetered. If he fell, he'd find himself impaled on the novihomidrak-forged tips hidden just below the dark surface of the water.

25

Siva stretched as she came out of sleep and, for a moment, she believed she was at home. Scratchy sheets covered the twin-sized mattress she slept on, and a thin, tightly woven blanket topped it off to help keep in her body heat. Her father might be the primieret on Nungh Two, but she was just another mouth to feed.

Her dreams had been mixed between memories of her home world and the ravagers of this world. A winged angel often swooped in to rescue her and carried her into other dreams. Right before waking, she'd been trapped in darkness. When the door opened, Prince – no, King – Henris stood before her with open arms she didn't want to go into. But she had no choice, and accepted his embrace.

As she tried to break free from those dreams, she found it hard to keep her eyes open. Somewhere amid the struggle, she recalled Henris asking a man to sedate her so she could sleep for now. She hadn't wanted drugs or to sleep, but Henris had insisted. Insisted so much that she began to believe that Sapere Falin's life might depend on whether she allowed the injection to be given to her.

Falin never regained consciousness as far as she knew after they'd taken him from the box unit on back of the truck, but his breathing and the occasional groans of pain indicated he was still alive. If Henris had any means of saving Falin, then she would allow herself to be sedated so they could focus on saving the sapere.

There would be plenty of time to ask Henris what he was doing out here. The one thing that had been clearly evident in the moments after he'd opened up the doors was that he was indeed working with the ravagers. Now, Siva had nothing but questions she wanted to put forth to him.

How was he part of this? Had he intentionally sabotaged their wedding?

Right now, those were her top two questions, and she used them to find her way out of the drug-induced fog back to this world that felt like her own but wasn't. She couldn't believe she'd gone from one war to another.

She'd been allowed to change into a tank top with spaghetti straps and a pair of shorts with no significant length to them before being given the injection. She'd been told that her clothes would be taken away and new ones provided. Those now sat folded on a nearby straight back, armless chair that looked as if it would be uncomfortable to sit in for any length of time.

As for her knife, that had been taken away from her before she'd been untied. The barbarian novihomidrak had told one of the ravagers about it and apparently they had been worried about her using it on King Henris if she got the opportunity. If she didn't like his answers, then, yes, she might use the knife on him. An over-exaggeration, maybe, but she wouldn't get angry until she spoke to him. Maybe his answers would be very logical.

Right now, she wanted to go check on Falin.

Her body seemed willing to move, though a little heavy, but her mind still felt dull, and sitting up sent her into vertigo. Siva glanced up to the camera discreetly mounted to the ceiling in the corner and wondered if anyone was watching her. How strange this world. At one moment, it lacked technology and seemed so simple, but then in another it showed great advancement. What was the truth?

Siva stood. The bed creaked behind her as she gained her feet. She remained in place for a moment to see if her legs would hold her. Blinking, she hoped she could pull everything into focus. As much as she wanted to shake her head, she didn't, fearing it would send her head spinning.

When she believed herself capable, she took a step toward the chair with the clothes. She didn't stagger or fall which she took as a good sign. Making it to the chair and picking up the clothes boosted her confidence a bit, and she made it to the trifold dressing screen which shielded her from the camera's view so she could change.

The windowless room was lit by three long LED bulbs embedded into the ceiling and covered with opaque white covers to further diffuse the light along the muted grey-green walls. Aside from the bed, chair, and dressing screen, there was no other furniture in the small room. Siva hoped someone would come and get her before she had to resort to using the bedpan placed beneath the chair. She wished she'd been provided with a means to clean herself, even if it was a bucket of water and a washcloth.

Behind the screen, she took her time getting dressed. The last of the sedation drugs were clearing from her system, and she still felt a little wobbly. By the time she was dressed, though, her head felt almost normal. But before she could come back around the screen, a tendril of nerves wound its way through her stomach. What would happen next? Where was Rake? Was he okay? What had happened to Keystone? He needed a sapere to heal him. The barrage of questions on her mind strengthened every fear trying to escape and run through her. She breathed deeply, allowing herself to feel her worries, and slowly the nervous sensations faded. Not that they weren't there, they just weren't as loud.

She'd not heard anyone come in while she was dressing, and she remained alone in her room. She had no proof that the camera was on. For all she knew, it might not actually be plugged into anything capable of receiving the video feed. On Nungh Two, there were several businesses that did that in order to save money. However, those with food always had connected cameras to protect their merchandise. Theft of food carried a swift penalty, especially when backed with proof.

Had her father made it home? Was he waiting for her? What would he do now to help their world now that her marriage to Henris hadn't occurred? Could the negotiations still be salvaged?

On the one hand, Siva wanted to hope that Henris had been searching for her and just happened to find her among the ravagers. Maybe they had respected his status as king enough to allow him safe passage. No, even that didn't sound right to her own mind. The only logical reason why they didn't kill Henris on sight was because he was working with them. That didn't mean she was in danger, and certainly so far she'd come to no harm, but that didn't mean the contract negotiated between their fathers still held. Had Henris even wanted to marry her, or did he feel obligated like a pawn just as she had? Would he seek a different marriage that would strengthen his position now that he was king?

She had to stop these questions. They were rolling through her mind and building more unfounded fears in her mind. She really needed to speak to Henris and get his side of the story.

Walking to the door, she realized she was about to find out if she was a guest or a prisoner. If the door was locked, she was the latter, but, if she were allowed to leave the room under her free will, she'd feel much more at ease with the situation.

The metal felt cool in her palm. She turned it.

It didn't open.

Siva stepped back from the locked door and looked up into the camera. Could they hear her?

"Hey," she said, waving her hands at the camera. "I'm awake, and I'd like to see King Henris."

Did anyone notice? Had someone heard?

"Henris," she shouted a bit louder. Maybe a guard had been posted outside the door and would hear her. Would the guard be one from the palace or a ravager?

Where was Rake? She'd feel so much safer with him.

"Hey," she said, raising both arms over her head in front of the camera. "Someone want to come unlock the door?"

A moment later, she heard the click of a lock being turned and the door swung open. She hoped to see Henris but she expected a guard.

She never predicted to see the one person who stood squarely in the doorway as it swung open: her father.

26

Rake held firmly to the spikes to use them as poles to steady himself even though they wobbled in the muck beneath him. Blood drenched the inside of his shoe and made it feel heavy, while the wound pulsed and stung. He wanted to fly out but in this tight space he wouldn't be able to pump his wings into flight even if they weren't covered with sludge. If he'd had feathers covered in this, it would have been worse. As it was, in time he might be able to shake and wash the oily goo from his scales, but it would take time.

This was a bad idea. Everything about this had been set up as a novihomidrak trap, and he knew it. Now he couldn't even trust where he stepped. This whole thing had been set up by someone who knew what a novihomidrak was, their weaknesses, their arrogances, and they'd had a novihomidrak willingly help them. Rake couldn't help the idea that someone also knew him personally, knew about his wings, and knew that he had gone through the Crossover ceremonies to make him just that much better and that he wouldn't go down easily. He wouldn't go out without a fight either.

There could be another trap set beyond what he'd already discovered. Two explosive devices, two layers of spikes with one seen and one unseen. It would be foul for Rake to not assume that this black yuck he waded through also didn't have another purpose other than just being disgusting. Since the traps seemed to come in pairs, there had to be something else waiting for him to trigger it.

Or that might be what they wanted him to think, expecting him to see the pattern only to set up something different that he wouldn't see.

Now he was second-guessing himself. That was dangerous, deadly even as he heard Cal's heartbeat, still frantic but slowing.

The sludge hadn't filled this area until the explosive device on the trapdoor was triggered. This was definitely a well-set trap, but it had to take more than just the barbarian's doing and knowledge.

No, this would take someone who thought about strategies to defeat an enemy, and did so frequently. Ravagers didn't plan like this and they certainly couldn't imagine the consequences of their actions or how another would react in order to build this multilayered ambush. That left very few people who could not only devise this but had the means to carry it out. The names on that short list didn't make Rake happy, and he didn't want to believe that any of them could conceive of the damage they were trying to inflict. The death of one novihomidrak was already on this person's hands, and, if this pit was an example, that person wanted more. Would it be enough for an angered dragon to spin this world off from the Onesong as well?

Since Ruckus and Keystone hadn't returned to help, Rake assumed they were also incapacitated. He had to pull Cal out of this mess so he could find Ruckus and Keystone before they were also used as pawns in additional ploys.

How high would the death toll go?

His injured foot pulsed as he continued to make his way toward the center of the pit. He led with that foot now, allowing it to be cut into a couple more times. The damage was done, so the least he could do was hurry along as best as he could and allow more injury to happen to the weakened foot.

As he made another move forward, the toes of his boots hit a body. Bubbles surfaced through the black ooze. Reaching beneath the surface, Rake seized a handful of cloth. He tugged it up.

Cal hung limply face-down as Rake tried to get a better hold. His stretched wings pressed against the spears, not allowing for Rake to get under Cal enough to lift him.

At a gurgle beneath him, Rake saw more bubbles coming to the surface, which jiggled as the ooze began to rise. The pit was filling.

Rake turned to try to pull Cal along, maybe get the novihomidrak to a better spot, but Cal stopped short with a yank.

Rake felt his heart speed up at the sight of a chain looped from a cuff around Cal's wrist. It wasn't thick, but it was holding Cal firm.

Despite the feel of the sludge sliding under his wings, Rake folded them along his back and tried to reach the chain. If he could just loop his talons around it, he could free Cal.

The pit was filling quickly with additional sludge. Rake hit another spike, driving it deep into his heel. Howling with frustration and rage, Rake had to free himself and, in the effort, Cal slipped away from him.

Rake clambered to retrieve Cal. The ooze had made his arms slick, and he had no counterbalance. Fear kept him from moving his feet too far apart.

Cal jerked away from him and, as Rake heard and felt a heavy clunk going on beneath him, Cal started to sink in increments. The chain, which had activated another deadly snare, was pulling the novihomidrak down to the bottom.

Unable to reach the chain, Rake knew he had to get to it and fast. Cal hadn't sputtered and spewed the ooze from his lungs which meant he wasn't even trying to breathe. It was only a matter of time now until Cal's heart stopped.

Rake raised his head toward the blue sky. "Crap," he muttered before taking a deep breath and diving into the sludge to go beneath Cal. Blind with his eyes closed, he used his hands to follow Cal's body over the novihomidrak's chest along to the arm on the far side away from Rake, then down his arm to the cuff and chain. Rake slashed, breaking the links.

His feet had come off of the submerged boards he'd been standing on, and now he had to twist himself upright and put his feet somewhere in order to stand. Not only would he have his weight but Cal's as well. Rake hoped he'd get out of here with only the one injured foot. Odds were against that right now.

He took the chance, hefting Cal up. His feet landed on the

sunken boards which had once been the floor and walls of the building. The pit had filled to his waist and become more oily. The odor of it had changed and now reeked of kerosene. He flicked his hand to clean it as best as he could, then rubbed it over his face trying to clean away as much of the muck as he could from his eyes, nose, and mouth. It would take more than one swipe, but he had no more time.

Rather than trying to walk, Rake flipped Cal over and began to swim with Cal. They had to get to the side. If the pit filled faster, Rake might be able to climb out.

He smelled smoke in the air. The Humline trembled, showing that danger approached, but Rake had already figured that out the moment he'd begun to smell the kerosene. He was drenched with it, as was Cal. They both bore injuries.

The Onesong quickly culled weakened novihomidraks. Only the strong should survive.

Rake had to prove he was strong. He was just in a really bad position.

His wings caught on spikes and he had to move a little backward before he could go forward again. Rake glanced back over his shoulder as he continued to swim. Ravagers carrying torches were indeed approaching.

"Stay back," he growled.

Would the ravagers be frightened by the low threat, or had the barbarian bolstered their confidence about how weak their prey would be? Carry the fire, light the pit, no more worries.

The pit had stopped filling, or seemed as if it had, leaving Rake about a foot down from the edge. He tried to lift Cal out, but, without sure footing, all Rake did was sink into the sludge. He braced his feet against the walls, but that didn't help him gain any leverage.

Grumblings above came from ravagers trying to encourage one another to get closer and drop their torches. Fire was bad, but the novies were worse. What to do?

Rake knew his time was growing short quickly. It would only be a moment before one of the ravagers decided to throw their torch to see what would happen. When the kerosene lit, then more torches would follow.

Having no choice, and knowing this was the widest space he had, Rake grabbed Cal beneath the novihomidrak's arms, and Rake spread his wings. Kicking with his feet, even though painful, he had to gain ground in the sludge. It helped him to lift. Then he pumped his wings. Spikes caught along the edges, and some of their tips shredded through his scales.

Damage done. He had to keep going.

Oily goop splattered off his wings as they fought to drag him and Cal out of the pit.

Rake held his breath.

A torch was thrown.

Then another. And another.

Fire ignited across the pit.

Rake held Cal. They reached the ground, his injured foot landing first.

Feeling the fire come up over him from the oil trail left behind them, Rake dropped Cal and came down on top of the novihomidrak. He bent his head in until his chin was against his chest, wings wrapped over both of them. Oil burned along his wings. The scent of burning kerosene crawled with black smoke through every crevasse it could and stung in Rake's eyes.

The fall had ejected sludge from Cal, and he began to spew more of it, purging it from his stomach, lungs, and throat. Rake had no choice but to let it come out and keep it from the fire. He stayed firm. A moment longer and this would all be over.

The fire stopped crawling over his wing's scales, though he still heard the flames raging in the pit.

Rake raised his head to peek out. Ravagers, several with torches still in their hands, trembled as they moved backward. They must think him a demon rising from a fiery pit. He was. Their perception was correct.

He felt his dragon teeth descend, face morphing under the cover of his wings. Then he spread his wings and roared at the ravagers, longing to rip each one of them to shreds for the pain they had caused him and what Cal had endured.

The ravagers ran.

Rake knelt beside Cal and checked his breathing and pulse. Cal was in bad shape. The novihomidrak's face had been battered. The breathing was all wrong, and Rake wondered if ribs were broken or maybe a lung punctured. Considering what Cal had just had inside him, would the novihomidrak become septic and unable to receive a sapere's healing?

Rake had no time to waste. He scooped Cal up in his arms and took flight.

27

The sight of her father, Ozlem Candemir, with two ravagers holding upright polearms behind him, stunned Siva at first. She quickly shook it off and pulled her father inside the room. Then, she went to attack the guards holding him.

"Siva, wait," he said firmly, landing a hand on her shoulder. "I have much explaining to do."

But his words came too late. The ravagers prepared for her attack, and one moved around Siva to stand between her and her father.

"Stand down," Ozlem said.

Siva thought the order was for her, but she saw the ravagers move back and raise the tips of their polearms once more. She turned and saw that the ravager who had gotten behind her was trying to put distance between her and her father.

"It's all right, Murk," Ozlem said to the ravager. "She

doesn't understand yet. She's just trying to protect me too. Go wait outside."

The ravager looked between Siva and Ozlem, then left the room and closed the door behind him.

"Father," she said, rushing into his arms. "Are you all right? You weren't hurt, were you?"

At first, he seemed happy to hold her in his arms. Then he pushed her away with a certain amount of shame in his actions and on his face. "Oh, Siva," he began. "I hope you can forgive me."

"Wait, what? Forgive you?"

He glanced around the sparse room, and Siva sensed that he wished he had a window to look out of. He often liked to go to a window when he had a pressing matter on his mind. The one at the primieret's palace that still existed without grates or bars was high up and gave a view of a valley wasteland. It wasn't much to look at, rather a deep reminder of what their world had become, but some days when the light was right it seemed as if hope had come to that valley. Ozlem often said that looking out there helped to widen his mind to new possibilities.

But now, the memories left her with a sinking sensation in her stomach because it meant that he had bad news to tell her.

Siva straightened her stance and tightened all her emotions into a ball to shove away deep inside her. At this moment, her father didn't need his daughter, but rather a soldier ready to take orders.

He noticed and shook his head, guilt once again flooding his features. The last time she'd seen him this distressed over giving her news was when her mother had passed. "You're a good daughter, you know that?"

Not only was she a good daughter, she was his only child. He had nothing to compare it to.

"I know you long to help our people as much as I do," he continued. "I should have shared the plan with you earlier, but I needed your actions to be innocent. Your life may have depended on it."

"What are you talking about?" She might have to go sit down in the chair if this discussion got any heavier.

"Siva, our people are lost. That became evident the day that I first came to Myeller for negotiations. This world was so plentiful and peaceful. Or I thought it was, until I first saw the ravagers attacking. It just so happened that a female was captured by King Rolant's novihomidrak."

Rake. It had to be.

"The female was questioned, and she was released," he said. "After that, I knew I had a bargaining chip." Ozlem turned in place to face her as she sat. "There was a man, if you could call him that, who lived on our planet while I was growing up. He was invincible. No weapon could harm him. Because he looked so strange, he generally stayed away and kept to himself. Every now and again, he'd come down and demand livestock and other goods he needed to survive. If the town he entered denied to turn over his request, he slaughtered them all until they gave him what he needed – or he would just take it. Rumor had it that he was a demon, but I knew better because I'd followed him when I was a boy to where he lived. I wanted to know the truth, and we talked. I showed him kindness where he'd had none before."

Siva had many questions she wanted to ask, but held silent. Her father's gaze had drifted to the grey wall beside her and now had a far-off look. Without benefit of a real window, he'd make one in his imagination.

"This man looked exactly like the ravager who'd been captured. I now knew I'd found his race of people, and the more I learned about the novihomidraks, the more I realized that this man was a novihomidrak," her father said. "When I returned to Nungh Two and went out to speak with him, he told me that he knew what he was and that he had doomed our planet. There is no way our world can survive. Can you understand that and imagine how he must feel knowing it is his fault?"

"That doesn't explain this," Siva said raising her hands, though she wasn't sure she truly indicated the area around her because she didn't know where she was. This had all become very confusing. "What are you doing? What is this all about?"

Ozlem glanced at her with a soft smile and a knowing nod. "You want to know what happened to the negotiations, if I sought to use this man to aid our cause."

"I suppose that's a great place to start."

"As did I. It had been my hope to bring him here to speak to the ravagers and get them to listen. Instead, he found his people. Memories surfaced."

"Memories? Father, if a novihomidrak remembers his past, it can be dangerous. It can break their mind."

Ozlem nodded. "I heard the same thing. He was already under such duress that his mind was already strained." He went back to staring at the wall before he continued. "He was already broken before. Finding his people healed him, gave him purpose once more."

"His purpose? To bring the ravagers together and give

them weapons beyond their own technology to help them kill even more people, to level cities to the ground?" Siva wasn't certain she could believe what she was hearing from her father. Did he not know what was going on out there?

"It has a purpose, Siva. We will be able to help our people."

"I'm not sure I understand. How is helping the ravagers meant to aid Nungh Two?"

"These people survive in harsh conditions."

"Are you really thinking that they can relocate to Nungh Two while we bring our people here?" Siva asked, praying that wasn't her father's line of thought. "Let us thrive on a healthy world while they slowly die without even having a chance?"

"They don't know that, and our world could still last for a long time. They could have generations of peace by themselves."

"The air is poisoned, and the land isn't far behind. They won't have a chance. And yes, the planet could last as a dead world for a long time. I can't even believe you'd consider this."

"Our people survive. Isn't that what matters?"

"Not at the expense of other people's lives."

"They aren't people, Siva. They are savages."

"You would consider even doing this to the novihomidrak you had the nerve to follow and ask questions of? You'll give him up too?"

He paused and took a moment to give her a solid look. "Yes. I was elected as the primieret to save our people. No one told me how to do that. This is my decision."

"Well, it's a wrong one." She glanced away from him. "I won't support it."

"You don't have to. I don't need you to like this."

"You'll have the death of a people on your head. Can you live with that?" Siva asked.

He dropped his gaze to the floor and gave an angry twitch of his head. "They will outlive me and most likely you too. I know that my grandchildren will be safe. To me, everyone is getting the best of the situation. At my death, I will no longer care what happens to them. In time, when your children are safe, you will see that I made the right decision. That will be enough for me."

Siva honestly didn't know what to say to that. Catching her mouth hanging open, she closed it and struggled to breathe while trying to think of the right next thing to say.

The door behind them opened, and Henris walked in.

"The ravagers know they are not getting a perfect world, but they understand they are getting a world all their own," her father continued. "That is paradise to them."

Before Siva could ask Henris if he agreed with this plan, Henris came over to Ozlem and placed his hand on her father's shoulder. "I'm afraid that she doesn't yet see the brilliance in our plan. I'm afraid we'll have to illuminate her."

"Henris, what are you going to do? I can't believe you would agree with this," she said, even while not believing her own words. She knew that Henris fully backed this plan. How could he not? He'd been fighting the ravagers all his life, and it had only gotten worse. She had known from the beginning that the whole purpose of the treaty between her world and his was not only to help her world but to help his against the ravagers.

"Please, Siva," Ozlem said in one final plea to make her understand before they enacted whatever they had planned in order to illuminate her, "you said you would do whatever it took to save our people. This is the only way."

"I refuse to believe that."

"The planet cannot support the lives of three civilizations. They are suited to eke out an existence in harsh environments. This makes the most sense."

Siva lowered her head, feeling as if her heavy heart sunk too. "In order to sell them the lie, you had to buy it first."

She wondered what would happen if she just kept her head down and walked by them. Would they let her go? Determined to try, she started toward the door. She didn't know where she was going or what she would do, but she couldn't remain here anymore. Out there, there was an answer to this whole problem. She wouldn't find it by staring at the brick walls of their decisions.

Henris seized her arm and yanked her back toward him. "A little time to realize how life survives no matter what, and then we will finalize our marriage, and you will accept that all this has been for the best."

He dragged Siva toward the door and yanked it open.

In that moment, Siva glanced to her father hoping for his help. She saw no sympathy there.

"Murk," Henris said, thrusting Siva toward the ravager. "Put her in the pit."

28

Finding Ruckus' ship abandoned dealt a serious blow to Rake's plan. Smelling the traces of the barbarian inside was even worse. Rake set Callous down gently on his bed in the room that still carried the fragrance of Siva. Considering Cal's state, Rake doubted the novihomidrak smelled anything beyond the scent of his own blood.

"Hang on, buddy," Rake said, wishing he could offer more to Callous than words.

What the unconscious novihomidrak needed was healing, not words, anyway. The sapere was supposed to stay here. Along with Siva. How had the barbarian gotten into the ship, which seemed intact. It had to mean that Siva and Falin had gone outside for some reason and the barbarian entered and waited for their return.

Rake stormed through the cargo area of the ship to the

pilot's cabin and dropped down in the seat to glance over the controls. Holding his hands up, the gesture felt like he was already given to helplessness as he didn't find any one button that said, "To fly ship, press here." There were so many gadgets and gauges, none of which Rake needed himself in order to fly. This console before him made flight seem impossible.

He had his wings, and, whenever he'd needed to get to a planet, he took the Wells. Rarely did he ever ride in a craft, and recently he'd made more trips in Ruckus' ship than he had on any other world. Now, when he needed someone to fly the ship, there was no one.

Granted, none of that would have mattered if there was a sapere here to heal Cal as had been the plan.

His only choice was to fly Cal all the way back to Plashia. The novi had barely been able to make the trek here. Carrying an unconscious person was a lot harder than one who was conscious and could help to hold on.

He thought of carrying Siva to Plashia and how she'd clung around his neck, her body, warmed by the frights the day had brought her, against his and the thunderous sound of her heartbeat in his ears. Cal had been the exact opposite, his body growing colder and heartbeat fading.

Cal wouldn't last the flight if Rake had to make it carrying him.

Rake would have to do his best with flying the craft. If he failed and crashed it, Cal wouldn't survive that either, but it might be a lot quicker death than what he'd suffer while Rake flew through the air currents. Rake had to try.

Wishing he'd watched Ruckus closer as he prepared the ship to take off, Rake remembered hearing the sounds of toggle switches being flipped. How many? There were so many silver stick toggles, not to mention several switches.

This was impossible. He might have better luck trying to find out where Falin went. Maybe he and Siva had abandoned the ship and hidden somewhere. They might not be far from the ship, and all he had to do was call out to them for them to come out.

The Humline might as well have been laughing at him for as much as it shivered.

Rake looked once more at the console, deciding to try all the switches if he had to. At least then something would go really right or really wrong and he'd have done something and gained information.

But when he flipped them, nothing happened. Nothing at all.

He pushed a red button he could only imagine would do something. One didn't place a red button in the center of things if it didn't have some reason. Nothing happened there either.

Once again, he held his hands up helplessly and sat back in the chair. What was going on?

Then he saw it. A single wire dangling from the casing beneath the console. Because of the wire, the panel didn't fit back on correctly. Rake reached down and pulled the panel off.

Beneath, the shredded wires resembled a mangled salad.

This was bad. Beyond bad. Now, Sapere Falin remained Cal's only hope.

Rake ran back to Cal's room and dug around until he found a couple clean shirts and a bin that could hold water. He used the first shirt to clean as much of the sludge away from Cal's face as he could. Tossing that shirt into a sink, Rake washed, put fresh water into the bin, and dropped the clean shirt into the bin. This he carried to Cal's bed and set beside his head, pushing it down into the pillows so that hopefully it wouldn't tip if Cal started to regain consciousness and thrashed about. There wasn't much Rake could do about that, but, if Cal woke that far, maybe a splash of water would bring him to full consciousness. Twisting the shirt, Rake stuck one end in the bin and the other in Cal's mouth. Hopefully it would provide Cal with some water while Rake was gone.

"I will hurry," Rake promised with a gentle touch to Cal's shoulder as he turned to leave.

Outside the ship, he called out for Siva and Sapere Falin and got no response. Of course it couldn't be easy. Next step was to start to track them. He knelt and picked up their scent in the weeds. The barbarian had definitely captured them.

This he followed until he found tire tracks. Siva and Falin had been placed in back of the vehicle, and the barbarian drove off with them. Extending his wings, Rake knew it would be much easier to look for and track a vehicle from the air, and for that he was grateful. He'd never liked following a scent on the ground. It took much too long.

Rake took flight and saw the tracks led in the direction he'd expected, right toward the compound. Very likely, the engine he'd heard coming, the one which had made him lift his head involuntarily and had caused the explosion, was the vehicle Siva and Falin had been in. If only he'd understood the Humline's signal a moment earlier.

He couldn't stew over past events. He had to focus on now. Cal's life depended on it.

His mind, it would seem, didn't want to remain present. It wanted to know how the barbarian had gotten Siva's shirt. Rake had taken her from the palace in her wedding dress. She'd picked up a tee shirt and jeans along the way, and those were all the clothes she had. The shirt the barbarian had been holding had been worn by her several times to carry the scent of her so strongly.

Rake didn't like the possibilities it opened up, especially the one that wondered if Siva had been working with the ravagers all along. There hadn't been any signs of a struggle. Both Siva and Falin had walked willingly with the barbarian. That behavior wasn't strange for a sapere, but he knew Siva was a fighter. The only reason for her to go unforced would be because she had given the shirt to the barbarian so he could find her. No wonder the barbarian practically rubbed it in Rake's face. He'd wanted Rake to know that Siva had been working with him the whole time.

Forgetting to beat his wings, Rake felt his flight descend quickly. He recovered and shook his head angrily. He didn't want to believe that of Siva, but what other explanation could there be?

His flight felt so downhearted. He loved flying, but now … now he just wanted to curl up and let himself crash.

No, Callous needed him to fly and find Falin. It would do no good for Rake to give in to self-destructive tendencies, and all over a simple human woman. She'd gotten into his head, and now he was acting like someone else. Novihomidraks weren't impulsive like this. They listened to the Humline which was embedded in the Onesong. They walked in step with the desires of the universe. They weren't given to flights of fancy for their own desires.

So what was going on with him?

The tracks continued toward the complex, long enough to ensure Rake of their destination, and he knew he'd have to land soon and continue by foot to avoid being seen. He wondered if the ravagers had mended the spot in the fence where he'd previously burned through. Even if they had, he could always make another. Or a simple jump with a couple of flaps with his wings and he could scale the fence easily enough. The latter might be the best idea for it wouldn't leave evidence of his arrival.

He landed in the thin grove of trees just beyond the complex and waited for units performing practice maneuvers to pass. Organized ravagers seemed a foreign concept, and if Rake had previously been told that it was possible, he would have laughed. Now, he didn't know what to think. When he allowed his mind to creep there, it ended in heartache for him.

Falin. He had to focus on Falin. Rake tried to get a sense from the Humline about where the ravagers were keeping the sapere.

He ran for the fence, jumped, let his wings beat twice, and landed on the other side. Then, he took cover behind one of the buildings until he could assess whether he'd been noticed coming over the fence. He heard no calls of alarm.

The Humline was a mess of information. So much was going on, and lots of the events overlapped. Rake didn't know where to begin with all of it. How could he disseminate the messages he received in this tangled flurry?

The one thing he could be certain of was that chaos had begun to occur here. With the Humline so stressed and erratic, a major misalignment had occurred. No, worse than that. Evil had been spread to this world, seeded, and taken root. That had to be from an outside source. That finger pointed toward Siva. She and Henris had been set to marry to cement a treaty between her world and Myeller. But all Rake knew about that negotiation was that people on her world were starving and fighting over remaining resources. Myeller was to help ease that.

What if she'd brought the rot from her planet with her?

"Stop it," Rake whispered in command to himself. He had to quit thinking like that.

King Rolant hadn't been without a devious side, a trait which had grown after the death of his eldest son. Perhaps that same madness ran deep with Henris as well.

It had been Henris who wanted to use Siva's people as fodder. He'd said as much before the wedding. Her planet had people and advanced technology which he wanted to exploit. Maybe training the ravagers had been part of a plan to give the ravagers a minimal fighting chance. Henris wanted to play his own war games.

Would Rake really turn against Henris all to keep Siva in a good light? What was going on in his brain? She really had gotten into his mind. This must have been what Maylene sensed and tried to warn him about.

One thing for certain, he couldn't rescue Falin with such confusion in his mind. He needed a strong link with the Onesong. This folly of emotion had to be purged. Rake was, after all, a champion of the dragons of the Onesong. He couldn't be given to wanton human feelings. They didn't serve him. If nothing else, Maylene's cautions were meant to remind him of that.

She was right. Even having just lost her mate to tragedy on

this world, she continued the mission. Rake couldn't now let the work they had done falter all because he couldn't make sense of his own emotions. It was time to put them away.

Rake reached down and plucked a palm-sized stone from the ground. This one was smooth and oval as if it had spent a long time being buffed by water. In all other respects, it was plain sediment with a couple flecks of quartz that winked at him in the fading light. Quartz was good. Not only was it a natural amplifier, but it stored information as well.

He couldn't believe he was contemplating doing this, but he needed a sapere because a novihomidrak's life was on the line, and Rake couldn't clear the clutter of jumbled thoughts from his mind. He desperately needed drive and focus, not a doorway for chaos.

With a deep, resolute breath, Rake placed the stone against his forehead, crossed his other hand on top as well, and willed all of himself into the stone. This technique was the final one a novihomidrak mastered during the Crossover and had to be performed right before a short mission, yet one where the Crossing novi could be watched very closely. While the object chosen, a rock, in Rake's current case, held the emotions of a novi, this practice could make a novi lose their soul too. Mind, body, and soul always had to be contained together. Take one away and the other two had to maintain an unnatural balance. Too often, the force of this broke the body and allowed the soul to escape.

While that was the worst that could happen to a novi, anyone too close to the novi was also in danger. The technique focused the novi on the mission at hand, regardless of those who might be there to help. Oftentimes, people got hurt or even killed merely because the novihomidrak didn't have the emotional compassion needed to push someone out of danger. Only the quest and its success mattered.

Rake felt lucky that, when he'd performed this for the Crossover, he'd realized the person who'd gotten in the way of his mission was only a child and had thrust him into his mother's arms before finishing his orders for the Dragon Council. It had been too close, and he didn't know how he would have handled the knowledge that he'd breathed out an intense fire which would have vaporized the child. Even the sapere sent with Rake had breathed a sigh of relief when the job was done.

But there were no children who might get helplessly in the way here unless they were the offspring of the ravagers. Seeing how the ravagers had used their own children in ploys of destruction, Rake didn't think he'd regret taking their lives early before they could cause harm. It might save someone else on this planet later. Even the Humline knew that.

Rake felt himself cool, and a calmness entered in place of the tumultuous emotions which were now channeled into the rock. He removed it from his forehead and slipped it into his pants pocket.

Falin. Nothing else mattered now other than finding Falin and getting him to Cal.

29

The hallways of the complex were all painted in that same muted grey-green color. Save for directional lines which matched the hallways and little symbols at the ends, nothing broke up the murky sameness as the ravager guards urged her along in her walk of shame. Many ravagers in the corridors stopped to stare at her, usually scuttling to the sides to watch until she had gone by.

She repeatedly forced her mind away from wondering what they must think of her. It didn't matter much. Besides, she should be finding out what had happened to Keystone, Ruckus, and Falin.

And Rake. She hoped he'd gotten away. Had he found Cal first?

Setting her mind to searching for them as they led her to this pit, Siva found that every door along the way was shut.

Which meant she'd have to escape and come back in somehow. But how would she know her way around?

"Murk, is it?" she asked the ravager beside her. "What are these? Is this your language?"

"Move along," he grunted.

"Yeah, I know. I'm going. But I'm still curious. You can at least tell me what they are as we walk along."

Did ravagers have the capacity for reason? They must – right? – if they could be organized into a sort of military.

"Please, I want to understand," she said.

"Pictures," he said as he nudged her hard around a corner as if he didn't want her to get a good look at the next directional sign.

That didn't stop her from trying though as she took a good look at the image of a box with a tiny X at the bottom just a little off center which featured on the directional they were going. It didn't look like a good sign. The pit, Henris had said. A pit with a dead person, the X, lying in the pit. At the next one, she tried to see if any of the other directionals offered more hope. There was a four-by-four block of X's, which she took to mean military exercises, and another of shirts hanging on a line – laundry or uniforms, she supposed. The last, an upside-down L which had a smaller and reversed transposed L beneath that, she had no idea what it meant but it gave her chills. Something about it looked like gallows on top and a handgun beneath as if they were simplified drawings that a child would use to illustrate such weapons.

Or perhaps it referred to big guns and little guns, like an armory.

The pictures changed along the way, but she stopped trying to put too much meaning to them since the box with the X at the bottom always seemed the worst one to imagine.

As it became a constant in all the symbols that they passed, it began to feel like a dooming drumbeat.

Rake, where was he? Did he have any idea where she was? Would he come?

Cold dread exploded through her as she realized that he worked for Prince – no, King – Henris. Surely that meant Rake wouldn't be coming to rescue her.

Rescue her? What an odd thought. She couldn't believe it had even raced through her head like that, completely unbidden. Since when had she needed someone to rescue her? Is that what she considered it now?

This line of thinking made her angry. And yet, the thought that he wouldn't even be there to help her saddened her, shaded with disappointment. If Rake couldn't – wouldn't – help her now, what could he do to help her planet.

None of this ended well.

That made it feel all so hopeless.

The ravager bent and began to unscrew a valve which sealed a lid onto a shaft similar to the one she and Falin had explored outside the ship. She wished she could go back to that moment now and never leave the ship.

The hinges were silent as Murk raised the hatch and let it fall back with a heavy thud. The smell of sewage wafted from the opening and Siva recoiled from the odor. Everything about this moment said the pit was well used.

"Get in," Murk grunted as he jabbed his finger toward the hole.

"I'm perfectly willing to go back and tell Henris he's right," she said with a step backward.

Murk snagged her by the back of her neck, pulling hair in the process, and shoved her toward the hole. "In."

Siva felt tears gather in her eyes as she staggered forward and fell against the corrugated rim. As she glanced back at the ravager, he seemed to have no pity for a woman's tears.

"In," he growled for a third time, and the tone clearly indicated there wouldn't be a fourth. He stepped forward as if physically stating that he'd throw her in if she didn't go now.

Siva scrambled onto the ladder and began to descend into the darkness below. What if something else lived in the pit, another prisoner? Hungry and still strong enough to bite and fight. Starvation made people go to extreme lengths.

With her father, she'd toured prisons on her world where sometimes the prisoners had resorted to cannibalism. There wasn't food to support those who'd done misdeeds, so these practices had gone on undeterred. The unfortunate ones were those who got away, sometimes with chunks of flesh taken out of their arms or legs. Most died of infection later. Those who survived though were easy marks for additional attacks.

She wasn't ready to deal with that reality here and now. The thought of becoming someone's meal had terrified her then, and rightly so, and did so again.

Her feet struck the ground and Siva fell away from the ladder. She stared to the light at the top as if it were a slim glimmer of hope that the ravager, or even her father, would call her back out. She prayed this was just a threat and not something that would become her reality. Please, please, let her father only show her this to let her know how bad it could be, like when he'd taken her to the prison to show her the lives of those who'd broken the laws. Please let him appear and call her out. Please …

Murk closed the hatch, leaving her in blackness. She heard

the valve turning, the screw tightening into place. She hoped it wouldn't be the last sound she ever heard.

For a moment, Siva didn't breathe so that she could listen for sounds around her. She heard nothing else in the darkness with her. That didn't mean there wasn't something dead down here, but at least nothing rushed out to devour her. She tried not to think about the smell or what had caused it, though she knew it was most likely animal waste, whether it be from a human or a ravager.

As a way to orientate herself, she reached out for the ladder and took ahold of it with one hand. With the other, she stretched out in search of walls around her. The corrugated tunnel shaft had ended somewhere about the time where the light no longer fell inside so this part of the hole was wider.

The walls were further away from the ladder than the span of her arms. She'd have to release the ladder in order to find the walls. Her chances of the ladder being set right in the middle of the pit were slim. It probably rested closer to one of the walls, but which way? She'd have to release the ladder to go in any direction. In the darkness, she might stumble, fall, or be unable to find her way back to the ladder. So many terrors attacked her thoughts at once. There might be additional shafts leading now only out from where she stood, but down.

No, certainly her father wouldn't allow Henris to put her down here if she had the possibility of being harmed, or if death were a real threat. She had to believe there was still a measure of safety here. They meant to scare her into going along with their plans, not kill her.

It didn't stop her breath from being shaky.

She stretched, reaching out even further, hoping one set of

fingertips would find cool rock while the other left the round metal of the ladder. Within a moment, she felt nothing under any of her fingers. Keeping her arms outstretched, she stepped sideways. If she could keep moving in a straight line, she wouldn't lose the position of the ladder.

Slowly, she crept her way across the floor, moving faster away from the direction she'd come, but slower into the unknown. Siva didn't want to jab her fingers against the wall when she did find it.

The pit stretched onward. It felt like she was moving forever. Everything was black. Her arms were growing tired.

Then, she felt her fingers nudge smooth rock. She placed her palm against it. Yes, it was rock, though not quite flat or even round like stacked stone. She collapsed against it and took in deep, relieved breaths. Certainly she couldn't have moved too far away from the ladder, but maybe more than she thought. It was nice to know there was a boundary to the darkness, and in a strange way it made her feel not quite alone.

After a restful moment, she began to work her way along the wall. It felt so smooth with these rounded dips, and she knew she'd felt something similar to this before: the walls of the tunnel outside the shrine, those which Rake had made with his dragon breath.

Yes, this pit had been made by dragon breath. Had the barbarian novihomidrak done this?

Or, an even worse thought, had Rake been helping Henris all along and made this pit too?

She'd been so silly. He'd probably been assigned to watch her all along, to determine if she would go along with the plans Henris and her father had made.

Siva moved sideways along the walls, trying not to imagine Rake's dragon breath carving them out. Her boot hit a pile a soft sludge, and the odor of disturbed sewer came quickly to her.

"Defecation corner," she said softly. The sound of her own voice in the darkness seemed to fill it, then vanish as if eaten by the blackness.

"Hello?" she called out, hoping she wouldn't get a reply but wanting to hear how the sound was there and gone in an instant. It felt so weird to have such a momentary presence that vanished quickly as if it had never been there.

Almost like a human life. Was that how it felt to a novihomidrak, who she knew had much longer lifespans? How could they do what they did, knowing that the people they fought for would be like a sound lost to space?

She made her way back the other direction and found a corner. Since she hadn't stepped further into the muck, she couldn't say honestly that it was a corner over there, only an assumption. Still, it made her wonder if this pit was more rectangular than square.

She started along the new wall she'd found when the familiar screech of someone unscrewing the valve to the hatch reached her ears. Certainly they weren't letting her out already. She'd barely been down here, and it hadn't been enough time for her to learn her lesson.

Unless, they were now putting a ravager down here with her.

Would it be someone to fight her or someone who deserved punishment? Either way, the safety she had in being alone was about to end.

She turned and put her back to the corner. She'd hid in the darkness for as long as she could.

The hatch lifted, and Siva recoiled from the bright light shining down from above. It forced her to shield her eyes against the glare. She saw the reflecting light off the metal of the ladder only a short distance away.

Then a body fell. At first, it was a brown mass against the light at the top. It darkened as it fell. With a thump, it landed and remained unmoving in the thin sliver of light which outlined its shape.

The hatch closed, and the lid tightened once more.

Siva knew she'd be better off possessing the high ground when whoever had been thrown in woke up. She hurried to close the distance to where she'd seen the ladder and began to climb.

It wasn't comfortable, but she twined her legs through the rungs so she could sit until the lump of a person regained consciousness.

30

Rake could pass himself off as a human, but he'd never be able to appear like a ravager. Worse, many of the ravagers knew him from their many encounters. Many believed him a winged demon, a notion he was more than willing to submit to. It was, after all, exactly what he was.

He'd realized this deep truth when he'd done his Crossing ceremony and allowed himself to become the near-mindless creature he'd turned into for the last ritual. Under normal circumstances, he was like an animal and driven by instinct backed by information from the Humline. But then, during that last task, he had gone beyond just being an animalistic novihomidrak.

Since then, he'd done the one thing he didn't believe any other novihomidrak, with their primal arrogance, had ever thought to do: study the other champions.

Novihomidraks were but one champion for the Onesong.

There were soulcolists, those who collected the souls of

the dead and returned the energy to the All, as they called the Onesong. Those who learned to manipulate energy efficiently were adopted into the Black Nights, a group of self-proclaimed ninjas because they moved in the shadows and worked in the darkness.

There were also the champions as chosen by the unicorns. Those who bonded with unicorns were there to save the world much in the same way that novihomidraks did, but they were stuck on their world and couldn't travel the Wells. Only those who had the purest of hearts could bond with the one unicorn who chose them. But even those with the best of intentions can falter and let chaos seep in. Those who resisted or turned away from chaos would become Winctonichts, or Sacred Knights. Unfortunately, they always remained at the whims of the unicorns and, if all seemed lost and hopeless, the unicorn could break the bonding and turn their champion into a mindless killer.

It seemed as if the Onesong pushed each of its champions into a metamorphosis which made them more and more brutal.

Rake hadn't had the opportunity to meet any other hyped-up champion and he knew that, as a novihomidrak who had completed the Crossover, he was a rarity even among his kind.

And he was just as much of an assassin as any of the higher leveled champions.

Ravagers fled, blindly running in all directions as Rake scattered terror through the compound. He raced along, trying to get Falin's scent from any of the buildings. He slashed any ravager who crossed his path, leaving them bleeding and dying in their own entrails on the ground, not caring if he stepped in the mess he left in his wake as he headed for the next building.

Sometimes he flew into ravagers as they tried to escape. He let his wings beat back opponents who tried to stop him.

In the back of his mind, he knew that chaos had to be creeping at the door of his mind, looking for a way in to overtake him. Let chaos try.

His hands drenched in ravagers' blood as his talons slashed away at them. It felt warm at first, then cooled and dried quickly, nearly completely before he reached his next victim. It would be amazing if he'd be able to catch Falin's scent over the coppery odor of all this blood.

His dragon lids were down, casting everything with a dark brown hue as if he were wearing the sunglasses some people wore on other worlds of the Onesong. Except, instead of merely shading his eyes from intense sunlight, his lids also provided a clarity to his vision which allowed him to see minute details others would miss. He'd see ripples in cloth as a ravager started an attack, or a shift of the foot indicating whether the ravager would flee or fight. He could see great distances too, enough to see the arrow released from the bow before he heard the twang from the bowstring. Easy to avoid after that.

Rake caught Falin's scent in a cargo van, and he moved toward the vehicle. The back doors were wide open, and Rake knew Falin had been pulled from within. Footprints suggested another ravager had picked up the sapere's feet and that they had carried him. There were other footprints too, but they didn't matter.

Or did they? Those smaller ones, scuffled in the dirt ...

No, only the sapere mattered.

He turned to follow the way the sapere had been carried off.

"Rake, what are you doing?" Henris' familiar voice called out with heavy authority.

Rake knew he should obey, pivot, and respond. Yet his feet marched on after those who had carried the sapere.

"Rake!"

"Where is Sapere Falin?" Rake swiftly turned and asked. As he faced King Henris, his hand raised to show off the talons drenched in blood.

It did make Henris take half a step backward.

"Are you injured?" Henris asked.

Rake realized that Henris might suspect he was hurt, covered in all that blood as he was, and in need of a sapere's healing. It might not be a terrible ploy, as Henris knew how terrible a wound was to a novihomidrak. This way, he might be taken to Falin immediately.

"Yes," Rake said. The word felt clipped on his tongue.

Henris looked momentarily confused and dismayed. "Where is Sapere Hig? Wasn't he with you? Or Sapere Andaris?"

Rake couldn't really recall what the other saperes had gone off to do. It was something important. "They went back to the shrine."

"They did?"

"Sapere Falin is here. He is the one I need." Rake resumed walking after Falin's scent, leaving Henris to catch up.

"Rake, is something wrong with you? Who did this? We can't follow Falin. The ravagers have him."

In the back of his mind that Rake realized Henris shouldn't be here with the ravagers either. Barely, the question of why Henris was here reached a more cognitive part of his thoughts. Realizing this was all very wrong wasn't inhibiting his mission though. Later, after he found Sapere Falin and got him back to Cal, then Rake could undo this ritual and figure it all out.

"I can't let you go any further," Henris said. "It's too dangerous for you, especially if you are injured. You should return to the shrine and get healing."

"I can't. I need Falin."

"Falin isn't here."

Rake spun around to face the king chasing after him. "Do not lie to me, Henris. I can smell him here."

"Falin was here, but he's not anymore. You're too late."

As Rake stepped closer to Henris, he saw guards closing in to protect their king. Though he doubted their weapons could hurt him, they could hurt Henris by mistake. Besides, Rake knew he was likely to get more – and faster -- answers if he weren't too aggressive with the king.

"Falin has been taken where he is needed. You should've never brought the sapere here. But we can make him into a valuable asset since he is here. It's the only way I could save his life."

"Where is he? What will be done with him?" Rake felt the tingle of other questions at the edges of his mind, but he couldn't make sense of them in his current state. The ritual might not have been a good idea. Only Falin mattered. Falin to heal. Everything else could be dealt with later. Deepening his voice even further, he growled again, "Where is Sapere Falin?"

Henris succumbed to the enchanted question. "He's in being prepared to become a sapere to Thralic."

Rake searched the Humline and learned that this unknown spoken name was the barbarian novihomidrak. The process of changing a sapere's allegiance was complicated and dangerous. They could break his mind so that he would never be the same person again. But if they wanted him to serve the barbarian, maybe they didn't even care.

"Where?" Rake's voice filled with the sound of rage and frustration that he felt at not completely being able to understand. The last time he had done this ceremony, his mission had been straightforward. He thought this would be as well, but now he was finding out different, and his mind wasn't holding everything that he needed to know.

"In bunker C-12."

That meant nothing to Rake. "Show me."

Henris called a command to his guards, who fell in line around them, and Henris started to move through the compound.

Henris' tension faded a little as they walked along, though Rake sensed Henris making motions with his hand down by his side.

Falin. Rake headed toward Falin. That mattered.

The uneasy pressing at the edges of his mind, that was inconsequential and not needed in this mission.

Rescue Falin and take the sapere to Cal.

A heartbeat quickened behind Rake as one of the guards took a sharp intake of breath. Rake turned, sensing danger upon him. Too late, he saw the mace coming toward his head. He tried to block the blow with his arm but was too late in bringing it up. The spiked end of the mace slammed against his temples with a crunch. Rake dropped, feeling the hazy fog of his mind settle over his body, and he was unconscious by the time he hit the ground.

The state didn't last long. Novihomidraks who let themselves fall so easily didn't live long with another novihomidrak in the vicinity. Rake recovered quickly, finding himself upright and being dragged down the corridor by two of the guards with their arms beneath his armpits to hoist him. Maybe they were taking him to the novihomidrak to finish the job. His hands were down at his sides and tied about his waist. He merely had to tighten up the muscles in his biceps and he'd handicap at least one of their arms each. He doubted either guard would be effective at fighting him in such a state, and yet he could use their bodies as weapons or shields. He continued to remain limp and peeked out of half-closed eyes. He didn't want to give any indication that he returned to consciousness. This gave him the element of surprise.

Rake looked at the intersection maps, which used pictures rather than words to indicate what was in each direction. Rudimentary, but it probably worked well for the ravagers. Their spoken language was broken at best, disagreements often caused by miscommunication with words which resulted in frequent skirmishes, and Rake doubted they'd ever even considered a written language.

But which way was Falin? It wasn't like any of the images showed one man standing over another in a ceremonial type fashion. Nor did they indicate which bunker he was in. He might be in bunker C-12, and they might be dragging Rake to witness this ceremony.

"Where are you taking him?" a male voice with a hint of an

accent called out. "This is a dangerous creature to have here, don't you think?"

Footsteps behind Rake stopped and pivoted as if the person was facing the speaker. "Did you know that certain novihomidraks can literally melt rock with their breath? I thought I might test out a couple of theories. It's said that trapped novihomidraks will do anything to survive," Henris said.

The newcomer gasped. "You don't mean to stick that creature in with my daughter, do you?"

"Just testing a theory," Henris said in a slow, lingering way.

Rake heard a crank turning in the short distance. The sound along with Henris' conversation confirmed that Rake wasn't going anywhere near Sapere Falin. A diversion from his mission was unacceptable.

Time to end the charade.

He clamped down on the guards' arms. Stomping a foot down on the floor, he leaned his weight onto the forward leg, dragging the surprised guards downward. Then Rake twisted and spun them off their feet.

Henris and the other man jumped back with a start while Rake rushed toward them with the guards in tow. More of Henris' surrounding guards braced themselves hesitantly.

Rake recognized several of them beneath their helms. It would've served Henris better if he'd circled himself with guards who didn't know who and what Rake was. Instead, their moment of questioning if they really wanted to attack Rake when they knew it would do no good was all that Rake needed to escape.

Rake spun around again, rotating the guards he held into the others. The arm of the guard in front snapped, but, whether that was his arm breaking or a joint popping out, Rake couldn't quite tell. The man fell, towing Rake toward the ground with him. But Rake released him and let the guard fall. In the next delicate dance, Rake stepped over the fallen guard without stepping on him, but the other guard he still held didn't manage as gracefully and Rake landed his boots in the man's stomach. Sharp cries and grunts of pain followed.

But with so many people congregating together to get out of Rake's way, the hallway suddenly felt congested.

No, it was something more than that.

Another novihomidrak.

Rake spun around, hauling the guard, complete with staggering and shuffling feet, with him.

Too late though. The other novihomidrak had come up behind him and seized Rake around the neck. Rake tried to ram the guard into him. The guard's shoulder popped as the man resisted getting into the middle of a novihomidrak fight. The pain had to be excruciating, but Rake couldn't let go. The only way he'd ever get free to go find Sapere Falin was by fighting his way out with every means necessary. Cal's life depended on it.

The arm tightened around his throat.

Rake drew out his talons and slashed at the barbarian's forearm with his free hand.

It didn't leave a scratch.

Or Rake didn't feel it rend any flesh. Cutting into novihomidrak hide was a sensation one didn't forget. There was no growl of pain from the barbarian, Thralic, either. Only the further tightening of bone and muscle against his windpipe.

Rake slashed down with his arm, intending to land in the

soft flesh of Thralic's inner thigh. All humanoid species were sensitive there, and, even with the toughened skin of a novihomidrak, it still hurt to be hit or pinched there.

Nothing.

Impossible. How could this novihomidrak be impervious?

There had been experiments with novihomidraks, trying to make those who were special creatures born from the dragons to be even more dynamic than they were. Was this barbarian …? Could he be one?

Why didn't Rake know?

Rake's head began to swim. He felt his eyes roll.

Why hadn't he sensed this from the Humline? Was he not meant to understand?

Was his existence in the Onesong about complete?

Blackness faded over Rake and he drowned in the darkness. The next thing he felt was himself falling. It seemed like forever. And then he struck rock bottom.

31

The metal rungs of the ladder bit into Siva's legs even though she frequently shifted. She felt like the indents in her thighs now had indents. How long had she been sitting on this ladder waiting for the unconscious person below her to wake up? Far too long. If the person who'd been thrown in with her wasn't dead when he or she was dropped, the fall might have snapped the person's neck.

She hated to give up the slight advantage that the ladder gave her, but it only seemed right to go and check on the person. It had to be a man because Siva had been given the courtesy of climbing down the ladder rather than dropped. Henris might feel it was important to get a male who might fight back down into the hole quickly. If he, and it could be Sapere Falin, were injured, then she should do something to help.

If she could. It might already be too late.

Once her feet touched the solid rock of the floor, she dropped down onto all fours and crawled through the darkness. She swept out with her arms to feel around for the body. It had to be around here somewhere.

Panic started to fill her as she realized the body wasn't anywhere near where she recalled it landing. She stretched out her leg and hooked the ladder with her foot to orientate herself. From there, she pivoted around and stretched out as far as she could with her arms, even extending through her torso despite it putting her off balance.

The body wasn't there.

Realizing this to be the truth, panic spilled into her as if she were an empty glass being refilled. She scuttled back toward the ladder and grabbed onto the railing.

Anything that could revive and move through the darkness so silently had to be ... well, something deadly. If that were a novihomidrak, then seeing in the darkness was no problem. She was probably being watched right now. If that novihomidrak were the barbarian, dropped in here to teach her a lesson as Henris had hinted, then she might be in more danger than she wanted to think about. Her instincts told her to fight. She'd been trained to do just that.

But this was a novihomidrak.

"Who are you?" came a low growl from somewhere in the obsidian blackness.

The voice surrounding her compelled her to answer. "Siva Candemir of Nungh Two."

The forthcoming silence held so long that Siva's hand started to feel slick on the ladder. She moved her hand to the next rung up, but the coolness of the metal didn't last long beneath her palm.

"You smell familiar."

It was a novihomidrak down here, cloaked from her sight. All of them currently on this planet knew her though. From somewhere wading through the fear gathering in her mind, Siva realized that the barbarian novihomidrak spoke differently. Plus, he knew her too. The fact that they'd encountered each other settled in with the realization that this couldn't be the barbarian. So, if it wasn't any of the novies she knew, who could this be?

"Cal?" she asked into the darkness. "Are you Callous?"

It made sense that Henris might dump him in here. Well, sort of. If she and Cal were together, it would make it easier for the novihomidraks to rescue them. Had Henris thought of that? Or were she and Cal being used as bait to lure the others in?

"Who are you? How do you know Cal?"

Siva's lips quivered. She wasn't being attacked yet, but the voice made it sound like she was close to being targeted. Because her father was primieret of Nungh Two, she'd been trained in diplomacy, but it had never been as important as her combat training. She always felt her skills as a peacemaker were never up to par. If they were, maybe she wouldn't be in this situation to begin with.

"Answer," came the growl a tad bit deeper than before.

"I told you. I'm Siva Candemir. I don't know Cal personally, but I'm a friend of Ruckus." She picked Ruckus' name because she knew the two novies traveled together.

Yet, there was another novihomidrak who she didn't know, who could have also picked up her scent from the area: Maylene's husband. Though they thought him dead, what if he wasn't? What if Maylene only thought he'd died.

"Who are you?" she dared to ask.

She hated knowing that her eyes were wide open, even feeling the air against them, and yet seeing nothing. Worse was knowing that, with his dragon lids, he was probably staring right back at her and could see her with near perfect clarity. Did he notice how she trembled? Could he sense her fear? Did he know how much worse he made it by remaining silent? Did he care?

"You can stop clinging to the ladder," the voice said though not in the low tones as before. "If I wished you harm, there is nowhere you could go. You could not escape me. But I have no desire to hurt you."

This voice she recognized much more. "Rake?" Her own voice broke.

Again, silence.

Siva released the ladder and stepped out into the darkness. It was the best sign of trust that she could offer up. But why didn't he know her?

"Rake, is that you? It's me, Siva." Maybe he'd been injured, received a concussion that had given him memory loss. Maybe that was why he hadn't answered with his name. Maybe he didn't know who he was.

"Do you know Sapere Falin?"

"I do. He was captured with me. I haven't seen him since," she said quickly. Falin might be the only memory Rake had. She tried not to feel the sting of knowing that Rake had no memories of her. It wasn't as if they'd known each other very long.

But she could still feel the protective shield of his wings around her as he saved her from the bullets aimed at them. She'd never felt so safe, so cared for than in that moment.

"You are having trouble seeing. Let me see if I can fix that. Close your eyes. Lazator."

She barely had time to shut her eyelids before hearing the strange word and seeing the blaze of yellow. She slowly opened her eyes, squinting against the stinging brightness. Then she caught sight of Rake standing against the wall.

He looked angry, and remained poised as if to pounce if she made the wrong move. If he did, she knew what the outcome would be, regardless of her training. Against the likes of him, it meant nothing.

Yet, he was also filthy and dirty, possibly covered with blood stains, and he reeked like the oldest of the poverty streets on Nungh Two. Maybe he'd taken a hit to his head. Could novies lose their memories?

"Rake, what happened to you?"

Whatever internal struggle he felt passed right over his face. He seemed to debate whether to tell her.

"Your heart quickens," he said. "Why?"

Siva wondered if she dared to take a step forward. She didn't. "I'm worried about you. We're friends. Do you remember that?"

Another strife took place inside him. "We might very well be," he said after a long moment. "I'm ... focused ... right now."

"What does that mean?" When he didn't answer after a moment, she said, "Rake, if this is one of those novihomidrak abilities I don't know about it, I don't understand. You're going to have to explain."

"You know that I'm a novihomidrak?"

Siva burst out with a smile and even a chuckle. "Yes." But the humor quickly faded as she realized it was confirmation that he really didn't remember her. "What's the last thing you recall?"

He softened slightly through the shoulders as if letting down his guard. "I haven't been injured. I performed a ceremony to suppress my memories and help me to stay on the task at hand." Rake glanced around. "And this is a little off task and a bit of a problem."

None of that made sense to her. Worse, her instincts let her know she should be afraid. That her life was in jeopardy.

"A problem complicated by the fact that you know me and what I am," he muttered. With that, he began to pace along the walls, studying them as he went.

"What's that suppose to mean?"

He paused in his stride, and his hand clenched down at his side. He pretended like neither of the actions happened. "I very much doubt the Council would find me at fault though. The ends justify the means."

"What is that suppose to mean?" she said, her voice nearly reaching a shout.

He stopped, facing the corner. "It means that I could get out of here, but only one of us is going to survive."

"So because I know you are a novi, that changes things?"

"Yes."

"Well," she said, not knowing what else to say that would help their situation, "if you were going to get yourself out, how would you do it?"

He turned to face her. "I'd use my dragon breath to melt the rock."

"Which would burn me as well."

"Agonizingly."

As if he needed to add that word! She glanced down at her

feet. "I don't suppose you could control the amount of dragon breath you use?"

"It will pull the oxygen out of the air. You'll suffocate." He tipped his head. "I will revive, however, once they open the hatch and air flows in."

"Even if they don't open it for several years?"

"Yes."

That scared her more. Maybe she didn't understand novies as well as she thought she did.

"We are creatures meant to survive," he said.

"I know. I just never realized what all that would entail."

"I have to complete my mission."

"And to do that, you need to be out of here."

He nodded. Siva's mind scrambled for another option other than him using his dragon breath. There had to be something.

"You could dig," she said with too much desperation in her voice. "Your claws tear through things easily."

Rake glanced at his fingers, turning his hand as he did so. "I have wings, so technically they're talons. Yes, they're great for defense, but digging through stone this hard, and already melted smooth by another novihomidrak, would be awfully slow work. We'd do better to see if they open the hatch soon."

His eyes brightened a little as that spurred a thought. "Have they brought you food?"

"No."

"How long have you been down here?"

Long enough that she'd started to feel the pangs of hunger. Not that she would complain, not yet at least. She was far from starving, and always had been, unlike many others on her planet. It helped her to recall that she too had a mission and that she needed to remain focused. If his ceremony to do that had made him forget about her, then she would do well to repress the emotions she felt for him.

Still, she had his question waiting for an answer. "Long enough to realize they aren't bringing me anything. Henris put me down here to teach me a lesson. But he can't break me. I've already starved for my people. It might spoil his plans to know that I'm willing to die for them too."

32

The woman knew him, and that made all the difference.

Rake watched her cautiously and half wished he hadn't performed the ceremony to narrow down his thoughts. At first, as he'd watched her in the dark, her heart beat fast from fear. Then, when she'd realized who he was, it quickened because of familiarity. Her breathing changed as well. She had deep emotions for him.

Worse, she seemed familiar to him as well and bounced uncomfortable sensations off the wall the ceremony was to provide his mind. This shouldn't be happening.

Cal lay dying and one woman now hampered the only way out he had. If she hadn't known him, then it would be easy to make the decision to use his dragon breath. He wasn't even sure why he'd hesitated while she clung to the ladder thinking that the slender metal would protect her from whatever lurked in the dark.

Something had stopped him. He'd convinced himself that it was because he was searching for another option that wouldn't cause anyone any harm. But now, he'd wondered why the Onesong would put this woman in his path and nudge him with feelings he couldn't comprehend. Those tiny footprints next to ones he knew belonged to Sapere Falin. And now she'd proven that she clearly knew him.

It stopped him from brushing her life aside to complete his mission.

The Onesong had to be testing him.

But why do this as a novihomidrak's life hung in the balance? It didn't seem fair.

The ceremony to bring clarity to his mission had done anything but that. Worse, now he had doubts about the validity of his actions.

No, the wrongness of all this came to a head when she said that she was willing to die to spite Henris.

She couldn't sense it, but their predicament was getting worse by the moment. The hatch above them was sealed airtight. In creating this pit, Thralic's dragon breath had sealed all the cracks and crevasses that normally formed in rocks, and the work to make the pit was new enough that new breaks hadn't formed as the earth naturally shifted. That meant the air they were breathing was getting thin. Even without using his dragon breath, it would be a short time before they suffocated.

There were other gases down here too, ones that could be downright toxic, from the decaying waste matter of ravagers put here before them. None of this bode well.

He might be doing her a favor by not letting her succumb to the sickly air. By saying that she'd die for her people, she was practically giving him permission to take her life. Even while she stood there defiantly with her hands on her hips, her tee shirt snug against the rising and falling of her breaths as she glanced around for another solution.

How did she know Henris? And why had he placed her down here?

Before he could ask, she pivoted so quickly that her ponytail flopped over her shoulder. "Magic," she said. "You lit the room with magic. I don't suppose you can do a spell to get us out of here, or spin the hatch, tear it apart?"

She obviously didn't know as much about novihomidraks as it had first seemed.

"No," he said flatly.

She looked at him as if she suddenly didn't believe him. He didn't need her faith in him, but he expanded his answer anyway. "For a novihomidrak, magic comes from two places. First is the world the novi is on. Some planets just don't hold much magic. Second is their novimather. Dragons can hold abundant power, but, if they've had no wish to share it with their creation, a novi could be powerless."

"Does distance affect that? I can't imagine dragon mothers always remain nearby."

She'd had a very perceptive question. "Imagine your body as the Onesong. Your toe doesn't understand that there is a brain in the body, but both exist, and information travels rapidly from one to the other. Like the very moment you stub your toe, you know there is pain."

Even though he'd given an answer, she turned on him now. "You novihomidraks! Are you always so pompous when you teach someone?"

She knew more than one novihomidrak. Others might

know about her. Harming her now was completely off the table.

"Why are you staring at me like that?" she asked.

He swayed from side-to-side on his feet.

"Rake?"

His mission. The Humline demanded he move, that he free himself now. Go!

The woman stopped him.

"You are the most dangerous creature I face right now."

Siva – she had said that was her name – laughed at him. "Me? You're the novihomidrak." As she scoffed, she turned away and looked back at the hatch, leaving him with the distinct feeling that she didn't believe him.

"Where's Sapere Falin?"

It was with another scoff that she turned her face toward him once again. Her lip pulled into a sneer. "Rake, do you really believe I know the answer to that? I've been down here most of the time since we were captured."

Then she softened. "All right. I will admit if I'd just gone along with what my father and Henris wanted, I wouldn't be here now. I might even be in a position to help. All I can promise is that if Henris opens that hatch, I will beg him to let us go. I will agree to whatever he wants so long as he lets you out with me. Then you can get back to your search for Sapere Falin and help Cal. And if he doesn't let you out with me, I will find a way back here to open the hatch for you just in case you can't get free yourself. It's the best that I can do."

The thought of what Henris would make her do to fulfill such a bargain made Rake's blood boil. He couldn't fathom the reason why.

Unless, she was the reason that he'd done the ceremony to begin with.

That made more sense than any other explanation he could dream up. But what did it mean? He'd heard her heartbeat quicken when she realized it was him. Did he have feelings for her too? She was a human, a mere blink in the lifespan that he would experience.

Yes, he had definitely locked away the memories if only for that fact right there.

How ironic that the one woman he had feelings for would end up down here in a pit and nearly be killed by him. Should he be glad that he'd hesitated?

"Well?" she asked expectantly.

He didn't remember her saying anything that required a response from him. As he found himself staring dumbfoundedly at her, he watched the disappointment in her eyes grow.

"I'm sorry," he said trying to recover. "I was a bit lost in thought. Did you ask me something?"

"I had asked if you found Cal and how he was."

Strange. If she'd said Cal's name and he hadn't heard, considering how focused he was to be, his pull toward her must be strong indeed. It made him want to dislike her even more, but, if he'd gone to such extremes, the feelings for her he had suppressed must be powerful. It was hard to hate that.

But since she knew about novihomidraks, the truth would be the best answer for her. "I did find Cal," he said. "He's barely alive. But his only chance to survive is if Sapere Falin gets to him soon, if it's not already too late."

"Then we really need to get out of here and can't wait on

the chance that Henris will open up the hatch soon. We need a better plan."

Once again, hot anger slammed in his chest and he pressed it back. Irritation at her would do no good.

"Do you have a suggestion?" he asked.

Siva looked toward the hatch, then she pointed at it. "It might take a while for your dragon breath to melt the rock, but what about the metal? Someone already had to make that somehow, right? If you melted it, it would drop down here and leave a hole."

She did have the start to a plan.

"Falling hot metal is still bound to splatter. I can't guarantee that it won't burn you," he said.

"Spread your wings. I'll stand far back behind you. Yes, it might still splatter, but at least then it could only hit my legs or feet, and even then the chances are slim. I can take that risk."

"And the heat?"

"It won't be as bad and last as long. I trust you can do it quickly."

There was one last consideration he had to tell her. "It'll probably melt part of the ladder too, if not all of it. Even if it doesn't, it'll be too hot for you to climb for quite a while. A patrol could come along and find the hatch melted."

"If you think you are leaving here without me, you're wrong. After the metal gives way, you'll fly both of us out of here."

Rake nodded. "Done."

With a determined stride, she crossed over to stand behind him. "Let's get this done. Then we'll find Falin and get him to Cal."

He was in total agreement with that. With a shrug, he extended his wings. "Let's do this."

Gathering the noxious air in his lungs, he began to breathe toward the hatch. Slowly at first, then harder. He saw it begin to turn red.

He also felt the heat rising.

When he inhaled for a second stream, the tang of heated metal burned along his tongue and back of his throat. Already it got hot.

Behind him, he heard Siva start to choke. He spared a glance over his shoulder to find her holding the collar of her tee shirt over her mouth and nose with one hand while waving at him to continue with the other. He wasted no more time.

The metal heated red hot, a visual for the rising temperature in the pit. Rake heard Siva coughing harder and doubling over from it. Each breath had to sear her throat and stab in her lungs like knives. How much could a human endure?

Not much.

A strange feeling arose. If he'd performed the ceremony because of his feelings for her, then he should feel nothing for her now. And yet his emotions weren't entirely dead for her. He had concern, but it seemed like a light touch rather than a firm grasp. Was this how he'd feel about any other human in this situation, or was it only for her?

Rake hated this confusion. Yet, what could he do?

The reddened metal dripped from the ceiling, burning over the metal rungs of the ladder and hissing as they melted and oozed to the floor.

Rake turned just as Siva stumbled. He caught her before she hit the floor. With her in his arms, he flew out of the hole.

33

At first, the air had been so horrible to breathe that it made her cough, and the coughing made her gasp for air. She couldn't tear herself out of the cycle. Her eyes stung. Nose and throat burned.

Then, warm arms wrapped around her and a cooling breeze pulsed against her skin. Her feet were lifted right as she felt herself sinking.

A moment later, it was all over, and she could breathe again. Relief flooded in as Rake whispered her name. She didn't understand why he was acting distant and even cold toward her. Something didn't feel right, but she couldn't identify it.

She opened her eyes to stare directly at Rake's face as he set her back on her feet. She felt her heart flutter a bit, and his brown eyes dipped. He'd heard her reaction and, when he realized that she knew, his mouth twitched as if he might smile.

Then, he was back to being cold and distant, stepping back away from her. "You shouldn't come with me."

"You're wrong. I should. Henris isn't going to like it when he finds out I've gotten out of his pit. He could easily decide to punish me another way."

A struggle played across Rake's face as if he were trying to remember something. "I can't take that on as my problem. I have to find Sapere Falin and get him back to Cal."

He started to walk away and Siva followed. Fortunately, the hallways were probably too small for him to open his wings and take flight. The best he could do was run away from her.

But maybe Rake was right. Her father was here, and she might not agree with what he was planning with Henris, but he was still her family. She didn't want to abandon him. He just needed to see that his actions were not the best for Nungh Two, not in the long run. Being primieret had always been important to him, but certainly this was not the way he wanted history to remember him.

It wasn't as if Rake needed her help either. Rake, a nearly immortal creature, could take care of himself. If anything, he'd only be protecting her. It might land them in a situation where they – no, Rake – gets delayed again and Cal would die because of it. Or maybe Sapere Falin would be harmed and left unable to help Cal.

She stopped following Rake through the grey hallways and watched him pace away from her. She would wait a moment until he was gone before deciding on her own direction.

But after a couple of steps, Rake stopped and turned to look curiously back.

"Are you coming?" he asked.

Her feet seriously wanted to move after him, but she knew that she couldn't. Couldn't, or wouldn't? She'd made up her mind to be independent, to move separately from him. What would that make her if she followed after him so easily now? The heavy pulse in her throat ticked away the seconds of her indecision.

Rake's dark eyes softened ever so slightly as he moved a step back to her. "I'm sorry." There was a flash of anger across his features which he hid away quickly. "I shouldn't have said that it wasn't my problem."

"You didn't. You said you didn't want to take it on as your problem, and you were right. If Cal's hurt, of course you need to get him to a sapere and Falin is the closest one. You should go."

"I have to get out of here. He's not in this building. The least I can do is get you out of this building, maybe even get you out of the compound. Cal's at the ship. He should have someone at his side."

That was a plan she didn't hate. She nodded and followed Rake. Once he saw her following, he turned and started to jog. Siva picked up her pace as well and soon they were both running. Rake slashed a couple of unsuspecting ravagers as they rounded a corner, taking them out without a sound.

"The others will pick up the scent of blood. We should hurry," Rake said.

But they were already close to the doors.

"Do you know what building Falin is in?" Siva asked as they arrived outside.

"C-12, but they all look the same, and I can't determine any differences or any markings."

Siva thought of the markings on the wall at each

intersection. She'd asked Murk what they meant, but he hadn't said. Maybe he didn't know how to translate them to her. "Are the ravagers smart enough to count?"

Rake shook his head. "Not that high. Not unless they'd had someone educate them."

"Which we have signs of here. Someone – Henris – has been teaching them how to be an army." She didn't want to think that her father may have also had something to do with teaching the ravagers.

"But one doesn't have to know how to count to attack and kill people."

That much was true.

"Do you know what they were doing with Falin? He was hurt in our battle before I fell unconscious. His arm was broken. He'd need medical attention," Siva said.

"They want to convert him to being a sapere for the barbarian novi," Rake said as he nodded with dawning comprehension. "They have to break his mind in order to do that. They'd want restraints, maybe even some sedatives."

Siva caught up beside Rake as they jogged so he wouldn't have to speak back over his shoulder to her. "Break his mind?"

"Saperes are seared with the magic of the dragon who creates them, but it's more than just that dragon's magic, it is their lineage. Saperes are as loyal to the entire breed of dragons as the one who blessed them, and to the novies of the same lineage. Novies don't often trust saperes of other dragon breeds from their own."

"Does it hurt, this searing which you also say is a blessing?"

"Intensely."

The shiver that went through Siva almost made her foot catch on the ground to trip her.

Rake slowed and raised his head as if to listen. "The bodies I dropped have been found, and there are repairs going on where I came through. It's too dangerous for you to try to get out another way. They're on guard now."

"I shouldn't have come with you. I'm slowing you down."

"No, it's a good thing you're here. I didn't think about Falin being injured, or what might help them convert him. We just have to find out which building is for healing."

"They use pictures."

"I know. I saw the images on the wall. But they are crude and could be easily misinterpreted. I suppose I could maim someone and see which way they go for help," Rake said.

"Assuming they went for medical help and not backup."

Rake's shoulders dropped. "If I could just get Falin's scent."

"What about the scent of medical supplies?"

"All I can smell is the gun powder for ammunition."

"Come on, Rake. There's got to be something. Cal is alone and dying while we are doing nothing."

"Don't you think I know that? That's why I performed the ceremony to focus so that I could quit thinking about you."

Siva came to an abrupt stop. She didn't know whether to be angry or astonished. "Because of me?"

Now, she wished she hadn't come with him.

"Sorry. It's all frustrating, and it's too much to explain. As you said, Cal's life is in the balance. I've found myself in a worse situation because I can't think straight. They're trying to break Falin's mind, but I think I've gone and destroyed my own with my actions."

Siva grabbed Rake's hand and pulled him alongside a

building. Then she took both his hands in hers. "Panic does no good. Don't give rise to your fears. Stop listening to them. Breathe."

A shudder went through him as if releasing the stress he'd been feeling. His eyes drifted partially closed as he took in a deep breath and exhaled it.

"Your dragon vision," she said. "Look for tracks."

His eyes were brighter, filled with hope, when he glanced back at her. He blinked down his dragon lids. One moment they had been gorgeous brown eyes like any human, and the next they were so dark they were nearly black, even the whites of his eyes. He stepped around her and began studying the ground.

"This way," he said after a moment. Then he began to run once more.

Siva followed, but she didn't need dragon vision to see that they were following heavy, lumbering tracks surrounded by several others. Someone in pain had been escorted in this direction.

What had happened to Falin in the time they'd been separated? Was he all right, and would he be capable of helping Cal? What if she and Rake arrived too late?

Rake slowed just before they got to the doors, and Siva halted so she could stay back while Rake entered first and dealt with anyone they might encounter inside. As she did so, she glanced up to the stones above the door. Cut into the stone was a dot, then two more dots separated by a small span between them.

She reached out and grabbed Rake's arm, pointing up at the marking above them. "How do you relate numbers to someone who can't count well? You break it down."

"One, then two. Twelve," Rake said, glancing up. "Compound building twelve."

"So this is the building, right?"

"Let's hope so." His voice stressed that he knew time grew short as well. Yanking the door open, he rushed inside.

Siva followed after a momentary pause, coming through the door just as Rake was dropping the last of the ravager guards to the floor. Their fresh blood smelled right at home along with the scent of antiseptics, sterile medicinal compounds, and tools.

"There's magic here," Rake said, his head lifting. "Let's go."

Magic? And he could sense it? He'd told her that he didn't have much magic, so what did he mean that he could feel it? Did it mean they were already too late?

Siva pushed her feet faster, trying to catch up even as Rake pulled away from her. He had to be feeling the same panic as she did. Maybe he even had it worse.

Rake slid as he ground to a halt. He lashed out with one hand, catching his talons into the wall to aid him into slowing. Siva gaped at the slashes left in the stone, but only had a second to marvel at them before Rake kicked down the door by where he stopped.

He entered first.

Ravagers quickly surrounded him. Rake dropped to his knees as the ravagers prodded him with long sticks, blue sparks coming out the ends and into him.

That was when the screams began.

Nearly immortal didn't mean invincible.

34

The walls of the medical facility were painted in the same dull grey-green as the rest of the complex, but the room Rake entered had one cheerful difference: sunlight streamed in through the dirty, barred window and brightened the room naturally, even if it were a bit muted by the filth.

Beneath the window was a bed where Sapere Falin lay. Rake thought the sapere might be unconscious, but he couldn't be certain. Falin would need to be semiconscious at least for the ceremony.

The barbarian novihomidrak, Thralic, stood bedside near the window. Shirtless beneath the blue and white open-front robes of the Rhotri dragons, he already had his weapons called to hand: a sword and a bow. Those two items made him lethal in both close quarter fights and long distance. Thralic's blue eyes stared unconcerned at Rake. Undoubtedly, Thralic had sensed the other novihomidrak was coming, but felt no need to ready himself for battle.

The ceremony to begin converting Falin into being the barbarian's sapere had begun. As soon as Rake had felt the magic, he'd expected that.

He hadn't been expecting the shock weapons, but he supposed he should have. How better to defend against novihomidraks who would be coming to protect their sapere? Had there been one or two leveled against him, Rake might have been able to dodge and knock the weapons away from the ravagers. No wonder Thralic hadn't been concerned about Rake's approach when there were five shock weapons in the hands of ravagers near the door.

They were coordinated enough to strike him all at once. The surge of energy bit into him and thrust him to his knees before he could retreat or retaliate. He tried to shout for Siva to run, but his scream held no words. His hair began to stand on end and his wings involuntarily surfaced.

Then he was on his knees and being shoved toward the floor. His body moved of its own accord to try to escape, but that only served to move him downward. Once he reached the cement, he'd have nowhere else to go. Didn't his body know that?

Five shock weapons held to his back suddenly became four.

Were feet scrambling around him?

The tip of another shock weapon fell away.

His mind cleared enough to realize that Siva had jumped into battle. Rake heard her grunt, but it wasn't from pain. Instead, her breath braced her as she blocked an oncoming attack.

Rake tried to get up. If the ravagers raised their shock weapons against Siva, would she be able to withstand the brutality of the weapon? It would depend on how old the weapon was, how much of the electricity it retained after being cut from the dragon. He knew his hits had been painful. Being struck with so many didn't allow for a good gauge of the weapons' health. He had to assume that they were all at full power.

That could break a human's mind.

One touch, especially a short one, she might be able to stand. But Rake doubted the ravagers would be gentle. They had a particular aversion to humans. Considering how they'd been treated, what had started the conflicts between the ravagers and the people of this planet, he wasn't surprised they'd have no love for humans. But, being brutish, the ravagers didn't understand their own strength either. The combination said it could be fatal if a ravager forced her mercilessly to the ground with one of the shock weapons.

Only because of the clarity of his thoughts did Rake realize the removal of another shock weapon. Still, two were enough to keep him from moving very far. His body still arched away from the tips. Muscles protested while painful electricity spat into him.

Siva gave another shout. Rake tried to look up. What would he do if she were in danger?

A shock weapon clattered to the cement floor close to his hand.

Only one tip remained against Rake.

He seized the middle of the weapon's shaft and whirled it around. He couldn't tuck his wings away to roll over. He wished he could. But his wing did press against the ravager, so Rake knew exactly where the last one stood. He shoved the tip of the shock weapon toward the ravager.

The first thrust missed, but the rod tapped the ravager's leg. It distracted the ravager enough that he released the pressing force on his staff.

Rake rammed the weapon in a second attempt and struck the ravager.

The shock of the weapon came as a surprised shout from the ravager who toppled backward. Not only did the ravager drop his weapon, which Rake seized onto, but he stumbled into another ravager and sent them both crashing to the floor.

As much as he longed to jump to his feet, the best he could manage was a slow, lumbering lift of his body. Aching muscles seemed to swear at him.

The battle in the room wasn't over yet.

Siva struggled to defend herself against three surrounding ravagers trying to get a strike in with their weapons. So far, she'd held them at bay, but they tightened in around her while she looked for attacks from the others in the room.

"No," Henris said from beside Falin's bed. He'd moved to stand between Falin and Thralic. Rake wasn't certain if Henris spoke to the barbarian, the other ravagers, or Siva. A good chance Henris also was talking to Rake. After all, it served in Henris' best interest that the novihomidraks didn't fight in the confined space, especially when shock weapons were involved, and Rake now wielded two.

Siva moved, ducking and twisting, and coming up with a kick. When she finished, all three of the ravagers had been knocked backward, one landing on the floor, and she held two of the shock weapons tucked under one arm and the last one in her hand. She leveled it at Henris.

"You will not be doing this ceremony. Sapere Falin needs to go with Rake right now," she said. "You, me, and my father will sit down like diplomats and solve the issues of our worlds, and there will be no more attacks from the ravagers."

A defiant look covered any shame over ordering the recent attacks that Henris might have felt. Still he looked as if he were about to give in.

Until Thralic pushed Henris aside.

The barbarian charged Siva. She turned, raising the shock weapon.

Thralic hit the tip of the weapon completely free of fear.

Electricity sparked.

Siva dropped the other two shock weapons to brace her full stance, holding the tip against the barbarian. Thralic opened his mouth … and Rake saw that Siva was about to die.

It didn't matter. Rake could get to Sapere Falin. The way was clear for him to get through, especially with his wings extended already. He could easily get through the remaining crowd and retrieve Falin.

That was his mission. He needed to complete it.

Siva. He'd done the spell to keep her out of his thoughts. Clearly, she could defend herself.

She was only human.

Was that a thought for protecting or not protecting her?

He couldn't decide.

Thralic appeared as if he were in the middle of an angry scream. Blue welled up his throat, and Rake could see the glow of it reflecting off the barbarian's open mouth.

Siva would see it. He'd seen her fight her way out before. Her last move had nearly been poetic in form. She would see what was about to hit her and be able to dodge it.

She'd endured Rake's dragon breath down in the pit.

Yes, behind the protection of his wings.

It had always been behind his wings where she'd been protected. Even through the ceremonial spell meant to block his memories and help him focus, he remembered encircling her with his wings while the barbarian had fired upon them.

Cal needed Rake's guardianship now.

Rake bolted for the bed where Falin lay.

He wrapped his wings around Siva, dragging her down as Thralic's electric blue dragon breath emerged. Hot waves rolled off Rake's wings and shot out to the nearby ravagers as if seeking out the nearest source to strike.

Rake felt people diving around the room while he held onto Siva. She remained calm in his arms, trusting, while screams filled the room. Rake didn't dare raise his head to ensure that Falin was unharmed. The sapere, though prone, was behind Thralic and, unless the barbarian turned, that would be the best place to ensure Falin's safety.

The moment Thralic's dragon breath ceased, Rake swooped Siva up in his arms and flared his wings open wide. A calculated risk for Thralic might have been ready with his dragon talons extended to tear Rake's wings. But either the barbarian hadn't thought of it or Rake had been faster. His left wing slammed against Thralic, knocking the novihomidrak down onto the bed across Falin's legs.

Swiveling, Rake set Siva on her feet beside him, then he reached for Thralic.

If Thralic hadn't had his talons out before, he did now. He clung to the mattress as Rake pulled him up, shredding it and sending padding spewing out as if it were a waterfall.

"Watch it," Henris commanded from somewhere nearby. "Don't harm the sapere."

Rake felt the magic in the room drop as the ceremony to convert the sapere failed.

Thralic thrust back on his legs, adding strength to his backward push by extending his own wings and giving them a flap which slammed Rake to the side.

Allowing all his aspects to show, Rake extended his wings too and circled the barbarian with his talons out. He pushed the humans back out of the way as he moved. The closer to the grey walls he could get them, the safer they would be.

But Thralic countered and tried to maneuver his wings so the people, mainly Siva, would spiral into the center of their battle.

Thralic's wings were small, meaning he'd probably endured the Crossing on his own, perhaps by his own instincts. Being smaller than Rake's meant Thralic could much easier grab onto things close to him. He started by tipping over a stand which had been bedside, though the obstacle would do little to deter two fighting novihomidraks.

Rake fixated on getting Sapere Falin out of the room. If he could do that, Thralic was bound to follow. That would keep the humans safe. Rake had no doubt that Siva could handle Henris, especially without the overwhelming presence of his guards in the room.

Thralic and Rake continued to circle around through the room. At last, Rake made it over to Falin, but, before he could turn around and swoop up the sapere, Thralic seized Siva.

35

The barbarian's arms wrapped around Siva, squeezing and locking her chest so that she couldn't breathe.

Her last breath was filled with the musty scent of the novihomidrak. The odor that had come off him the moment he opened his wings had been that of dirty, aged leather. Rake's wings didn't have such a smell, and Siva's thoughts took off down an odd trail of what the difference could be. Might Thralic be older than Rake, much in the same way older people picked up a strange fragrance as they went into their elderly years?

Maybe she'd only noticed it here in her few days on this planet before her life fell apart as ravagers destroyed her wedding. There were so few people beyond sixty on her planet that she hadn't had the chance to be around many elderly until she'd come here. King Rolant had been over fifty at least, as were many of his staff and guards. Whenever one of them passed Siva, she noticed the odor that they carried on them.

It had always set her a little on edge. To her, people just weren't supposed to live that long.

And yet, here were these novihomidraks who would outlive all the humans in this room as well as any of their children and grandchildren.

What had she been thinking falling in love with Rake?

No, wait. Love? Was she really falling for him?

No, she's fallen. She might as well admit it.

He'd said that he'd done a spell to get his mind focused off of her. Did he feel the same? Was he in love with her?

All of a sudden, answering this question seemed to be the most important thing in the world. Nothing else mattered.

Except there were other important situations to attend to now. Cal was dying. Falin was the only one who could help. And, at the moment, Falin was unconscious, and people wanted to break the sapere's mind.

Siva wanted this situation to end.

She reached down with one hand and clawed the inside of the barbarian's thigh while her other hand came up and seized the hair at the base of his neck to pull with all her might. She might not be able to tear skin or give him a real injury, but she knew that novihomidraks felt pain – and she could inflict it.

Thralic tried to shove her away, an instant reaction to wanting to relieve pain. Only his brain overcame his immediate instincts and he recalled why he'd grabbed onto her.

She felt his talons brush against her. They tore her flesh as

Rake rushed forward and knocked Thralic back from her. He'd been listening to the Humline he often spoke about and had waited for the right moment. He'd seized it.

Now Siva was free, and the two novihomidraks were locked in combat.

She rushed for Falin, who remained unconscious. There was no way she'd be able to carry him out of here. Not by herself.

Glancing up at Henris, she wondered if she could turn foe into ally. "One of the novihomidraks who has come to help your world is dying. He needs the help of your sapere. Don't risk the fate of your world and let it become like mine. We can find another way to help everybody if you don't let the sapere die."

The horrible sounds of battle behind her nearly kept her from finishing, but she knew she must not look back. Instead, she kept her gaze firmly locked on Henris. She felt tears welling up in her eyes.

"Please," she added.

Henris' face tightened, but he acquiesced and slid his arms beneath Falin. "Thralic, make peace. We go."

Surprisingly, Thralic disengaged from Rake immediately and straightened his stature. It took a moment for Rake to relent his fighting stance, and, when he did, he wiped a trickle of blood away from the corner of his mouth.

Henris barked an order to have his ship readied, and one of the ravagers in the room ran off to inform Henris' guards.

Siva touched Rake's arm as they followed, with the additional ravagers following behind them. "Are you all right?"

He gave a silent yet solemn nod. His eyes still looked wary

and his body still hunched as if prepared to spring into action if needed. She suspected he wouldn't relax until Sapere Falin had healed Cal. He had a right to be distrustful. The royal family he'd pledged fidelity to while being on this planet had betrayed him. She couldn't blame him. Her father had betrayed her and she had her own resentment against him too.

More guards, Henris' men, fell in around them as the group made their way. Siva noticed several of the guards taking second looks at Rake in curiosity before averting their eyes. One man even reached out to touch Rake's shoulder before falling into step at his place near his sovereign.

As they headed across the compound, Siva's father emerged from the building where the pit was housed and rushed to intercept Henris. As he got close, he began to stammer, "Th-the pit. It's … Siva! Where's my daughter? The hatch … it's all … melted."

"Behind me," Henris growled under the stress of carrying the unconscious sapere.

Ozlem halted outside the collected ring of guardsmen, who continued to march on by, and tried to look around for Siva. His gaze brushed right over her at first as if he no longer knew what she would look like. Had she changed that much? Did she no longer look like his little girl?

Siva left Rake's side long enough to retrieve her father.

"What's going on?" Ozlem asked as he stumbled between the guards to enter their protective circle.

Siva was glad to see that the ravagers had moved off as the guards arrived. Maybe many of them had battled in the past, and Henris found that he could either be protected by his guards or surrounded by ravagers, but never by both. An uneasy and somewhat unsettling truce.

"It's a long story," Siva said. "We'll have some time to discuss it later."

Henris' ship was a sleek silver and twice the size of Ruckus' craft. Rather than having seats that ran as benches along the walls and left the center open for cargo, these seats ran in aisles. There was some confusion at first as Henris set Falin down onto the nearest seat and buckled the sapere in. Siva noticed the cast on Falin's arm, which she hadn't seen while the sapere had been resting in the bed covered by the light blankets. But now, it thumped mercilessly against the chair while Henris pulled the belting across. When he was done, Henris remained beside Falin and strapped himself into the chair beside the sapere.

Rake took the seat immediately behind Falin.

A couple of the guards looked dumbfounded as they stared down at the people sitting in their obviously assigned seating.

Thralic grinned at Henris, then pushed his way through the shocked guards to go to the back of the ship and take the seat that was placed at the center, raised up a couple inches on a small platform. Obviously, that chair belonged to Henris under normal circumstances.

After a small bit of shuffle, everyone got seated and just in time too as the pilot, dressed all in black, yet bearing the insignia of Henris' royal family, arrived.

Moments later, they were in the air. From his seat and still lightly dripping blood, Rake instructed the pilot toward Ruckus' craft. Siva sat beside Rake and hated that she waited for the moment of betrayal from either Henris, her father, or Thralic. It never came. But Falin did begin to regain consciousness, and by the time they landed, Falin was awake and trying to gain comprehension of all that had been going on. Rake growled to several people that it didn't matter, that all Falin needed to know was that Cal needed immediate healing.

Siva hung back while Falin was taken aboard Ruckus' ship, but she couldn't stay aboard. Henris either, not with Thralic still excited about sitting on Henris' chair. Instead, she waited outside and tried not to think of how she and Falin had been captured by Thralic. She enjoyed standing out in the open, fresh air and in the shade of the trees.

Henris sauntered over to her. At first, he stood there shifting his weight from foot to foot as if he were weighing his options and trying to decide what to say.

She decided to speak first. "The treaty is off, Henris. I won't marry you. I want to help my people, but not in the way you and my father were intending to."

"The ravagers can't stay here," Henris said. "Without that barbarian, they are nearly uncontrollable. He barely manages to hold them in line. They're all animals."

"After seeing your plans, I see you as more savage than any of them."

Henris looked as if he'd been slapped. He opened his mouth to say something, but Ozlem came out of the ship at that moment. "The ravagers, any of those who wish to go, will come to Nungh Two," Ozlem said.

Henris spun around, flapped his hand in the air, then let it fall to strike his thigh. "Great! Take them to your dying world. See how far it gets you with those animals. Come see me when you want to undo your mistake and bring your people to my world. Maybe I'll grant you mercy."

Ozlem came up to Siva and put his arm around her shoulders, giving her a side hug. "They are a hardy people, and we will take those who want to work hard. It won't be easy for our people or for the ravagers. It's going to take a lot of work. Thralic will explain what we want to his people. I've offered him a ship so he can go back and forth as intermediary. Some of his people will want to stay here."

"Henris will only continue to fight against them or make them his soldiers," Siva said. "What kind of life is that for them?"

"It's their choice, and this is their world. You don't wish to leave yours."

Her father was right. No matter how tough the journey ahead might be, she wanted to fix what was broken with her world.

Ozlem stepped away from her. "I'm going to follow Henris, try to have a chat with him. We'll still need supplies, more now if we're going to take ravagers with us. I guess we'll need to come up with a better name for them."

"How about citizens?" Siva said.

Ozlem smiled and nodded, then turned to follow Henris.

After a long wait where Siva thought she might go to check on everyone, Rake bounded down the ramp and came over to her. "Cal's going to be okay. He's got a lot of healing to do, but he'll survive."

"You're all healed up too?" Siva asked, noting that he was all cleaned up save for a couple dark stains on his shirt.

"Yeah." His lips tightened as he tipped his head toward

Henris' ship. "I'm going to go see if Thralic needs some healing too. We've got to start somewhere."

Siva watched him go off, and she breathed a sigh of relief. It was over and the healing was beginning. She looked up beyond the branches of the trees to the blue sky.

Someday, her planet would look like this again.

Someday.

EPILOGUE

Some days, the scars ached. Today was one such day.

Rake grimaced in pain as he bent to pick up the shovel that had fallen over. His sharp hearing heard soft footsteps walking toward him, so he stood quickly before Siva noticed his discomfort. He never wanted her to notice it. He was, after all, supposed to be nearly immortal. That didn't mean that age wasn't catching up with him.

He'd nearly finished laying the stone for the walkway through the garden they were growing. Long vines of squashes, watermelons, and cucumbers had flourished in the recent stretch of good weather and were now tangling together. At first, he'd tried to keep the plants separated, but that was a battle he quickly lost.

There weren't many battles these days, and he didn't mind losing one like this.

The skies were beginning to darken and the smell of rain was in the air. They'd have storms this evening, which wasn't so bad because he and Siva would cuddle together in their sunroom and watch the water stream off the glass awning he'd personally made with his dragon breath.

While he'd long heard her approach, it was time he acknowledged it.

He looked at her and smiled. As always, the first thing he noticed were her eyes. Silver had touched her hair, but her eyes were as bright as they had been when they'd met so many years ago. By the Onesong, he loved her intensely.

"I brought some cucumber sandwiches too," she said as she handed him the refill of water she'd gone to bring him.

"I see that," he said, glancing at the plate of small sandwiches she carried.

"Sorry it took me so long, but I went to take some out to the workers doing the repairs on the street."

By workers, she meant the ravagers who had come to Nungh Two to help with recovery and rebuilding of the planet. In exchange, they would be accepted and given rights as citizens, something Henris still wanted to deny them. Those who had followed Siva had come home, even as harsh as it had been at first.

But the planet was now starting to thrive. The hunger and wars the people of Nungh Two had known were now becoming a distant memory. Siva's father had retired several years ago, and had passed away peacefully knowing his people would survive.

"It looks like rain tonight," Rake said, glancing skyward through a brownish haze that lessened with each passing day. Soon, the sky would be blue again. Storms were good as they cleared even more pollutants from the air. "It might even be a little chilly. I suggest more comfort food tonight for dinner. Then we can nestle up together and keep warm."

Siva grinned. "I was thinking the same thing."

He couldn't help himself. He leaned down to kiss her.

Rake heard his voice called by a ravager at the moment he sensed another novihomidrak approach. Rake turned, seeing Urlin, a ravager they'd hired to dig out some of the hard stone in some new land they were clearing to build housing.

"Rake," Urlin said again, "this man say he know you."

It wasn't one man, but two, and behind them was a woman. None of them were human, but all were novihomidraks, and Rake recognized them right away. Except for the woman. He didn't know her.

"Cal, Keystone," Rake said, taking Siva's hand and leading her over to visit them.

Keystone glanced around. "Look at this place, would you? I hardly recognized it."

"All Siva's doing," Rake said proudly. "We figure that, with her initiatives, the sky is going to be completely clear in another decade. And, if you think our garden is going strong, you should see some of the community gardens. The ones we started are flourishing. If you're staying for a while, I'll take you over there to see them later."

Much later, he hoped, not wanting to give up his time with Siva and the incoming storm.

"Well," Keystone said, "I was planning on staying for a bit and hoping for a favor from Siva."

"From me?" Siva asked. She seemed a bit startled that a novihomidrak would request a favor from her.

"A couple, actually," Keystone said with a sly, half-hidden smile. He even gave a small shake of his head which rippled his long blond hair, and, even though Rake heard Siva's body respond to the sensual nature of the gesture, Rake wasn't jealous. He'd seen how humans reacted to Keystone's natural beauty and charm, so this was nothing new, and Rake knew that Keystone's heart had only ever beaten for one woman – his mate, White Swan.

"Well, are you going to say what these favors are?" Siva asked with growing excitement.

Keystone reached back to the woman behind him, took her hand, and guided her forward. "Primieret Siva Candemir, I'd like to introduce you to Temperance."

When Keystone blushed and Temperance smiled while lowering her eyes, Rake knew the two of them were in love. Keystone had found another mate. A theory Rake soon found to be true when Keystone asked if Siva would marry them on her world and in her beautiful garden, a place where new life had begun after devastation and tragedy.

"I would love to," Siva said. "It'll give me time to hear all about how you two met."

Keystone grew a bit more solemn, and he now released Temperance's hand to take Siva's while he put his other hand on Rake's shoulder. "I had lost faith and hope in true love until Rake told me about how his memories and emotions for you broke through his focus ceremony and how strong his feelings were for you after he released the spell."

Now Rake blushed. He'd never told Siva how intense the reaction had been when he'd finally taken the stone from his pocket and released the spell. But Keystone had felt it and come to check on him. In the talk that followed, Rake knew he had to be with Siva and help her repair her world. Negotiations and truces with the ravagers had followed, not only for Myeller but to help with the recovery of Nungh Two. In that time, everything he felt for Siva deepened until he knew he could not be without her. Keystone had given Rake the first push toward Siva and the last.

"I know," Siva said, smiling over at Rake. He knew the truth of her words, and he felt foolish for ever having thought that she was blind to it. She'd known the whole time anyway. Of course, how could she not?

"But there's another reason why we're here," Keystone said.

At this point, Cal stepped forward as Keystone released Siva and returned to Temperance.

"The two of you saved my life," Cal began. "Both Keystone and I have been healed because of you, me physically, and Keystone emotionally. We both are in your debit."

Siva gave a dismissive laugh. "As if you didn't come to help me save my world. I couldn't have done it without the novihomidraks."

"Come now," Rake said. "You were voted primieret by your people because of your great leadership abilities. That you did without us."

"Man, he is just going to ruin our whole surprise," Ruckus said, striding down the path toward them now. He looked at Siva. "My one complaint about Nungh Two is: it takes forever to park your ship and get through inspection. You'd think, of all people, I'd get a pass. I even told them I was best friends with the primieret, but did they care? No! I really don't think they believed me."

"I'll see what I can do," Siva said.

"So, what's the surprise?" Rake asked, not letting them off so easily. They had more of a reason for being here, and he was ready to hear it. The storm was almost here, and he wanted them gone so he could have some alone time with Siva.

"We want to put a shrine on Nungh Two," Cal said. "Falin spoke to the Dragon Council on our behalf, and he wants to come here as a Grand Sapere. Other saperes have pledged as well. This world is still fragile, and we want to come help secure its future."

"That's a good thing, right?" Siva asked, turning hope-filled eyes towards Rake. "That means the world is healing, I mean, if saperes want to come live here. Right?"

"It's a good thing," Rake confirmed.

Siva clung onto Rake in a strong hug while bouncing with excitement.

"I take it that's a yes to our shrine?" Keystone said. "But there's one more request."

Rake felt stiffness move through Siva as she settled and turned as if she were about to face bad news.

"This one request?" she asked.

"Oh, here we go," Ruckus said with a roll of his eyes. "Now it's going to get sappy."

Cal smacked the back of his hand against Ruckus' stomach. The two of them shared a grin, and Rake felt a zing go through the Humline. The Onesong had something in store for these two.

Ignoring them, Keystone pulled a little, carved white swan from his pocket. "I wish this placed in the shrine."

As Keystone handed it to Siva, Rake noticed that the carving wasn't complete. The swan was only half done.

"It's the last one," Keystone said. "The one I was working

on when I met Temperance. I no longer need to keep White Swan with me. Time heals hearts as well as worlds."

Siva stared at the swan in her cupped palms while tears brewed in her eyes. The emotions were too intense for her to speak, so Rake did it for her. "After what you've said, I think it's very fitting."

Siva cupped her fingers protectively over the swan and put her hand against Rake's chest near his heart as he took her in his arms. Time did heal. Rake could see that, whether he looked around at all the changes he'd seen in this world, or noticing how Temperance leaned against Keystone as if he'd become the central support to her life.

He felt Siva move to look once more at the swan in her hand. The scent of the coming storm felt strong enough to be a current beneath his wings. He'd taken flight and landed on a new world, one they were building together. He was right where he needed to be, right where the Onesong had placed him, and surrounded him with love and friendship. He'd found Nungh Two had offered him everything.

Not bad for a planet others had given up hope on.

Siva had believed. She'd always had faith in her world, and in him.

She glanced up at him with those bright and amazing eyes, the ones he wanted to stare into forever, as the first light drops of rain began to fall.

In carrying her away, he'd found himself transported. Now, he was thoroughly captivated by her and to her world, and the Humline sang with happiness.

A champion with a special destiny.
A crazy, old dragon.
A mission already failed once.

Can Moonhunter survive on his own?

AVAILABLE IN AUDIOBOOK

WWW.MORNINGSKYSTUDIOS.COM

THE FATE OF THE WORLD LIES IN HIS HANDS. BUT IS HE THE REDEEMER OR SOMETHING FAR WORSE?

PRAISE FOR TANGLED MAGIC:

"I highly recommend reading all of Ms. Blair's tales as she is masterfully crafting many universes to explore."

WWW.MORNINGSKYSTUDIOS.COM

A genie champion who wants to serve
an imagination dragon.
All that changes when a beautiful
woman steals his lamp.

READY FOR ANOTHER QUEST?

Sign up for Dawn Blair's newsletter to learn about new releases, hear about events, and more!

It's easy.

Go to **www.dawnblair.com/newsletter** to join the adventure.

Dawn Blair grew up on a ranch in a rural Nevada town. The old buildings provided inspiration for her imagination as she thrived on stories of unicorns, princesses, heroic knights, and hidden doors to other dimensions.

For as long as she can remember, Dawn has had a passion for storytelling. Though she started out writing, her creative life expanded into painting and illustration.

She loves creating worlds and spinning tales for people to enjoy. The best ones are the stories that surprise her as she's writing. She loves her characters doing the unexpected. She'll gladly tell you that the most exciting part about being a writer is being the first one on the journey.

Thank you for taking the time to join her on these adventures.

Find more about Dawn and her work at:
www.morningskystudios.com

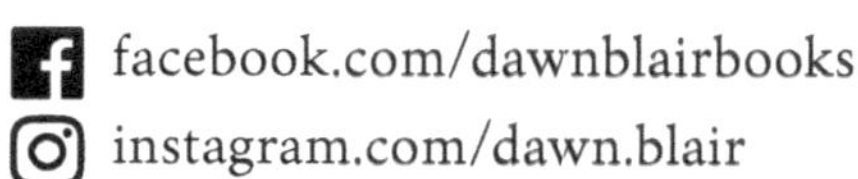
facebook.com/dawnblairbooks
instagram.com/dawn.blair

www.ingramcontent.com/pod-product-compliance
Lightning Source LLC
Chambersburg PA
CBHW030126010826
48973CB00002B/446